Bridge
  Julia in Ireland

JUL 2 2 1974

JULIA
IN IRELAND

Books by Ann Bridge

PEKING PICNIC
THE GINGER GRIFFIN
ILLYRIAN SPRING
THE SONG IN THE HOUSE
ENCHANTER'S NIGHTSHADE
FOUR-PART SETTING
FRONTIER PASSAGE
SINGING WATERS
THE HOUSE AT KILMARTIN
AND THEN YOU CAME
THE DARK MOMENT
A PLACE TO STAND
A FAMILY OF TWO WORLDS
THE LIGHTHEARTED QUEST
THE PORTUGUESE ESCAPE
THE NUMBERED ACCOUNT
THE TIGHTENING STRING
JULIA INVOLVED
THE DANGEROUS ISLANDS
THE EPISODE AT TOLEDO
FACTS AND FICTIONS
MALADY IN MADEIRA
MOMENTS OF KNOWING
JULIA IN IRELAND

with Susan Lownes:
THE SELECTIVE TRAVELLER IN PORTUGAL

JULIA
IN IRELAND

by

Ann "Bridge"

AF

MCGRAW-HILL BOOK COMPANY
New York   St. Louis   San Francisco

123456789 BP BP 79876543

Library of Congress Cataloging in Publication Data

O'Malley, Mary Dolling (Sanders), Lady, date
    Julia in Ireland.

    I. Title.
PZ3.05435Js3   [PR6029.M35]   823'.9'12   72–13049
ISBN 0–07–007736–3

JULIA
IN IRELAND

1

"JULIA WANTS to come up next week" Edina Reeder said, turning the sheets of a letter.

"Oh, how very nice" Mrs. Hathaway said. "Has that lawyer taken the flat in Gray's Inn, then?"

"Not so far—but there's pages more" Mrs. Reeder said, reading on rapidly. "Yes" she added after a moment—"she says 'The set is disposed of at last, quite satisfactorily'—that's all she says about it."

"I wonder what she will do with all that furniture—there were some lovely things of Philip Jamieson's, and some very *good* pictures" Mrs. Hathaway pursued.

"Store them till she decides where she's going to live, I suppose" Edina said, reading on. "Oh, listen to this—'Could I bring a friend up for the first week-end? Gerald O'Brien—he can't stay long.' What do you make of that?"

Philip Reeder lowered the *Glasgow Herald* and stared at his wife.

"Julia bringing a *man* to stay? I should have said that could only mean one thing" he said. "Thinking of marrying again. Does she say any more about him?"

" 'He sings very well' " Edina read out—"that's absolutely all she says."

"O'Brien doesn't sound much like an Italian opera-singer" Philip Reeder said, as usual at Glentoran getting up to put another couple of logs on the fire. "More coffee, Mrs. H.?" He refilled her cup. "I suppose he's one of the chaps from her office."

"No, I don't think Mr. O'Brien is in Intelligence, though she did meet him while she was working in Tangiers" Mrs. Hathaway said. "He was out there with the O'Haras, those friends of hers from the County Mayo; I think he lives near them."

"You haven't met him?" Edina asked.

"No."

"She seemed to be enjoying the Tangiers job when she came back for Christmas" Edina said. "She loves Morocco."

"Who wouldn't?" said Mrs. Hathaway. "Such a lovely climate, and such flowers! And I gather she has been remarkably successful in her work."

It was now just over two years since the widowed Julia Jamieson, whose husband had been killed on a mission to Central Asia, had been taken on officially by his Service, British Intelligence, and after a little preliminary training in the London office had been sent out to Tangiers, where she had many friends and contacts. Meanwhile her small son and his Nanny had been parked with her cousins at Glentoran, where there was a sizeable Reeder brood in the ample nurseries.

"Oh, do they say so? Do you see her bosses?" Edina asked with interest.

"I see Major Hartley sometimes, and Major Torrens occasionally" the old lady said.

"Doesn't look as if it would be much good Torrens starting dangling after Julia again" Philip Reeder said, "if she's taken up with this Irish chap." A Major Torrens was known to have pursued Julia with some vigour before her marriage to his senior colleague Colonel Jamieson; in fact Colin Monro, Edina's brother, who was also in Intelligence, had once complained that falling in love with his cousin seemed to be an occupational hazard in the Service.

"I don't think we ought to assume too much, Philip dear" Mrs. Hathaway said mildly.

"No, agreed—but you must admit that her actually *asking* to bring him up here looks a bit suspicious" her host replied. "She's never done such a thing before. Well, I must be off. Want anything from Tarbert?" he asked his wife. "You, Mrs. H.?"

"I don't want anything from, but there's a case of honey to go to" Mrs. Reeder replied. "The Argyll Hotel, please."

"Perhaps you would be so very kind as to look in at the Medical Hall and see if they've done my prescription—Dr. Lamont said he would drop it there" Mrs. Hathaway said.

"I'll do that—the bus isn't so good for bottles!" Philip Reeder said. He was familiar with the habit of West Highland bus-conductors, who act as carriers in a small way, of hurling parcels onto the roadside as their vehicle roars by at fifty miles an hour. "Is the honey in the hall?"

"No, in the cloak-room."

"Right." As he started towards the door it was flung open, and a small boy with a mop of reddish-gold hair rushed in. "Hullo, young Philip! Look where you're going! You nearly knocked me down! Hullo, Nannie Mack—would you and the little 'un like a run in to Tarbert?"

"Oh thank you, Sir, but I think not today. Master Philip has been a naughty boy."

"What's he done, Nannie?" Mrs. Reeder asked.

"He pulled up a plant in Miss Rosina's garden" Nannie was beginning when she was interrupted by a series of bellows from young Philip—"Want to go to Tarbert! Want to go to Tarbert!"

"Oh no you don't! Not if you shout like that" Reeder said cheerfully. "Pipe down, now—another time, when you've been good." He gave the child a light cuff on the head and went out, shutting the door after him. Mrs. Reeder almost laughed, the look of astonished consternation on the little boy's face was so comical—he stood staring at the door, and he put an incredulous hand up to the side of his head.

"Uncle Philip hit me!" he said, slowly.

"A good thing too" Mrs. Reeder said briskly. "You must learn not to shout, nor to pull up plants. Did you want anything, Nannie?"

"Only to see if you had any messages wanting doing in the village, Madam."

"Oh, no, thank you, Nannie; I was down before lunch."

"Then we'll just go and get our wool" Nannie Mackenzie said, and took herself and her charge off.

"Young Philip is getting to be a bit of a handful" Mrs. Reeder remarked. "Almost too much for Nannie Mack."

"It has been such a mercy for him to be up here with all your children" the old lady said earnestly: "You have done a good thing there, Edina. Alone, he might have been spoilt; as it is, I don't find him noticeably so. Does he get on all right with the others?"

"Oh yes, he's really no trouble; they've got quite fond of him. It's just that he's so fearfully sharp, he's taken Nannie Mack's measure, and plays her up for the fun of it. I'm sure he didn't pull up Rosina's plant to vex Rosina, but to tease Nannie Mack. He's really getting to be a proper little toughie!—he needs slapping down more often—and I mean *slapping!* Anyhow, if Julia's coming back for good she can take over. He knows better than to try any nonsense with her!"

"Oh, does she not spoil him?" Mrs. Hathaway asked; she looked a little surprised.

"Not the least in the world! Why, did you think she did?" Edina asked, surprised in her turn.

"I know that the fear of spoiling him is a thing that's constantly on her mind" the old lady replied.

"Well, she *doesn't*—if anything I should say she goes a bit too far in the other direction" Edina said judgematically. "Of course a boy does need a father; that's the normal way to keep their egos in balance." She got up. "You for your shut-eye, Mrs. H.? I'm going to the bee-room to separate the last of the frame honey."

Mrs. Hathaway got up too, collected her spectacles and her own copy of *The Times,* and set off on her rather slow progress towards her room and her afternoon rest. As she held the door open for her elderly friend—"Perhaps that's what Julia has in mind" Edina said.

As the day for Julia's arrival approached Mrs. Reeder displayed a quite unwonted degree of fuss about the advent of this long-known and much-liked cousin, who since their childhood days had always treated Glentoran as a second home, dashing up from England whenever she wanted at very little notice, dashing away again when some family emergency or, quite as often, the British Intelligence Service called.

"I don't think the Philipino had better come to the boat to meet Julia" she said one morning to Mrs. Hathaway.

"Oh, don't you? He does usually, doesn't he?"

"Yes, I know—but he bounces about and demonstrates so. I want it all to be quiet and easy, this time."

"I see" said the old lady thoughtfully. "Then I suppose you won't tell him beforehand that she's coming? Otherwise he will be *anything* but quiet, if he isn't allowed to go!"

"Yes—let it be a surprise, for once."

"But what about Nannie Mack?"

"Oh, I shall tell *her*—and say I can't take the child, so he'd better not know" Edina said firmly. And later that evening, in the day nursery, with young Philip safely in bed and asleep, she carried out this plan.

"Nannie, Mrs. Jamieson is coming up to stay again."

"Oh, how nice, Madam. Is she coming soon?"

"Yes, the day after tomorrow—by the steamer. But someone else is coming that day too, and there won't be all that much room in the car—so I think Master Philip had better not come to Tarbert to meet her this time."

Nurse Mackenzie looked doubtful.

"It will put him in a terrible way if he isn't allowed to go" she said rather gloomily. "But of course whatever you say, Madam."

"Then don't tell him; I shan't, nor let the other children know; and I'll tell Joanna not to mention it to Nannie Baird, or anyone." Joanna was the daily housemaid.

"Very well, Madam."

As she went downstairs—"Really, how ridiculous to have to plot and plan for the benefit of that tyrannous brat!" Edina said to herself. "It's high time someone took him in hand. I hope this O'Brien person is as tough as hell, if Julia does think of marrying him."

But tough as hell was hardly how Edina Reeder (or anyone else) would have described the small man whom she saw following Julia down the gangway off *The Lord of the Isles* a couple of days later. He was small—more than half-a-head shorter than tall Julia—and when introduced spoke in a low soft voice, with a rather marked West of Ireland accent; indeed his accent was the only marked thing about him. The mouse-brown hair, curling slightly above the ears where a hint of grey showed, the not-quite-brown, not-quite-hazel eyes, the wide mouth and blunt nose—everything was indeterminate, un-noticeable; an extreme contrast to Julia's height and beauty, and her mass of arresting auburn-gold hair. Edina studied him with incredulous astonishment as he helped the blue-jerseyed porter to stow the luggage in the car; he was very quick and efficient about that, she noticed, and about tracking down and retrieving a missing suit-case of Julia's. But how on earth? . . . that was her inner astonished question.

As they drove through the grey unbeautiful streets of the little town—"Where in the name of fortune do they get the name Macsporran from?" the newcomer enquired.

"I believe originally it was a euphemism for an illegitimate" Edina said.

"In Portugal they call them Espirito Santo" Julia put in.

At that, there came from the back seat of the car a burst of the most delicious laughter Mrs. Reeder had ever heard—rather high, bubbling, and prolonged; moreover, it was infectious—she found herself laughing too. And on the long drive back to Glentoran she became more and more pleased with her new guest; he was very observant, and constantly asked shrewd questions about the soil, and the crops.

"The roofs of your houses are so good" he remarked at one point. "Hardly any thatch." (In fact he almost pronounced it "tatch.") "Do the people put the slates on themselves? T'is rather a skilled job."

"Only when one falls off, if the estate joiner is busy" Edina replied, a little puzzled.

"They don't build their own houses, then?"

"Goodness no— we build the houses."

"On their own holdings?"

"No, Gerald" Julia put in. "There are hardly any individual holdings down here—it's all big estates. There are crofts up in the Islands, of course, Skye and the Lewes, but not down here."

"Is that so?" He was silent, reflecting. "No wonder t'is all so neat and tidy, then; I haven't seen a broken gate yet."

"Nor an old bedstead put in to 'bush out the gap'!" Julia responded merrily. "No—this isn't at all like the County Mayo, Gerald."

"Is this your land we're on now?" O'Brien enquired of his hostess.

"Not yet—when we get over the next hill" she told him.

But when the car crossed the summit of the next hill, and that astonishing view of sea and islands and blue mountains broke upon them, Gerald O'Brien forgot about gates and roofs close at hand—he gave a sort of gasp, and then was silent, staring speechless out of the car window.

"It is a view, isn't it? Didn't I tell you?" Julia said, leaning back to him.

"It's beyond all telling!" he answered simply. Edina was rather pleased; she set a good deal of store by that view herself.

Mrs. Reeder had made her dispositions with some care, with a view to the desired ease and quietness for young Philip's encounter with his mother. "Let him be playing on the lawn—I'll tell MacWhirter to put the croquet-hoops up" she told Nannie Mack. "We should be back at four or a little after. Then Mrs. Jamieson can see him at once, and play with him a bit, while the luggage is going in." And she instructed the other nursery party to go down to the sawmill and collect scraps of bark, so essential to the success of log fires, and not be back before 4:30 at the earliest.

So when the car swung up the long drive and emerged from between trees onto the open stretch which culminated in a broad space of gravel in front of the house, the Philipino and Nannie were on the lawn. He stopped playing to watch it; then when he saw his mother get out, he flung down his little mallet and ran at her crying "Mummie! Mummie!" He clutched at her coat, pulling her down to reach and kiss her face. But after a couple of moments his mood changed; he let go of his mother and turned on Nannie Mack, who was approaching to greet her mistress—"Wicked Nannie! You didn't take me to meet her!"—and started pummelling her with his little fists. Edina intervened. "Stop hitting Nannie, Philip. It was I who said you weren't to come to the steamer." At that piece of information the child picked up his croquet-mallet and set about Mrs. Reeder, crying "Wicked Aunt Ena! Wicked Aunt Ena!" Julia, in dismay, stepped hastily over and caught hold of the other end of the weapon—when suddenly, irrepressibly, Gerald O'Brien's laugh burst out, as bubbling, gay, and infectious as before.

At the sound the child turned—for the first time he saw the stranger; he dropped the handle of the mallet, and stood staring at him. Then, forgetting his fury—"Oh, laugh again!" he said.

Gerald did so—in fact he couldn't help himself—but as he went over to the little boy he said, in that soft voice—"Mrs. Reeder, I am so sorry!" And to the child—"I was wrong to laugh; t'is no laughing matter at all, a boy to be hitting the women; I'm ashamed of myself. I've said I'm sorry—what about you?"

"Sorry, Aunt Ena; sorry, Nannie" the child said at once, perfunctorily; then he turned to his mother. "Who is he?" he asked.

"He's Mr. O'Brien" Julia said.

"Will he stay here?"

"For a day or two."

"Now I've said I'm sorry, will he laugh again?"

"I shouldn't think so, till you've given Aunt Ena and Nannie a nice kiss, and said that you're dreadfully sorry you were so naughty" Julia said, severely. Obediently, the Philipino went through this ceremony; then the elders, helped by Joanna, busied themselves in taking the luggage indoors, and Nannie Mack in putting away the croquet things. "Bring over that ball, now" she told the child. "No, Mummie's going to have her tea now; and so are you, when the others come up. You may see her after tea, if you're good. Oh, I am ashamed of you, behaving like that in front of strangers! Whatever will Mr. O'Brien think of you?"

Poor Julia, over the usual ample tea in the hall, was secretly asking herself the same question. Philip Reeder's immediate assumption that if she was bringing a man to Glentoran it could only mean one thing had in fact been not far off the truth—the question of marriage had been raised between her and Gerald O'Brien. But Julia had been guarded and hesitant; she had insisted, as an indispensable preliminary before anything was decided, that he should take a good look at what she called her "encumbrance"; he, for his part, was equally insistent that she should come over to Ireland and see what he had to offer in the way of an establishment and surroundings, especially human surroundings. It was the sensible, civilised attitude of two people already mature who though deeply drawn to one another, were no longer of an age to be blinded by sense-enchantment, nor at the mercy of the selfish recklessness of young love. Gerald had never married; the fiancée to whom as a very young man he had been passionately devoted had been killed in a riding accident a fortnight before the wedding, and till he met Julia with the O'Haras in Tangier the idea of marriage had never again loomed at all large in his mind. Now it did, with an extreme urgency; so for both of them this first encounter with all Julia's closest friends and relations was a slightly nervous occasion. And beside her embarrassed distress at the Philipino's having made such a poor showing at the very first moment, Julia during tea was watching Gerald's effect on Mrs. Hathaway—Philip Reeder was out.

It all went quite smoothly, of course, except that when some caustic crack of Edina's brought Gerald's laugh out for the first time Mrs. Hathaway actually started a little; he turned to her at once with his ready "Oh I'm so sorry," and in a matter of seconds she was laughing herself. When tea was over Julia looked at her watch.

"The creatures take such ages over their tea, they won't be down for another half-an-hour at least" she said. "Edina, do you mind if I take Mr. O'Brien up the glen? The primroses are so lovely in this light."

Mrs. Reeder of course raised no objection, and the pair went straight out into the cool evening air, where the strong glow from the west did indeed give the primroses, massed under the sycamores on either side of the drive, an unusual depth of colour. "It *is* a lovely place" the man said, linking his arm through hers as they passed out of sight of the house.

"Yes, isn't it? I knew you'd like it. But now, Gerald"—she stopped and faced him, gently releasing her arm—"You see what I mean about the Philipino? It's frightening when he goes off the deep end like that—taking his mallet to Edina! What *will* he be like when he's older?"

"Perfectly normal, I should say," he answered, putting his arm round her and drawing her to one of the wooden seats that stood a little set back from the drive-way. "Sit" he said. "Oh my poor darling, you're all upset; but I don't think it's frightening in the least. Spirited healthy little boys do go on like that. The only thing it showed me, beyond what I'd expect, is how desperately he loves you, and how much he's missed you."

"But what ought I to *do* about it? One can't just let a thing like that pass."

"Oh, can't one? I think one could and should."

"Would you still say that if we were married, and you were his step-father, with real authority and responsibility where he was concerned?" she pressed him—she was quite wrought up.

He considered.

"No, I think if I had been in that position for a couple of years, and he knew me and trusted me, I should probably have given him a light *Ohrfeig,* there and then" he said at length. "I'm rather a believer in the *prompt* slap, or a good leathering when they're older; I think physical punishment, if it can be given immediately, is one of the wholesomest forms of discipline for all young creatures. But never anything delayed, or psychological, God help us!—no remonstrances, or 'What would your Mother think of you?' wretchedness."

"Nannie will have been remonstrating like mad, I expect," Julia said, beginning to giggle a little.

"Oh, that would not matter—he wouldn't pay any attention to that" O'Brien said cheerfully. "No emotional attention, I mean."

She stared at him.

"But you've thought all this out, Gerald!" she said in

surprise. "One would think you'd spent half your time bringing up children."

"I've spent a good part of it training horses and dogs, and
that's very much the same thing" he said gaily. "They're all
young animals, and what they all like is to know where they
are. Discipline makes them feel safe and comfortable; it's
all rubbish to pretend that any of them resent a good wal-
loping! I bet you the psycho boys who pour out all this stuff
about physical punishment damaging a child's ego have
never trained a dog to the gun—if they had they'd know
better! But sweetheart" he said in an altered tone, "you
asked me a question just now, a question with an 'if' in it.
Does that mean you've got any nearer to reaching a decision?"

She considered in her turn.

"No" she said after a moment—"Not nearer to a decision,
only nearer to the problem! In fact you may say we're *at* it—
and having my nose rubbed in it like that, all at once, made
me think what it might be like in actual fact. I'm sorry—I
didn't mean to start all that up again."

"Don't be sorry; you haven't re-started anything—with me
it never stops!" he said, with a comical grin that was oddly
allied to the tenderness of the pressure of his hand on hers.

"Oh Gerald, you *are* a darling!" she exclaimed, almost in
tears.

"Ah well, so much the better!" he said. "Don't fret, sweetheart; we'll stick to our full programme and you shall come
and see Rossbeg and all. I won't hurry you." He glanced at
his watch. "Yes I will, though—hadn't we better be getting
back? T'is nearly half-five."

As they walked down the drive to the house Julia was
half-aware that in fact this conversation with Gerald had
brought her nearer to a decision. His extremely firm, not to

say tough views on bringing up children—so strangely in contrast with the very low soft voice in which he pronounced them—had startled her; but the more she thought about it, the more it seemed to her that a marriage with Gerald might not only be "a good thing" for small Philip—it was largely in that light that she had always considered it—but the answer, the best possible answer, for him and for herself as well.

The after-tea appearance of the nursery party usually took place in the hall, leaving the library as a place of refuge for the master of the house and anyone else who had no taste for an hour of games, noise, toys and general hullabaloo. This was all in full swing when they walked in; the table had been cleared and pushed to one side, and the elder children were doing jigsaw puzzles at it; the smaller ones were building with blocks on the floor—Edina and Mrs. Hathaway looked on from seats by the fire.

"Oh, we *are* late, after all" Julia said, sitting down too. "I'm sorry, Edina."

"No harm—they were unusually quick today" Mrs. Reeder responded.

At this point small Philip came up to the group by the fire, leading a slightly bigger girl by the hand.

"Will the gentleman laugh for Rosina?" he enquired of his mother, indicating O'Brien, who was perched on the fender.

"You'd better ask him."

"Please, would you laugh for Rosina, because I pulled up her plant" the little boy said earnestly.

"Will I sing for her? That lasts longer" O'Brien said easily. He got up as he spoke. "Come over here" he said, taking the child's other hand, and led them across to a long leather-covered seat under the window. "There—one on each side; that's right." And without any hesitation he broke into a sort of recitative, half sung, half spoken.

> "Old Mother Duck has hatched a brood
> Of ducklings, small and callow
> Their little beaks are gold, their down
> Is mottled grey and yellow.
>
> One peeped out from beneath her wing
> One stood upon her back.
> "That's very rude" said old Dame Duck—
> "Get down! Quack-quack! Quack-quack!"

"Why was it rude to get on the mother duck's back?" small Philip interrupted.

"I expect it tickled. Anyhow, you don't generally stand on your mother's back, do you?"

"No—but I'm heavier than a baby duck."

"Oh do let him go on!" Rosina said impatiently.

"Well now, I've forgotten the next verse, but—"

"*Why* have you forgotten the next verse?" Philip asked.

"I should think because you interrupted him!" Rosina said. "*Do* shut up, Pino, and listen. *Please* go on" she said to O'Brien.

He resumed.

> "Now when you reach the poultry-yard
> The hen-wife, Mollie Head
> Will feed you with the other fowls
> On bran and mashed-up bread.
>
> I should get right inside the dish
> Unless it is too small;

In that case I should use my foot
And over-turn it all."

The ducklings did as they were told
And found the plan so good
That from that day the other fowls
Got hardly any food.

At this unexpected dénouement Philip clapped his hands. "The other fowls got hardly any food!" he repeated joyfully.

"Oh really, Gerald, what a terribly subversive thing to teach them!" Julia exclaimed. "Where on earth did you get hold of it?"

"It was an old Auntie of mine had it from her Scotch nurse."

"That's curious—my old Scottish Nannie used to tell it to me," Mrs. Hathaway said.

"Sing it again, sing it again!" Philip urged.

"No, we'll have something else" Gerald said. He went over to Mrs. Hathaway.

"It must be Scotch in origin, if you had it from a Scotswoman too" he said.

"I wonder if Nannie Mack knows it?" Edina speculated.

"Something else! Sing the something else!" Philip urged, tugging at Gerald's hand to pull him towards the window.

"Right you be—but there's no rush" the man said good-temperedly. Again settled on the window-seat he began to sing.

The others gradually drifted over to listen too, as he went on from one song to another—there were loud protests from all the children when the two Nannies came to shepherd their charges upstairs—"It *can't* be time yet!"

"Oh yes it is, and past" O'Brien said. "Now, put up your

blocks, Peanut. Is this the box? And you, Rosina." He went over towards the big table. "But what about the puzzles? Ah, I see you have them on trays—that's a great idea! But where do they go?"

"In the press here" he was told, and he helped to stack them in a solid oak press opposite the window. As good-nights were being said to the mothers and Mrs. Hathaway— "Will you sing to us tomorrow?" Rosina and Philip asked.

"For sure I will—if you go quickly now."

When the rising generation had all trooped out—"Oh, we forgot to ask Nannie Mack about Old Mother Duck" Edina said.

"So we did. We must do that tomorrow" Mrs. Hathaway said. "And Nurse Baird too." They were still talking by the fire when from the outer hall Philip Reeder came in.

"Good Lord, are you all down here still?"

"Yes, we were listening to Mr. O'Brien singing to the children, and then we just sat on. Mr. O'Brien, this is my husband, Philip Reeder." The men shook hands. "But let's go up now. Have you had tea, Philip?"

"Yes, I took it off the Halls."

Upstairs, rather to his wife's surprise Philip Reeder took the fresh guest off to his study for a drink; generally every-one sat together in the library, to which the women now re-paired. When, summoned by the dressing-gong, they emerged into the passage they heard peals of Gerald's treble laughter, and Philip's deep guffaws, coming from the study.

"They seem to be getting on all right, anyhow" Edina said.

This was confirmed when the master of the house came into his wife's room a few minutes later.

"That chum of Julia's is a most comical fellow" he said, sitting down and taking off his shoes. "You never heard such stories! And the way he tells them!—he's a born actor."

"He's a beautiful singer, too" Edina said. "But what do you make of him otherwise, Philip?"

"Oh, he's as sharp as a razor—no doubt about his wits. And he seems to have quite a good practice, too."

"Practice? Is he a doctor, then?"

"No, no—a lawyer, in some country town down there in the West, as he calls it. I asked him if he never thought of shifting to Dublin, but he said No, a small frog does better in a small pool." He laughed again at the recollection. "Actually I think he'd make his way anywhere," Reeder went on, "but of course he has his place there, and these horses that he's mad about."

"What sort of a place?" his wife asked, thinking, not for the first time, how much more fruitful men's conversations seemed to be than those in mixed company.

"Oh, two or three hundred acres, I think. He doesn't really farm—just hay for the horses and a few cows for the house; he has a man he calls a 'herd' who manages all that for him. And it seems he's a fanatic about his garden, too."

"Julia will like that."

"She'll never have a dull moment, anyhow, if she does marry him" Reeder said. "He's a most comical fellow" he repeated.

"What does he do with the horses? Hunt?" Edina asked.

"No, I don't think so; shoots and fishes, mostly. He breeds the horses and sells them. He seems to have some tremendous woodcock and snipe shooting; I shouldn't mind putting in a week over there myself. And you can take *carp* in the lake—I've never caught a carp." He went off to his dressing-room to wash, leaving Edina wondering a little what breeding horses and shooting woodcock would say to Julia, apart from amusing the guests that she would doubtless be eager to lure to Ireland.

In the library after dinner Reeder turned suddenly to his new guest with—"Now, what about a song, eh? My Missus says you're a great singer."

"No, quite a small one—but willing!" O'Brien said. He sat a little forward in his chair and moved his right hand gently to and fro in front of him; Julia wondered what he would choose for this party of strangers. He began with a song she had never heard from him yet, "Pretty Little Polly Perkins of Paddington Green"—in fact it was well chosen. As the light baritone voice wound through the song with its gay air, every word enunciated with beautiful clarity, Mrs. Hathaway involuntarily began to smile, and Philip to beat time with his hand. O'Brien came to the last verse:

> Soon afterwards she married, this hard-hearted
> girl
> And it was not a Wiscount, and it was not a
> Hearl,
> It was not a Barrynight, but a shade or two
> wuss
> T'was the bow-legged conductor of a tuppenny
> bus!"

Reeder burst out laughing. "Capital! Let's have another" he said. O'Brien immediately obliged with "Green Broom," and then went on to some of Percy French's Irish songs— the Irish as seen through the eyes of the Ascendancy, that is: "The Ballad of the Mary Anne McHugh," "The Girl from the County Clare," and so on; his voice brought out the mixture of the ironic and the lyrical which is in most of them perfectly. Philip Reeder laughed a great deal, and went on saying "Capital!" at intervals.

Next day he took his Irish guest out with him in the Land-rover. He had recently let one of the hill farms to a new tenant, and wanted to pay him a visit; and there was some new forestry planting to be inspected. Gerald continued to be impressed by the clean-ness and tidiness of everything. "Your new farmer keeps his haggard like a drawing-room!" he said as they drove away.

"His haggard?" Philip was puzzled.

"Where the cowsheds are."

"Oh, the shippon! Yes, I think he'll do. Must keep a place decent." After leaving the fresh plantings—"Is there much forestry done round you?" Reeder asked.

"Not close by—the Forestry Commission is doing a good bit up in the mountains behind Oldport."

"The private owners don't go in for it?"

"Not many; trees need too much capital, and tie it up for too long! Some of the landlords, who have spare capital, do plant a bit."

Philip was puzzled again. "The landlords! Aren't you a landlord?"

"Not really, no—I'm a native! What we mean by land-lords in Ireland are the Anglo-Irish, who own large prop-erties, and become officers in the British Army, and send their boys to Winchester or Wellington." He spoke quite without rancour—rather amusedly.

That evening there was not so much singing—Philip Reeder wanted to talk with his lively guest. But at last Mrs. Hathaway pleaded so earnestly that Philip gave in—"Yes, right-oh. I'd like some songs too."

"Do you know any Scotch songs?" the old lady asked.

"One or two. Would you like 'The Bonnie Earl o'Mo-ray?' "

"Indeed I would"—and Gerald sang that, and two or three of Burns' better-known ones like "Ay Fond Kiss." At last he embarked on—"There were twa sisters sat in a bower," with its curious recurring refrains of the names of Scotch cities. This is rather a test of any singer, and Gerald met it beautifully, keeping the refrain somehow separate from the song itself by singing it with a sort of dreamy expressionless remoteness, as if it were an accompaniment—as indeed it is—completely detached from the dramatic intensity of the verses. He came to the last one:

> When next the harp began to sing . . .
>   Edinbro', Edinbro',
> T'was "Farewell sweetheart" sang the string
>   Stirlin' for aye.
> And then as plain as plain could be . . .
> "There stands ma sister, that drooned me."
>   Bonny St. Johnstone stands on Tay.

"Goodness, it is *frightening,* the way you sing it!" Edina exclaimed.

"It's a frightening song" O'Brien said. "I always think nothing shows the difference between the Scottish and the English characters more clearly than their treatment of precisely the same story, of the jealous elder sister drowning the preferred younger one, in this song and in 'The Berkshire Tragedy.' That is practically opera-bouffe, with its jaunty tune and refrain, and the off-hand, almost comical, ending— 'The Crowner he came, and the Justice too, With a hue and a cry and a hullabaloo!'—tolerantly turning a tragedy into a joke."

"That is very interesting" Mrs. Hathaway said. "I never thought of it like that before."

Reeder asked for "The Berkshire Tragedy"—"I've quite forgotten it. It's years since I heard it."

"Philip, he can't!" Julia protested. "It's got *fifteen* verses, and he's been singing quite a lot already."

"Ah, quite right. Sorry, O'Brien. Have a drink."

Gerald had a whisky and soda, and promised to sing "The Berkshire Tragedy" first thing the following evening. Edina, over their drinks, asked him where he had had his voice trained.

"It never did have any real training" he told her. "More a lot of practice, really. I sang in the choir at school, and of course the organist, who acted as choir-master, told us to drop our chins, and get our consonants out clearly. But I always had any song firm, once I'd heard the words and the music three or four times, so I got put onto a lot of solos and anthems. And at college when we had musical shows I was usually roped in for a part."

"Don't wonder" Reeder said bluntly. "A memory like that for words *and* tunes must be a gift to anyone producing a concert or a show."

Presently Mrs. Hathaway said—"I don't want to be greedy, but could we perhaps have just *one* more, something gentler, to go to sleep on."

"But of course" O'Brien said; he thought for a moment, and then began to sing "Plaisir d'Amour," very low and quietly. When he had finished Mrs. Hathaway thanked him.

"That is soothing, although it's rather a sad song, I always think" she said.

"Ah, it's a sad song, all right. Count Fersen used to sing it with Marie Antoinette" said Gerald O'Brien.

2

GERALD LEFT a couple of days later, and this time Edina raised no objection to Julia's taking young Philip and Nannie Mack in to the steamer to see him off.

"*Why* have you got to go away?" the child asked, as they stood on the quay.

"Got work to do, my boy."

"What sort of work? Farming, like Uncle Philip?"

"No. Chasing bad people and helping good ones, mostly."

"What sort of bad ones? Murderers?"

"No, more usually robbers."

Small Philip's eyes sparkled.

"Oh, I'd like that! When I am bigger, can I come and help you chase robbers?"

"If you get very good yourself, maybe you might. No assault, mind—you couldn't chase robbers if you go in for that."

"What's assault?"

"Taking a croquet mallet to Nannie, and thumping your mother! No more of that, mind."

"Oh, I won't! Not never! When are you coming back?"

"Some time—when I can. Goodbye now, Peanut." He bent

and kissed the child, and walked a little way down the quay with Julia.

"He's a darling, really" he said to her. "Be gentle with him, my dearest."

"He's so good with you" she said wistfully.

"Don't worry about him—romp with him, come *out* to him! And now, when are you coming out to Mayo, God help us?"

"In about a fortnight, I thought, if Helen can have me then."

"You won't stay at Rossbeg?"

"Oh better not stay at first, do you think? Wouldn't that make a lot of talk? Let me stay at Rostrunk, and come over for the whole day, at a week-end, when you'll be free. I'll come twice, at least! And you'll come over to the O'Haras'."

"I will surely." He pressed her arm. "Don't worry about me either, my darling one. Whatever you decide in the end, I'll accept."

"You're too good!" she said, with tears in her eyes. "Look, they've got the gangway down; you ought to go."

"Ah, I will. Goodbye, my dearest heart."

While the party on the quay were making their farewells, Edina and Mrs. Hathaway, not surprisingly, were discussing Gerald's prospects in the morning-room at Glentoran.

"I must say I think she'd probably be wise to marry him—he's a wizard with children," Edina said. "It would be the making of that child to have him for a step-father."

Mrs. Hathaway sounded a little dubious.

"I don't think it would be quite fair to a man to marry in order to give one's child a good guardian" she said slowly.

"But Mrs. H. that needn't be the only reason, need it? I think he's a charmer—very much a person one could marry and be happy with. Don't you agree?"

"Yes, I think he is, in himself. It's"—she paused for words to express her hesitation. "It's Julia's terrible sense of duty that I'm afraid of" she said at last. "Oh, I wish Colonel Jamieson needn't have died!"

"Anyhow, she's perfectly right to go over and stay with these other friends, and have a good look at the house and everything. He's insisted on that—he told me so" Edina said.

"Did he? Well, that is very kind and wise of him. He is the *nicest* thing imaginable" the old lady said. "Only it would be such a different life for her."

"In her place I think I should be rather thankful to settle down to a bit of domesticity and peace and quiet, instead of this perpetual spying and sleuthing" Edina said vigorously—Mrs. Hathaway laughed.

Julia set off for Ireland a fortnight later, Lady Helen O'Hara having said that then would be a suitable time for her to pay a visit to Rostrunk. Philip Reeder tried hard to make her travel via Stranraer—"if you're *in* Scotland, it's absurd not to use a Scottish port"—but Julia professed a passion for the Dublin-Liverpool boats, to which she was accustomed, and did as she chose, as usual.

She had her normal comfortable little single cabin, a familiar cheerful stewardess brought her tea, as ordered, sharp at six; by seven-fifteen she had dressed and packed, and was tucking into an ample breakfast of bacon and eggs in the saloon—she had left her luggage in charge of an elderly steward, who had promised to take it ashore and secure her a taxi, when the gangways were down. "No roosh, for the train at Westland Row" he told her. Well, she didn't believe the Stranraer boat could have been any improvement on this, was Julia's reflection; no doubt about it, the Irish were most comfortable people to travel among. But what would they be like to live among? With this question in her mind she was a little watchful of her own reactions, which normally she was apt to ignore. She always enjoyed returning to Dublin, she thought, as she went up on deck—there was the Customs House, beautiful as ever in the early light. And when she had gone ashore, and the usual cheerfully chatty taxi-driver took her to Westland Row, and a friendly porter installed her in a smoking First in the Martinstown coach, Julia felt vaguely and irrationally encouraged.

She sat down in the back comer seat, lit a cigarette, and idly watched the other passengers passing along the platform to board the train—her attention was caught by one party which also obviously intended to get into the Martinstown coach; they stood waiting by the door till a porter arrived wheeling their luggage on a barrow. There was a man, tall, dark, handsome, and rather noticeably well-dressed—too well-dressed, Julia thought; two children, a boy and a girl, per-haps ten and twelve; and a woman, small and slight, with fair wavy hair—her clothes were as casual as the man's were elegant: she was bare-headed, and wore pale corduroy slacks, a rough sweater, and a loose fawn wind-cheater. But there was something vaguely attractive about her rather square pale face, with a wide forehead and a wide mouth, and still more about the dégagé attitude in which she stood, her feet far apart, looking up at the elegant man and laughing. She shooed the children and the porter into the train, where they presently irrupted into Julia's carriage—yes, only one seat was taken, Julia told the porter; while the fresh lot of luggage was being stowed in the racks and on the middle seats she continued to watch the pair on the platform. When the porter emerged it was the woman who tipped him; Julia saw him gape at the size of the tip, and then touch his cap, grinning. A whistle blew; the elegant man enveloped the woman in a warm embrace before she hopped onto the train as it started to pull out.

Julia's normal feeling of slight annoyance at the idea of a long railway journey with children in the carriage was only partly modified by her even slighter feeling of interest in the fair woman, who now came in and sat down, and pulling a cigarette-case out of her jacket pocket, offered it to Julia—"Oh, I see you're smoking—good" she said. She spoke with a very faint American accent. The children asked if they could have their books.

"Yes—they're in the small tartan grip; get them out yourselves" she told them briskly. When they had done so— "Now clear off" she said. "Find yourselves places in some other carriage."

"What if they're all full?" the boy enquired.

"Then you can stand in the corridor—but I don't suppose they are, for a moment. Scram!" his mother adjured him. Laughing, the children obediently went out.

Julia was highly amused by these proceedings, and studied the stranger with more interest. No, she was not pretty, and yet there was something akin to the compelling appeal of beauty in the colourless square face—the eyes, of a very light hazel, were beautiful, actually.

"I can't stand children on a train" the stranger now remarked calmly. "Children are always hell to some extent, but on a train they're somehow complete hell."

"They seem very obedient" Julia said politely.

"Well if children aren't obedient, they're just plumb unendurable" the fair-haired woman pronounced.

Julia felt that she would have liked to hear Gerald in discussion with this very positive person, who seemed to have solved her own child-care problems so satisfactorily. Presently they settled down, by mutual consent, to their newspapers; at lunch-time the children were recalled from their exile in the corridor to get down a hamper and eat an ample lunch of meat pies, tomatoes, cream-cheese with biscuits, and cake—perhaps being so very well-fed contributed to their cheerful docility, Julia thought, again amused. She too had a modest parcel of Glentoran meat pies, but gratefully accepted a tomato and a cup of excellent coffee, piping hot from a thermos. Over this they talked, the children having been banished again. The fair-haired woman talked well and easily—about recent plays in London and Dublin, and recent books by English and Irish writers; Julia was rather out of her depth, especially in the Irish part, but found her new acquaintance very good company. She was gay, and yet somehow detached—"neutral" was the word that came into Julia's mind; she gave quick amusing little appraisals of this actress or that singer, but they were all perfectly good-tempered—it struck Julia suddenly how unusual it was to be so amusing without a single harsh or even sharp judgement. About herself she vouchsafed no information whatever except that she had "a shack on Achill," to which they were on their way; Julia found herself quite glad that they would be together for the whole journey—Martinstown was the terminus.

In spite of her detachment and apparent casualness, the fair woman was quite practical; fifteen minutes before the train was due in she summoned the children, got them into their anoraks, made them stow their books in the tartan grip, and handing down the luggage out of the rack, caused them to carry the small pieces along the corridor and place them near the door; two heavier ones she took herself. By the time less active travellers began to bestir themselves, the small party was strategically placed for a rapid exit.

"Bye!" she said to Julia, as she left the carriage, and

"Goodbye—thanks for the coffee" Julia replied. When they had gone she got down her own luggage and put it on the seat; then she lowered the window and sat by it, to watch for Helen, who had said she would be meeting her.

Almost before the train had really stopped the two children sprang out, and took the pieces of luggage which their mother handed down to them; in a moment they were joined by a middle-aged man, short and thick-set, who lifted the heavier pieces out; when the fair woman followed, he too enfolded her in a warm hug, kissing her repeatedly—Julia watched with amusement. This new admirer was the greatest possible contrast to the Dublin one; he was at least twice his age, and as plain and scruffy as the other was handsome and elegant. Catholic in her tastes, Julia said to herself laughing, and waved to Lady Helen, who now approached with one of the two Martinstown porters; he came in and took her suit-cases, and she got out and greeted her hostess.

In the station yard the other party were stowing themselves and their luggage into a very ancient and shabby Ford. "Helen, do you know who those people are?" Julie asked, indicating them.

"I've never seen her before—he's Billy O'Rahilly" Lady Helen said. "Thank you very much, Mick" she said, giving a coin to the porter, and getting into the car.

"And who is Billy O'Rahilly?" Julie asked, getting in beside her.

"One of our poets!" Lady Helen replied, with a slightly ironic inflexion, as she drove off.

"Oh. Does he live in Achill?"

"No, he lives quite near us, our side of Oldport. Why on earth should you suppose he lived in Achill?" Lady Helen enquired, curiously.

"Oh, because she said she did, part of the time." Julie explained about her companion on the journey down, and her peculiar method with her children—"In fact I thought her frightfully nice" she ended. "Could she be his wife?"

"Billy's not married, that one ever heard of," Lady Helen replied. "For her sake I should hope she isn't, nor going to be—he's rather a dubious type, Michael says."

"Oh dear! Dubious in what way?" Julia asked; she had no very great faith in General O'Hara's assessments of people, as a rule.

"Oh, he's mixed up with all those parlour pinks in Dublin, the Lefty intelligentsia" Lady Helen said vaguely. "He has the most extraordinary people to stay. *And* he has the most hideously noisy motor-boat!" she added. "It goes like the wind, and fills all this end of the Bay with its roar when he takes it out." Some time later, after they had passed through Oldport, as usual collecting various parcels, as they were crossing a bridge she pointed to a grove of trees on the right of the road—"That's Billy's house" she said, "in that wood."

"Where does he keep his boat, then?" Julia enquired.

"In the inlet below the bridge, where the river runs out—there's a path to the anchorage along the bank. He doesn't use it all that often, thank goodness, but it's horrible when he does."

"How boring for you" Julia sympathised. She was a little disappointed that her amusing new acquaintance's local contact should be some one the O'Hara's disliked.

"Gerald's coming to dinner tonight" Lady Helen remarked, as they turned down the familiar lane to Rostrunk.

"Oh, good."

"He seems to have enjoyed his week-end at Glentoran. How did he and the Reeders get on?"

"Oh, they were utterly seduced by his singing, of course! —Philip especially."

"Philip *Reeder?*" Lady Helen asked, with a lift of her eyebrows.

"Yes, completely. As a matter of fact small Philip was too" Julie said; it was as well to get this over at once, she felt.

"Oh, he took to him, did he? I'm so glad. Gerald seems to have approved of The Peanut, as he calls him, too. I think he's quite ready to take on the job, Julia" she said, turning to her friend with a smile of great affection.

"Bless you, Helen. Yes, well we shall have to see" Julia said.

"Yes—'see' is exactly what he wants you to do. He's taking you down on Saturday—an early start, he said. He really is a most chivalrous creature, you know."

"I *do* know. But I must take my time, Helen."

"Of course. I won't pester you."

They all spent a pleasant and quite unembarrassed evening, and even General O'Hara, least tactful of men, refrained from any comment when Gerald O'Brien arrived at 8:30 A.M. on the Saturday to drive Julia down to see his establishment. It was one of those rare clear mild spring days which occasionally bless the West of Ireland at the beginning of April, and Julia's spirits rose. They passed through Martinstown, but some miles further on took a small turning to the right.

"Oh, is Rossbeg out here? I thought it was by Lough Balla" Julia said in surprise.

" 'T'is, but I want to show you something pretty first" he said. They were driving south-westward, and mountains rose ahead of them, above the gently undulating farmland; now they came to a river and followed it, and presently reached the strangest place Julia had ever seen. It was a village, the little white houses set rather sparsely, with a group of monastic ruins among them; but the river either divided into several, or was joined by others, she couldn't be sure which —anyhow there was water everywhere, crystal-clear and brimming; one had the impression that the whole place was afloat.

"Oh, how magical!" she exclaimed. "Do stop, Gerald."

"I thought you'd like this" he said, pulling into the side of the road.

"It's too lovely. What are the ruins?"

"Oh, an Augustinian Abbey—the Augustinians were great settlers all through the West. But there was a much earlier monastery here; sixth century, they say. This was always a holy place, and specially good to be buried in" he said gaily. "Come on and I'll show you."

"Can't we look at the ruins?"

"Another day. We don't want to get in wrong with Bridgie by being late for lunch."

Some distance beyond the floating village the road ran through woods. Gerald slowed down and pointed out to Julia small cairns of stones, some as much as two or three feet high, standing on the bank at the edge of the wood, or, where a track ran through the trees, at intervals along it. "Those are coffin cairns" he said. "Whenever a funeral is brought along the road or that track, the people bringing it put a stone on the cairns as they pass."

"Do they really? Why?" she asked.

"I don't know the reason" he said. "It's just a custom they have, when people are taken to be buried at the Abbey ruins. Maybe they do it at other places too, but this is the only place I've seen it."

Julia insisted on getting out to examine one of the cairns. "But Gerald, these stones at the bottom are all over moss!" she said, after peering at it.

"Ah, they would be. People have been doing this for ages —centuries, I daresay."

Beyond the woods they came out into open country, rather flat, where the underlying limestone emerged onto the surface of the soil in bare grey stretches, fissured into deep crevices—the "limestone pavements" which are such a strange feature of parts of County Galway and the County Clare; ferns grow in the deep clefts, and the bare rock is set with small bright flowers. Julia was enchanted.

"Gerald, what fascinating places you seem to live among! I've never seen anything in the least like this before."

"Did the O'Haras never take you to the Burren?"

"No—where's that?"

"Down in Clare—there's miles of this limestone there; in fact the Burren is practically all limestone. We'll go there one day; now we must get home." He turned east again, and they soon left the limestone and were back in farming country; presently, from a confusion of small roads they emerged onto a main one, and drove rapidly north. They passed through a small town, then again through woods; among these was set a noble gateway, with a pretty lodge beside it. "Who lives there?" Julia asked.

"No one, now; old Mary Browne used to—it's been in the Browne family for ever. But the money ran out; she was never much of a manager—and she had to go."

"The drive looks quite well-kept" Julia said. "Are you sure no one lives there?"

"How literal you are!" He turned a rather mocking smile on her. "Sure it's well-kept—it's a convalescent home for

T.B.s. I just meant it was no longer what it used to be and what it was meant to be, a family house with a woman in it. Now it's an institution."

She laughed. "And the T.B.s are un-persons! Yes, I see what you mean. I'm sorry."

Gerald now took a turning to the right, first through woods, then in open country again; at the foot of a low ridge was a gateway with a lodge, a modest one this time; he turned in and up a drive between tall slender oak-trees till they reached a grey stone house, like the gateway modest, and pulled up.

"Here we are" he said.

Julia got out and looked about her. Beyond the broad stretch of gravel in front of the house was a range of pastures divided by post-and-rail fences, which seemed to be full of horses; as Gerald appeared from behind the car a number of these galloped up to the nearest fence, tossing their heads and whinnying.

"Ah, my lovely boys! Were you missing me?" he said walking over to the graceful leggy creatures and fondling one or two of them, who nuzzled at his pockets; but as Julia moved to join him they flung up their heads and heels and galloped off again in a swirl of flying manes and tails.

"Gerald, they *are* pretty!" she exclaimed, genuinely delighted.

"Ah, they're shy," he said. She moved further along the fence; here the fields fell away steeply to flat, marshy meadows bordering a vast expanse of lake—"Oh, that must be Lough Balla. How huge it is!" she said.

"Yes, it's big all right; and from up here one sees most of it at once."

"Where's the garden?" she asked.

"The other side of the house, facing the sun. But come in now, and have a drink before lunch."

As they entered, Julia looked at her surroundings with almost painful interest. A long hall ran right through the house, its walls adorned, if that was the word, with rather withered stuffed birds, discoloured with age, and two enormous stuffed fish in glass cases; at the nearer end, immediately inside the front door, was a strange miscellany of objects: fishing-rods on racks, garden-tools, gum-boots and baskets standing on the floor, while from hooks hung raincoats, riding-whips and lunging-reins, and a variety of hats and caps, including a couple of sou'westers—everything was rather dusty. By contrast, some of the rugs on the unpolished wooden floor were, even to her not very expert eye, superb. Gerald threw open a door on the right, and they went into the drawing-room, which was full of light from a big bow window commanding the immense vista of the lake; the furniture was covered in fresh bright cretonnes, matching the curtains. "Oh, what a pretty room!" Julia said.

"I had it done up two years ago, when I let the house—Helen found the stuff for me, and got it made up" he said. "It was then I put in the bath rooms."

"Had you none before?" Julia asked; after her first sight of the hall she had begun to wonder about bath rooms.

"Only one terrible old thing, with a sort of wooden sentry-box at the end!" he said. "Now there are four—Helen said I'd better do the job thoroughly while I was about it. We put in central heating too, and all oil-fired—so if the girl oversleeps it doesn't matter, neither the house nor the water is cold! Now have some sherry."

The sherry-drinking again offered certain contrasts. Glasses and decanter were set out on a vast and very beautiful lacquered tray, which was, however, far from clean; the glasses did not match, but the Waterford decanter was magnificent, and so was the wine it contained.

"Gerald, what lovely sherry!" she said.

"I'm glad you like it. I get it from some people in Limerick who import it themselves; they know Spain well, and get good stuff."

"They do indeed!" She took her glass over to the window.

"Goodness, it *is* a view! What an extraordinary colour the Lough is, that sort of pale pastel-green."

"That's the lime on the bottom. The whole floor of the lake is covered feet deep in white mud, a deposit from the streams flowing in from all that limestone you saw."

"But the rivers at that place were as clear as crystal!"

"I suppose it doesn't show when it's in suspension in the water; but that's why Balla has that particular colour."

There came a knock on the door, and an elderly woman with red hair turning grey poked her head round it.

"The lunch is ready if the lady is" she said.

"Oh, don't you want to wash? Bridgie, take Mrs. Jamieson up to the spare-room bathroom."

Julie followed Bridgie up a flight of stairs, as dusty as the hall, and into a neat modern bathroom, complete with fitted basin and hot towel-rail.

"Mind your hands now. The water's awful hot" the woman said, as Julia reached towards the tap—and indeed, when she turned this on, the water gushed out in a cloud of steam. "The thermostat must be set too high" Julia thought to herself.

Luncheon provided more contrasts still. All the food was served on magnificent massive silver, which from lack of cleaning was as near as no matter black; the main dish, boiled chicken on rice, smothered in a thick bechamel sauce, was perfect, but the eggs en cocotte which preceded them were hard. "Oh dear, she always over-cooks the eggs" Gerald said gloomily, when Bridgie had left the room.

"They're awfully tricky to get just right" Julia said. "What do you cook on?"

"An Esse."

"Esses are very good. Do you have any trouble about getting the fuel?"

"Not if I remember to get it in before the snow comes! Otherwise the lorry can't get up the hill; one has to take a whole lorry-load at a time, from Galway."

The *crème brûlée* which ended the meal was so faultless that Julia was quite startled.

"Good Heavens, Gerald, but this is marvellous! Is your Bridgie chef-trained?"

"No, Helen came over and taught her to make this; she knows I love it. She came for three nights, and we had *six crèmes brûlées!*—and the last one was like this."

"I haven't eaten its equal outside Clare College, Cambridge" Julia stated roundly.

But the coffee, which they had in the drawing-room, was appalling. Julia wondered why Helen O'Hara had overlooked this essential, among her other efforts on Gerald's behalf, and made a mental note to send him an electric percolator as a present the moment she got near a shop.

"Now, would you like to see the rest of the house, or shall we look at the garden?" he asked.

"Oh, the garden!—the sun's so lovely."

They went out through glass doors at the far end of the long hall, on to a terrace with flower-beds set in the gravelled surface; from this, steps led down to a wrought-iron gate giving onto a walled garden—through it Julia caught a glimpse of neat plots of fruit-bushes, a strawberry-bed, and flower-borders just showing the early green of what would later be phloxes and lupins. But as they started down the steps they were intercepted by a tall grey-haired man.

"Mr. O'Brien, Sir, would you come to take a look at Belinda?"

"Oh, all right, Mac. Where is she?"

"In the haggard, Sir."

"Do you mind? It won't take a moment" Gerald said to Julia.

"No, I'd like to come." Julia rightly guessed that Belinda was a cow; she would like to see how the haggard at Rossbeg was kept, she thought, and followed Gerald up the steps, along the terrace, and out into a small farmyard where stone-built sheds, pig-styes, and hay-ricks stood in a pleasant confusion.

"Here she is, Sir, in the cow-stable."

In the sweet-smelling gloom of the shed stood a large brown-and-white cow; MacGarry, the herd, stooped down and pulled skilfully at her large udder—a few feeble drops dripped down onto the dung-stained straw.

"She only gave three pints this morning, and only four last night."

"How long is it since she calved?"

"Seventeen weeks, Mr. O'Brien."

Gerald also stooped and felt the udder carefully.

"No, she's not withholding it; she has no milk there" he said. He walked round and felt the animal's muzzle. "How old would she be now, Mac?"

"Well, we bought her for five, and it's four years now we had her."

"Nine. Well, say ten—she might be a bit more than five when she came. No, she shouldn't be failing yet—old Ellie was giving her two gallons when she was fifteen."

"Ah, that was a great cow! You'll not get many like her. Anyway, Sir, shouldn't we be getting another? Miss Collis is complaining she hasn't enough milk for butter."

"Yes, we'd better. When is the next fair? Oldport on Wednesday? Right, take her into that, and get a cow. Micky Tom Billy can get rid of her, and you buy the new one yourself." He walked away.

"Do you make your own butter, then?" Julia asked.

"Yes, Bridgie's a great hand at butter, especially since I got her an electric separator."

"Where is your dairy?"

"Oh, my dear girl, we don't have a dairy!—this isn't Rostrunk! The separator's in the scullery, and she makes it there; there's heaps of room."

Julia found these tidings rather encouraging. From the state of the sherry-tray and the silver dishes at lunch she had begun to wonder what degree of cleanliness would obtain in Bridgie's scullery, but if butter was made there, it would be clean; she remembered with a pang how delighted her husband had been with the Irish phrase, quoted to him by Lady Helen—"You can't fool butter." Boiling water and scrubbing-brushes invariably surrounded every phase of the sacred ritual of butter-making.

They went down to the garden which lay, in its high walls, "facing the sun," as Gerald had said; it was exquisitely trim and neat, with flourishing plots full of vegetables, and huge old-fashioned earthen-ware seakale-pots. "Oh, do you grow seakale? How lovely!" Julia said.

"Yes, masses of seakale, and tons of asparagus! We're just near enough to the coast to send the lorry for a load of rack when we need it, and seakale and asparagus both love rack."

"What is rack? Some sort of seaweed?"

"Yes, that common kind all over little bobbles that grows

everywhere right on the shore. Come on, there's nothing out here yet. Come and see the rest of the house." He started up towards it again; but as they reached the top of the steps he glanced at his watch. "It's later than I thought—I said I'd take you to tea with the Fitzgeralds at Kilmichan, so we'd better be making a start."

"Who are the Fitzgeralds?"

"Some sweet old neighbours up near the far end of the lake; I want you to see them—they're a type that's dying out fast."

They got into the car again, Julie taking a polite farewell of Bridgie, and once more out on the main road spun rapidly northwards, catching glimpses as they went of the pale-green expanse of Lough Balla on their right. A turning beyond the end of the lough led them to the village of Kilmichan; as they passed the small group of cottages Julia said—"Oh, there's a post-office! *Could* we stop? I forgot to get stamps anywhere this morning, and it will be shut at Oldport when we get back."

Gerald accordingly pulled up at the minute post-office, and went in with her.

"Well if it isn't Mr. O'Brien! You're heartily welcome!"

"It's nice to see you, Mrs. Spicer. How are you?"

"Great, thanks be to God."

"Mrs. Jamieson wants some stamps" Gerald said. When her needs had been supplied—"It's up to the House you'll be going?" the post-mistress said.

"Yes. How are they all?"

"Mr. Richard and the Mistress are great. Miss Oonagh is a bit weaker than usual. Did ye hear that Mr. Richard got us a van? Affie's bicycle was busht altogether, so Mr. Richard wrote up to Dublin and said he should have a van and not be riding about in the wet—and we have the van!"

"Splendid—I'm very glad" Gerald responded heartily.

"Ah, Mr. Richard's a grand man. 'Tis pity he'd ever die!" Mrs. Spicer said firmly, as they left.

"Who is Miss Oonagh? And why is she weak?" Julia asked as they got into the car.

"She's Norah Fitzgerald's sister, who lives with them; she's rather dotty, so I suppose 'weaker than usual' means that she's in one of her bad fits."

"Oh dear, how wretched for them" Julia said, with genuine sympathy.

"Oh, they don't mind—they take things as they come" Gerald said cheerfully, as he swung the car into another of the drive gateways that Julia was coming to think of as a special feature of the West. They went up a long drive, and into a wood of tall trees, dense and dark—"That wood on the right is bewitched; if you go in you may never find your way out" he said.

"What can you mean?"

"Fact. I went in once, just to try it, and I was utterly lost; spent hours trying to get out. Thank God the keeper happened to come along, and he brought me back onto the drive. 'Twas terrifying, I can tell you."

"How did the keeper know his way?"

"Ah, he had the dogs. Nothing will send him into the Big Wood without them."

Julia pondered this in silence, wondering what form of witchcraft it might be that affected human beings but not animals. But just as she was about to put a question about it the drive emerged from the wood and broadened into a vast gravelled space in front of a tall grey stone house, with curved steps leading up to the front door.

"Oh Gerald, what a lovely place!" she exclaimed.

"Isn't it? And but for Norah and her quick wits it would

be a heap of ruins now" he said, pulling up at the far side of the gravelled expanse. "Wait now while I tell you. D'you see that row of little windows right at the top, under the parapet?"

"Yes—attics, I suppose."

"I daresay. Anyhow in the troubles Richard was away, and there was only Norah and Oonagh in it, and the boys in the village got very drunk one night, and decided to come and burn the place down."

"But I thought the Fitzgeralds were so popular" Julia said in surprise.

"So they are—so they were then; 'twas just silliness, and the potheen in them, and hearing how many other houses were getting burnt. Anyhow old Barney, the gardener, heard their talk, and saw how tipsy they were getting, and he managed to slip up and warn Norah."

"And what did she do?" Julia asked, with eager interest.

"Opened all those little top windows, and put a maid at each one, holding a broomstick out of it—crouched down, so they wouldn't be seen; and she herself loaded Richard's gun and stood at that big window over the front door—she locked poor Oonagh away in a room at the back, so she wouldn't do anything silly. And when the boys came up the drive—they were carrying the trunk of a small tree they'd cut down, to ram in the front door—she roared at them— 'We're armed! See the guns at the windows! The very first one of you that sets a foot on the steps, we'll shoot him as dead as a maggot!'

"Well 'twas getting dusk, and the boys saw the broomsticks and took them for gun-barrels; she had the lamp on behind her on the landing, and they could see the light shining on the barrel of Richard's gun, no mistake about that!

And they came to their senses and turned round and went back the way they'd come."

"How splendid." Julia glowed. "But do you think they'd really have done anything to people they knew so well, and liked?"

"Sure they would! Look what they did to Moore Hall, the far side of the lake! There was no one in that, and they filled the ground floor with hay, and poured petrol on it, and burnt the whole place to ashes—furniture, portraits, silver, everything!"

"How ghastly!" She reflected. "But were the Moores perhaps not so well liked as your friends here?"

"NO!" He almost shouted the word. "No one in the world had done more than old Colonel Moore to get the people their rights, and the land, and decent conditions; 'twas with the Government and their own class that they were unpopular! No, it was what I say—just the drink in them, and a sort of emotional silliness, really hysteria. Our worst and our oldest enemy" Gerald said sadly. "Come on—let's go in."

3

JULIA FELT a lively curiosity to see the heroine of this remarkable episode. An elderly maid-servant opened the door, led them up a short flight of stairs, and ushered them into a large room which seemed crowded with people and with furniture, in which small glass-topped tables full of medals and curios predominated; through these a tall woman with auburn hair turning grey, and a worn handsome face, came forward to greet them with loud cries of pleasure—"Ah my dear Gerald, here you are at last!"

"My own self, Norah! And this is Mrs. Jamieson."

She was closely followed by a small man, clean-shaven, with neat features and a conspicuous neatness about his dress and his whole person, whose words of welcome made Julia guess him to be her host, the "Mr. Richard" whose immortality was so much desired by the Kilmichan post-mistress; the introductions, like the room, produced an effect of some confusion, with person after person pressing up to greet Gerald and to wring her warmly by the hand, often saying— "Never mind now who I am; you'll get us all sorted out later." At last Richard Fitzgerald took matters into his own hands, saying in his precise tones—"Norah, let Mrs. Jamieson sit down and give her a cup of tea"; as he spoke he took his new guest by the elbow and steered her to a chair next to a very little old lady dressed in black, saying "Mary, this is Mrs. Jamieson, who is staying with the O'Haras at Rostrunk; Mrs. Jamieson, let me present you to Lady Browne." This lucid formality Julia found rather soothing; she shook the old lady by the hand, rightly assuming her to be the late owner of the house which was now a sanatorium for T.B. patients, who had managed so badly. She cast about for a polite remark to open the conversation; one could hardly say "Where do you live now?" which was what she rather wanted to know. However the old lady spared her the trouble by asking most unexpectedly—"Do you want a fur coat? I've got a lovely one that my son-in-law gave me; it's mink!"

"I don't think I could afford a mink coat" Julia said, rather taken aback.

"Oh, I would sell it very reasonably. It's much too big for me; I'm sure it would do for you. Tommy—my son-in-law—bought it big so that it would go over other things; but the whole point of a fur coat is surely not to have to *wear* a lot of other things?"

"How right you are!" Julia agreed warmly, relieved to be on this safe generalisation. But her relief came too soon.

"Then will you come and see it one day? Quite soon? I want the money to get a new pony for my little cart. I have a cottage down near the Killaries." She fumbled in a large black handbag with an enormous silver clasp, and pulled out a black morocco card-case which actually contained that rarity in the modern world, visiting-cards, one of which she tendered to Julia—only to draw it back again. "Oh no— that's where I used to live; I'll scribble my new address on it." More fumbling produced a silver pencil, with which she scrawled rather than scribbled "Ponticum Cottage, Lough Sayle, County Galway."

"It was called Hawthorn Cottage, but there are no hawthorns, so that was silly" old Lady Browne pronounced briskly. "But it's smothered in ponticums, so I changed the name. The O'Haras know the way there; he comes to fish in the lough sometimes, and he always brings me a fish. Very proper, the General is!" said the old lady, with a sudden cackling laugh.

"Now Grannie, you know perfectly well that by good rights General O'Hara ought to bring the fish to *me*" said a very tall pale young man, who had come up to them, tea-cup in hand, and now positively loomed over the little table by which they sat. "The Lough is mine."

"Oh, perhaps legally—or more likely your father's" said the old lady sharply. "But what good would trout be to him out in Ceylon? And a young man like you can catch your fish yourself. No, what the General does is quite right. I'm sure you agree with me, Mrs. James," she said turning to Julia.

"I think General O'Hara has a great sense of propriety, as you said yourself just now" Julia said, wishing she could find some way of escaping from this uncomfortable companion. As before, her sharp-eyed host soon came to her rescue.

"Mary" he said, coming up and taking the old lady's cup, "come to the library with me; there's a friend of yours waiting there for you. You will excuse us, I hope?" he said to Julia.

"Oh yes, Richard" the old woman said, getting to her feet with surprising agility; a sparkling expression of delight spread over her wrinkled old face as she walked off beside him. The young man sat down in her chair, carefully adjusting his long legs to avoid the little table.

"Now he will give my Grandmother whisky, which will make her *quite* impossible" he said resignedly. "But then he will send her home with the chauffeur, so that will be all right; he knows I've got to go to the Young Farmers' Dinner in Oldport tonight. Was she trying to sell you the fur coat? It isn't mink, you know."

"She did mention it" Julia said; somehow the young man was not in the least an uncomfortable companion.

"I thought so. It doesn't belong to her either; my mother *lent* it to her the last time she was at home, because it was an unusually cold winter, and my grandmother kept the cottage so icy. She has very little sense of *meum and tuum,*" he added, with a cool grin. "Oh, I ought to have introduced my-self—the name is Terence White. Are you really Mrs. James?"

"No, Mrs. Jamieson" Julia said, laughing outright.

"I thought so. I mean, I thought your name wouldn't be what Grandmother said it was."

"Old people are apt to be forgetful" Julia said politely.

"Yes. Hers is a peculiarly selective form of forgetfulness; but she is also a little deaf—*not* wholly selectively!" he added.

"I hope she likes living in the cottage?"

"Oh yes—she insisted on it. I suggested she should come and live in a wing of Kinturk, but nothing would induce her to, although there is central heating that would have kept her warm for nothing. She said she wanted to live on her own land."

"Is the cottage on her own land, then? Much land?"

"Thousands of acres!" the young man said, laughing. "Lough Sayle is mine, as I reminded her; but a long stretch of the sea-coast belongs to her, unfortunately."

"Why unfortunately?" Julia had no hesitation in plumping out the question to this cheerful young man, who was so remarkably frank about the peculiarities of his relations. For the first time, however, he hesitated a little.

"Oh—well—foolish old ladies who have absolute control of a lot of property are liable to get into the hands of unscrupulous characters" he said. "And we have plenty of those about in these parts." He got up. "Let me get you another cup of tea."

"Oh, thank you" Julia said, rising too. "I think I will try to see a little more of my hostess." And she followed Master White over towards the table where Mrs. Fitzgerald presided over a massive silver tea-service on a vast silver tray.

"May I take a chair by you?" she asked.

"Oh yes, do—I've hardly seen you. Did Richard rescue you from old Mary?"

"Well, he came and took her away" Julia said, amused, studying the fine resolute face—yes, she could see Norah marshalling her maids with broomsticks at the attic windows, and loading her husband's gun to threaten the tipsy intruders. But why "as dead as a maggot?" Maggots always seemed so revoltingly alive. She must ask Gerald—and later, as they were driving back to Rostrunk, she did.

"Oh, it's just an old country saying. I don't know its origin —you're right, it's not as flatly accurate as most things country-people say. What did you make of the Fitzgs.?"

"I think he's an *absolute* charmer—and she looks a splendid person; I didn't get much talk with her. Couldn't we go again some time when they're alone?"

"Yes, we can and we will" he said, pleased at the suggestion. "I saw you talking to poor old Mary Browne."

"Yes—I thought she was rather pathetic."

"Goodness, *why?* It's the last word most people would use about her."

"Well, isn't she fairly dotty?" Julia asked. The man burst out laughing.

"No, only uninhibited—to a degree you find incredible!" he said. "She's really quite sharp, especially where cash is concerned."

"Her grandson didn't seem to think so" Julia said, a little defensively. "He spoke of her as a foolish old lady, who might easily fall a prey to unscrupulous people; he seemed quite worried about it."

"Oh, Terry White said that to you, did he? I wonder what's been going on?" he said, half to himself. "But rest assured Terence wasn't worrying in the least about his grannie's financial position, only about her lack of public spirit! —which is only another aspect of a lack of inhibitions," he said gaily to Julia. He looked at his watch; they had passed through Martinstown and were in the green undulating country on the approaches to Oldport. "Do you mind if we stop and have a drink in the town?" he asked. "We're in good time, and there's someone there I might learn a bit from over a drink."

"Josie, I suppose" Julia said easily. "Yes, let's. He'll know whatever there is to know, and quite a bit that there isn't."

Gerald looked at her, a little surprised.

"Oh, you know Josie Walshe, do you? I shouldn't have thought the O'Haras patronised him much."

"He produces Michael's supply of Guinness, and I go in there sometimes to pick it up. Helen leaves her messages there too. I think she quite enjoys him," Julia said easily. "Anyhow I do."

So they pulled up under the modest sign of "Walshe's Hotel" in the wide grey street, and went in. The small bar, as usual in the evening, was fairly full; Mr. Walshe greeted Julia with his usual warmth. "So you're back from Africa,

Miss Probyn! Well well—it's good to see you again. And bless my soul if it isn't Mr. O'Brien! It's an awful while I didn't see you."

"I've been abroad too, Josie," Gerald said, shaking the publican's hand, "having a holiday. And I'm wondering if I mightn't have stayed a bit too long" he added, in a lowered tone, leaning over the bar till his head was close to Josie's greying curly one.

"Come into the snug—Miss Probyn will want to be able to sit down" Mr. Walshe said loudly. "Mary Ellen!" he shouted, in a stentorian roar, as the others edged their way through the crowd of farmers with glasses of Guinness in their hands towards the far end of the bar; a door here opened in front of them, and Walshe's tiny sweet-faced wife appeared in it.

"Do you look after the bar a minyit; I want to give Miss Probyn a chair in the snug" the landlord said. "Miss Probyn, what will you take?"

"Oh, just a gin and vermouth, please Josie"—and "Same for me" Gerald added; Mrs. Walshe opened another door on the further side of a small dark passage, and they passed through into a little room with a table and several wooden chairs—the "snug," a great feature of Irish pubs. Its one window gave on the garden; a fire of turf and logs burned brightly in the grate. After a hurried "You're heartily welcome" to her new guests Mrs. Walshe hastened off to her duties in the bar.

"I never was in here before" Julia said, moving over and looking at the bare garden. "I wonder why they have sparrow-wire over the window?"

"I can tell you that—to keep the jackdaws out" Gerald said.

"*No!*—how extraordinary. Do you mean to say they'd come into the house?"

"Come through every chink, and make an appalling mess" —but just then Mr. Walshe entered carrying a small metal tray with three glasses of gin and vermouth. "Have a chair, Miss Probyn—and you too, Mr. O'Brien." Julia sat down at the table and took the offered glass. "Here's luck!" the host said, raising his.

This ritual over—"Well now, Josie, what news have you for me? Has our poet been very active lately?" O'Brien asked.

"Well he was, but 'twas little enough that came of it in the end."

"How was that?"

"He got after one or two back the Bay; Jimmy Kelly would have agreed right away, but there wasn't enough space on his holding. So he got Joe Carey and Peter Sweeny to come in too." Julia pricked up her ears at this. "Back the Bay," she knew, meant westwards down the long arm of the sea at the head of which Rostrunk stood; Kelly and Carey and Sweeny were all close neighbours of the O'Haras.

"So what happened?" O'Brien asked, offering Mr. Walshe a cigarette, and lighting one himself; Julia was already smoking.

"Lady got to know of it somehow—from Norah Sweeny it could be; she works up at the House odd times—and she told the General, and he roared them out of it."

Julia and Gerald both smiled at this description of General O'Hara's methods.

"I'm not in the least surprised; it was foolish ever to try that on" O'Brien said.

"Well that's the way it was. So now Billy's looking for some place else."

"You don't know where?"

"Well he does be tearing around a lot in that boat of his, but it goes so quick, he's gone before you'd see him."

"Well let me know if you hear any more, Josie."

"I will, Mr. O'Brien, Sir."

On their way on to Rostrunk, Julia asked Gerald what all this was about, and what O'Rahilly wanted "space" for on the Bay? He drew into a gateway and pulled up, and turned and looked at her.

"Do you know, I think you'd better not hear about it from me, since the O'Haras are now directly involved" he said. "Ask Lady Helen—she will tell you."

"How can I have heard enough to know anything to ask her?" Julie objected.

"Ah, how can you? Well, you'll have to say 'twas something you overheard being said about O'Rahilly in Josie's. You'll manage all right," the man said easily, starting his engine again.

In fact Julia didn't even have to ask. She left it for that evening, though she was seething with curiosity at all this mystery-making—for why on earth should what Terence White had said to her about old Lady Browne have prompted Gerald to stop in Oldport and pump Josie about O'Rahilly's activities? It was all most puzzling. But next morning, as she and Lady Helen were sitting in the drawing-room sewing and chatting, the well-known odious roar of the motor-boat came in through the open windows; to her surprise her hostess sprang to her feet, letting the sheet on which she was putting a patch fall to the floor, and hastened across to the big bow to look out. "Surely he can't be coming down here *again?*" she exclaimed.

He wasn't—when Julia joined her at the window they saw the white plume of the wave from the speed-boat flash across

the blue gap between the two headlands, and disappear towards the North.

"What is it, Helen?" Julia asked.

"Oh my dear, that revolting man! Do you know what he's
trying to do now?"

"No—tell me."

The story when it came fully justified her friend's anger,
Julia felt. Jimmy Kelly, through O'Rahilly, had been offered
an enormous sum for his "holding," a modest farm stretching along the sea-shore and extending perhaps a quarter of a
mile inland; it was wanted by developers, identity unknown,
to build a large hotel with a beach, a swimming-pool, a
restaurant, "and a discothèque!" Lady Helen said indignantly.
Julia began to gurgle with laughter.

"Goodness, how did Jimmy pronounce discothèque?" she
asked.

"It wasn't Jimmy, it was Norah—and it isn't funny!" her
hostess said, rather vexed; then she began to laugh herself.
"Well yes, it is, in a way—'Something in the order of a disgotax' was what Norah Sweeny said to me—'Would you
know what that might be, Lady?' " As usual Helen O'Hara
reproduced the local speech perfectly. "But you must agree
it's a horrible idea. Of course the tourist industry is madly
important, but we're getting plenty of tourists, and no one
wants the sort of tourist that that kind of set-up would attract, except these greedy dollar-snatchers in Dublin—even
the Government is against the idea."

"Oh, do you know that for certain? That's rather useful."

"Yes, Michael went up to Dublin and saw the Tourist
Board people—his namesake among others—and they don't
want it in the least. But it's rather difficult to stop—you see
it isn't exactly *illegal* to build an hotel, and they offer these
poor wretched people such a fantastic amount of money that

once it's been dangled before their eyes, the authorities would be rather unpopular if they snatched it away again by refusing planning permission. You wouldn't believe the sums that were mentioned to Carey and Kelly and the Sweenys by that wretched man. Of course he's acting for someone—Billy hasn't got a bean—well, except his house and that boat."

"How does it stand now?" Julia asked.

"Oh, Michael was able to stop it. You see he owns all the land between the Bay and the County Road, and he told Billy he would never let them have a foot of it to build an access road on—of course the lane would be impossible for that sort of traffic. And water—they could only get that from the Lough, and he owns that too, so he's in quite a strong position here. But we don't want that kind of development *anywhere* in the West. You do see that it's a horrible idea?"

Julia did—perhaps even more practically than Lady Helen. Since her return to Morocco on her Intelligence job she had seen the results of the handiwork of developers there: the flimsy villages of châlets and bungalows being run up on the beaches round hotels, dance-halls and casinos, and the effect on the local inhabitants of disproportionate wealth and un-dreamed-of indecorum being flaunted before their eyes—bikini-clad women coming to the doors of their *nualas*, the tent-like reed-built structures in which most of them lived, and asking to buy meat for their *dogs* from people who only ate it four times a year. There was demoralisation from high wages, too easily earned, for a short part of the year, and un-employment for the rest of it; there was understandable dis-affection and discontent; there was actual injury to the local morals. And that this situation might be reproduced here in Ireland was definitely a very unpleasant idea indeed.

"Yes, it's appalling" she said. "And I see that it's not too easy to prevent, for the reasons you've given—unless one could somehow get after the developers themselves, and make them see reason and lay off. You've no idea who Billy is acting for?"

"None. Michael asked him, of course, but he wouldn't say. Said he'd undertaken not to 'divulge' it," Lady Helen said with a contemptuous accent on the word 'divulge.' "And the people Michael saw in Dublin didn't know either—in fact they had no idea that this was going on till he told them about it."

"Of course if they applied for planning permission I suppose their identity would have to come out" Julia said thoughtfully.

"Yes, but then it might be too late."

Gerald had arranged to come and collect Julia on the day of the fair in Oldport when the cow Belinda was to be sold and a replacement bought—she had never been to a fair, and wanted to see one. "Well, wear gum-boots" he said.

"Why on earth, if it's fine?" she asked.

"You'll see!" he said, with his rather sardonic grin.

So on Wednesday he came and picked her up; it was a fine day, with alternate clouds and sun, but no rain—Gerald glanced at Julia's feet, and saluted her gum-boots with "Good girl!" Out in the lane, beyond the cattlestops which protected the O'Haras' premises from their neighbours' animals, he slowed down.

"Well, did Lady Helen tell you what Billy's after?" he asked, switching off the engine.

"Yes, she did indeed. It's a really wicked idea" Julia said energetically. She went on to recount the main facts as she had heard them—"In fact, you see, it was really Billy whom Michael 'roared out of it'! But Gerald, don't you think that the vital thing is to find out who *is* behind him, and get after them?"

"I don't see, at once, *how* you can do that, if he won't say" the man said.

"Well, I have an idea about that."

"What is it?"

"Well, if you, or anyone, has any sort of hold on Josie, and could force him to tell you the truth, I think he's quite likely to know. After all, he is in the hotel business himself.

"Oh, have more sense, darling! One can't really call Walshe's here in Newport being 'in the hotel business' in the way that Billy's developer associates must be."

"No, I know one can't; that isn't what I meant" Julia said calmly. "But I do call the Ailesbury Hotel in Dublin the hotel business, in anyone's terms—and Josie has had a half-share in that for a long time."

"Good Heavens!" the man exclaimed, thoroughly startled. "Are you sure? Who on earth told you that?"

"Josie himself; he volunteered it, quite casually, once when I was over here before—oh, a goodish time ago, now." Gerald began to laugh.

"Well, you're the one for getting people's secrets out of them, without really trying!" he said.

"Yes, but getting other people's secrets, not his own, out of Josie mightn't be so easy, especially if he was hoping for a cut at the cake himself" Julia said. "That's why I wondered if you had any sort of hold on him, or might know anyone who had."

"I don't fancy that would work" Gerald said at once. "Josie's much too sharp, and he could be nasty if anyone tried something of the sort on and failed. You're far more likely to twiddle it out of him yourself, and find out by your normal sleuthing tactics." He started the engine. "We'd better be getting on; Belinda and MacGarry should be there by now."

The small town of Oldport, when they drove into it, was an extraordinary sight. The wide main street was full of animals: mostly cattle, though a few horses were being led up and down. Gerald swung up a side-road towards the big church on the hill. "Oh, are we going to Confession or something?" Julia asked.

"No, but we might conceivably be able to park."

Others had had the same idea; the large gravelled space in front of the church was fairly full of cars, but Gerald managed to tuck his Minx into a handy space, and they got out and walked down into the hurly-burly of the town again. The whole place was swimming in manure, through which men in tweeds and oil-skins walked about, prodding animals knowledgeably, occasionally asking the price of one, and on hearing it walking contemptuously away; only to return later, and after prolonged argument a deal was occasionally concluded—this was invariably sealed by a drink at one of the pubs. " 'Twould hardly be legal else!" Gerald told Julia, with his mocking grin. The noise was deafening: cows mooing, beasts lowing, pigs squealing; this was the permanent background to occasional stentorian shouts of "Come back here, now!" from a vendor to a recalcitrant buyer. Gerald carefully examined a couple of heifers but made no offers— "I'm not buying today" he said carelessly. Presently they spotted MacGarry and Belinda in the distance, on the far side of the street; they crossed it where they were, and then strolled casually down to where poor Belinda stood, when master and man discussed an offer that MacGarry had received in low tones.

"Yes, well if he'll give you another twenty shillings, close with him" O'Brien said. "Now I want you to come up here and look at these two heifers—leave her with Martin. He'll be back in half-an-hour, tell anyone" O'Brien said to the boy, and they walked slowly up the dirty street again, till the two heifers could be pointed out to MacGarry. "You do the buying; you'll get one cheaper than I shall" Gerald said, thrusting a thick wad of folded notes into his herd's hand. " 'Tis the little yellow-and-white one I want—you can go to thirty-three for her."

"Thirty-three? That's a terrible price for one that didn't calve yet" the man said, looking worried.

"Ah, but she has a drop of Jersey blood in her; a little and not too much—did you notice the smoky look of her round the muzzle? And take another look at her, Mac. Do you remember that old yellow-and-white bull of McGrath's, that threw such wonderful milkers? I bet she has some of his blood in her; the marks on her quarters, the yellow and the white, are exactly the same as his were."

MacGarry screwed up his eyes and peered at the animal across the crowded street.

"So they are, begob! Well fancy Mr. O'Brien remembering that, after all this time! I'll do the best I can, Sir."

"Right. We'll come back presently and see how you got on. Don't go after her till we've left you a minute or two; but then, don't lose any time."

"Right you be, Sir."

Gerald and Julia walked on.

"Tired?" the man asked.

"Well, I wouldn't mind taking the weight off my feet for a little while" Julia admitted. "Could we go and have a drink somewhere?"

"The pubs will be fearfully crowded, and some of the clients a bit rough, if they've done several deals!" he said rather doubtfully. By now they were not far from Walshe's, and suddenly Julie spied the fair woman she had met on the train endeavouring to make her way through the crowd to go in.

"Oh, do let's go in to Josie's'—I don't mind a few rough clients!" she exclaimed. "I do want to see her again."

"See who?"

"That woman with the fair hair—oh, she's gone in. She was on the train when I came down."

"Who is she?"

"I don't know—but Josie will! Do let's, Gerald."

"Very well" he said, rather reluctantly, and they too made their way into Mr. Walshe's establishment. The bar was so crowded that this was by no means an easy task; they had literally to push their way over the threshold between men with glasses of drink in their hands, all talking very loudly —in no time a glass of Guinness had been spilt down the front of Julia's burberry. In a moment Josie appeared, making his way with the skill of an eel or a weasel between the crowd of bodies.

"Come into the snug now, Miss Probyn; Mrs. Martin's in it, but you'll be better in there. Tst! Tst!" he exclaimed disapprovingly, seeing the brown fluid still trickling down her —"Mary Ellen, give me over a cloth." His wife threw it to him, and he dabbed rather ineffectually at Julia's garment, and then made a way for them to the door at the far end of the room, and led them through it, with a firm "No you don't now, Peter John!—I have ladies in here," to a youth who tried to push his way into the passage.

In the snug the fair-haired woman was sitting at the table, looking rather gloomy, a glass of whisky in front of her; she rose at their entrance.

"Oh hullo" she said, to Julia. "How nice to meet up again." She held out her hand.

Mr. Walshe was still trying to wipe Julia down; she took the offered hand over his head.

"Hullo" she said. "Oh Josie, don't bother with my burberry; I'll take it off—it smells rather." She did so, and the landlord hung it up on a hook on the wall.

"Does Mistress Martin know Miss Probyn, then?" he asked.

"Yes, we travelled down from Dublin together."

"And this is Mr. O'Brien, Mistress Martin. Miss Probyn, what will I bring you?—and you, Mr. O'Brien?"

"Whiskey, please Josie," and "I'll have the same" Gerald said—Mr. Walshe bustled away. When he had gone—

"Not really Miss Probyn" Julia said, also seating herself; "Josie never can remember that I was married. Mrs. Jamieson now. My husband is dead" she added, out of a vague wish to clarify the position, which seemed fraught with possibilities of confusion.

"Well, a husband can do worse things than die on one," Mrs. Martin said crisply, startling her two hearers—on seeing their astonished faces—"Sorry I said that—forget it" she said. "It's just all that row outside, and the drinking, has upset me a little."

"Oldport pubs are always a bit of a rough-house on fair days" O'Brien said soothingly. "But you couldn't know that."

"No. All the same, I don't think Billy was being exactly a ball of fire to suggest this as a place for us to meet, and *today*" Mrs. Martin said, still a little crisply.

"Oh, are you waiting for Mr. O'Rahilly?" Julia asked, with a polite show of interest that was by no means feigned. "Perhaps he forgot it was fair-day; poets are supposed to be vague! Anyhow, I'm glad it has let us meet again. How are the children?" she asked then, still politely.

"Fine, thank you. They just love it on Achill; there's such a lot for them to do. Ray goes out with the fishermen—after basking sharks, sometimes; that thrills him to pieces. And Annette picks mussels off the rocks with the girls—if the tide's wrong for that, she goes and helps the old woman in the tweed and amethyst shop to sell her things to the tourists. It's just perfect for them."

"It does sound very nice indeed" Julia said. "I'm so glad."

"Yes. I love Ireland—I fell for it the very first time I was brought here, and I wanted them to like it too. Besides, I think it's right for children to get to know their own background, as early as possible—after all, they are partly Irish."

"As they're Martins, isn't the County Galway more their own background than Mayo?" Gerald observed.

"I don't think so—why should it be?" Mrs. Martin asked, looking puzzled.

"Oh, the Martins were one of the Twelve Tribes of Galway—haven't you heard about them?" He launched into an account of that curious piece of Irish history.

"That's very interesting," the fair woman said. "Well, I'll take them to see it all, some time. But I guess we'll go on staying on Achill—I don't think there's anywhere in Galway that has so much for them. And it's all Ireland, anyway."

Josie now appeared with the newcomers' drinks—"Sorry I was so long, Miss Probyn." Then he informed the fair woman that "her gentleman" was waiting for her in the bar.

"Oh God, do I have to go back into that ghastly racket?" she asked, almost desperately.

"Surely not" Gerald put in. "Can't Mrs. Martin go out by the side door, Josie?"

"The side door be's usually kept locked and bolted on fair-days, Mr. O'Brien."

"Fair enough, Josie—I see that. But just today I think it would be best to bring Mr. O'Rahilly in here and let them both out that way."

Mr. Walshe's obvious surprise that his new customers realised the identity of Mrs. Martin's "gentleman" made it clear to both Gerald and Julia that he had been displaying a landlord's tact in manoeuvring to keep O'Rahilly out of the snug; saying "I'll do that thing, Mr. O'Brien" he bustled out.

"O thank you" Mrs. Martin said to Gerald. She downed her whiskey and gathered up her bag and gloves. "I really *am* grateful" she said, shaking hands with him—and to Julia "Come and look me up on Achill, Mrs. Jamieson" she said. "I promise I'll not be so silly next time." She slipped out into the passage, and in a moment Julia and Gerald heard first a roar of voices as the door from the bar was opened, and then the sound of bolts being withdrawn and shot home again, as the other pair made their exit.

"Well, what do you make of that performance?" Julia asked, lighting another cigarette. "She wasn't a bit like that before."

"I deduce that the all-too-present and wholly unlamented Mr. Martin is a heavy drinker, and that she has suffered from this failing of his so much that the sight of Josie's bar today brought on a sharp attack of hysteria," Gerald said thoughtfully. "Poor soul. You must go and see her" he added after a moment.

"Oh, I will. But it's so extraordinary that anyone can be so utterly different at two different times," Julia said.

"People *are* different when they're in a state of hysteria," O'Brien said.

"I wonder if Josie knows anything about the husband?" Julia speculated.

"Well you won't get anything out of him today, about

that or anything else, he's far too busy." He looked at his watch. "We'd better be going ourselves—MacGarry will be wanting to start home." He unhooked her burberry and held it out to her. "Better put this on to protect your suit— we've no excuse for not facing the bar."

"Goodness no." She slid her arms in, buttoned the garment up to her chin, and put her bag inside it under her arm; then they made their way out through the thronged and noisy bar. In the street they walked down to where MacGarry was standing with the yellow-and-white heifer, this time with no concealment; there was no sign of the cow Belinda.

"Yes, he gave me another thirty bob" the man said, in answer to O'Brien's question. "That was a very decent price, Mr. O'Brien, Sir."

"It was indeed, Mac. And what did you have to give for this pretty little lady?"

MacGarry put his face close to Gerald's ear:

"Thirty-wan, Sir!" he hissed.

"Well done—you'll see, she'll be worth every penny of that! Well now, go in and get yourself a drink; Martin can start leading her home, and we'll take you in the car till you catch up with them. Walk her gently, now, Martin."

"I will that, Sir."

"We'll come with you across the bridge" O'Brien said. "You don't mind walking that far?" he asked, turning to Julia.

"Not a bit. She *is* a pretty thing, Gerald," she said, as the boy led the creature down the street.

"Yes. Now we must settle what to call her."

"Daffodil" said Julia promptly.

"Excellent! She'll soon turn into Daffy or Dilly, but what harm? They're both pretty names."

They escorted the boy and the heifer till well beyond the

town—"out of the way of temptation," as Gerald said; when they became one unit in a stream of animals being led or driven along the road towards their new homes; they went back and collected the car and MacGarry, and drove him out till they overhauled his two immature charges. Then Gerald took Julia back to Rostrunk. On the way—

"Well, now you've seen a Connaught Fair" he said, "what do you think of it?"

"It's given me a certain sympathy with Mrs. Martin" Julia said.

4

IN SPITE OF her professed sympathy with Mrs. Martin, Julia decided to postpone her visit to that lady till she had seen Josie Walshe again, and perhaps picked up a little more information about her background, and also, with any luck, about Billy O'Rahilly and his activities. Two days later General O'Hara's stout was pronounced to be running low, and Julia instantly volunteered to drive in and fetch it.

"Oh darling, *could* you?" Lady Helen said. "Then I could finish pricking out those primula seedlings." Helen O'Hara grudged every hour spent away from her beloved garden.

So Julia took the small car, and paid a visit to Walshe's Hotel; she was early enough to find the landlord alone in the bar, but not too early to have a drink with him—afterwards she went to the Post Office and rang up Gerald, and made an appointment to meet him in Martinstown the following day.

"No, no need to come all the way out to fetch me; I'll come in on the bus. Wait at the station; the bus goes there. No, I haven't got a lot for you—just some odds and ends."

As Gerald held open the door of his car for her in the station yard next morning—"Now, where do we go to talk?" Julia asked.

"The Mall, I thought."

"The Mall?" She looked surprised. "Where in the Mall?"

"In the car, under the trees" he said, as he got in beside her.

Martinstown shares with Perpignan in Southern France the curious and delightful feature of a river running straight through the town, spanned by several bridges, with a broad tree-shaded street on each side of it; in Martinstown these streets are of simple and modest, but rather elegant Georgian houses—the whole bears the title of The Mall. Sitting under the trees, looking down the broad vista of water, foliage and architecture, Julia exclaimed "How clever you are, Gerald! This is enchanting."

"Yes, I like The Mall myself. And no need to keep one's voice down. Now tell me your odds and ends."

"Well, the husband is an American, but of course of Irish extraction, and of course from the County Galway—Josie knew all about that, naturally. " 'His Grand-da kept a small shebeen' " Julia quoted.

"Does he drink?"

"Well I couldn't very well ask that, and Josie wasn't very forthcoming. 'Ah, he always does himself well, that one' was as far as he went, for what it may be worth. What had really impressed Josie was that Mr. Martin has become enormously rich."

"What in? Oil?"

"No, property. It seems he owns a whole string of hotels 'in those islands near America—what's this they call them? —some name like the Bananas.' I suppose Josie meant the Bahamas" Julia said.

"He certainly did!" Gerald said, startled. "Good gracious!"

"What's so exciting about that?" Julia asked.

"Simply that he must be the Martin part of Sherwood

Martin, that huge development company that's running up hotels and starting casinos and *plages* all over the world; but especially in the Bahamas." He thought for a moment or two. "It seems as though we don't need to look much further for who is behind O'Rahilly and his pestilential schemes" he said at length. "I wonder if she's in on the whole business."

"Oh, surely not! she apparently *hates* her husband" Julia objected.

"So she may—but with husband and boy-friend in on the same racket, it's stretching probability a bit to think that she can know *nothing* about it, wouldn't you say?"

"Oh dear" Julia said, on a big sigh. For some reason this possibility disconcerted her very much; it fitted so badly with her strong impression, formed on that long train journey, of the great *nice*-ness of the fair woman.

"I don't think I will go to see her in Achill, after all" she said.

"Oh, I think you ought to. She can't be in a very happy situation, on her own showing, and she obviously wants to make friends with you. She may be rather lonely."

"Ye-es. Perhaps that's why she took up with Billy in the first instance" Julia said. "All right—I will go."

Before doing so, however, Julia bethought her that she had better send a card announcing her arrival, and realised that she had no address for her new acquaintance. Normally now, in Britain, in such circumstances, one looks in the local telephone book; but Mrs. Martin's name didn't appear in the Achill section. So Julia used the grape-vine. She rang up the big shop at The Sound, the place where a bridge carries the road across the narrow strip of sea which makes Achill technically an island, and made some enquiries about tweeds, which she wanted to look at anyhow; then she enquired casually if they could give her a Mrs. Martin's address.

"Ah, she lives out in a little small house near the Amethyst Hotel" she was told.

"But how do I write to her?" Julia persisted.

"Mrs. Martin, Achill, will find her right enough. Sure everyone on Achill knows Mrs. Martin—she's a grand woman."

This Julia found interesting as well as useful; the Post Office was only a few doors from the shop, so she accepted the information as reliable, and sent off her card. A couple of days later, on her return from a walk, Lady Helen greeted her with—"A Mrs. Martin from Achill rang up, and said that Tuesday would be perfect—that was all she said. Who is Mrs. Martin?"

"Someone I met with Gerald at the Fair" Julia white-lied; if she mentioned the train, Helen was only too likely to remember her enquiries about the fair woman whom they had seen driving away from the station with Billy O'Rahilly. "I want to get some tweed for Edina, so I thought I could kill two birds with one stone. She invited me to look her up" she added.

"Oh well, if you're going to get tweed at the shop, ask if they've still got some of Mrs. Geraghty's; they had a lovely bit of hers in that beautiful plum-coloured dye she has the secret of" Lady Helen said. Most conveniently, her interest in the local tweeds deflected her attention from the subject of Mrs. Martin.

Of course when Tuesday came Julia was told to borrow the small car, and drove herself up the familiar road to Achill. She paused at the big shop at The Sound, which sells pretty well everything in the world as well as the tweeds for which it is renowned, secured a suit-length of Mrs. Geraghty's famous plum-coloured tweed, hand-spun, hand-dyed, and hand-woven, for Edina Reeder; there was another lovely one, golden-tawny, like dead bracken in the sun—she got a length of that for herself. Then she drove on across the island towards the Amethyst Hotel. The far, mountainous end of Achill is still wild and desolate; from the edge of the cliffs one can look down, sheer eleven hundred feet, to the sea tossing below, and watch the ravens rolling and playing, like children on a feather-bed, on the ascending air-currents—an astonishing sight. The low-lying part is where people live: Achill has three or four fair-sized hotels, some small groups of shops, and a spatter of houses between them; but it was all a *natural* growth, Julia reflected as she drove along, called into being by the needs and wishes of the local people —even the numerous guest-houses reflected the inhabitants' desire for more accommodation for the wealth-bringing tourists. No planners had laid out a scheme to develop the place —that was why everything was so charmingly haphazard; and though no one could call all the buildings beautiful, they were mostly in the local style, and nothing was arrogantly large, or modernistic in construction.

At the hotel the porter directed her at once to Mrs. Martin's "shack," which was what in Connaught is called a "country house," one of the local thatched white-washed one-storey dwellings, with a corrugated-iron addition at one end —to house the bathroom, Julia guessed; a tank on a metal water-tower, standing a little way behind the house, confirmed this surmise. The whole establishment lay up a small by-road, and a space before it had been levelled to permit cars to turn; in front stretched the great view of the Atlantic, with part of Clare Island showing as a blue hump away to the south.

Mrs. Martin came running out to meet her when she pulled up, and greeted her warmly as she led her indoors. Julia was curious to see how this stranger would have furnished this very Irish dwelling, but it had been done with considerable skill and a sense of fitness:—a plain deal table laid for lunch, and wooden chairs, in the middle of the room; a tall range of bookshelves and a press against the far wall, a long low hearth-stool in front of the turf fire; the only things at all out of keeping were those essentials to modern life, some comfortable arm-chairs ranged round the hearth, and a television set. Even the drinks, she noticed with approval, were not in that modern horror, a cocktail-cabinet, but were standing on another high narrow deal table between the windows. The fair woman asked what she would drink—when Julia opted for whiskey her hostess earned her further approval by asking—"Do you take ice with Irish? I always do, though it's supposed to be the wrong thing, I know."

"As a matter of fact, I do too, if I can get it" Julia answered smiling. Her hostess darted towards a door in the partition at the end of the room farthest from the hearth; Julia followed her.

"May I see?" she asked, and looked into a neat kitchen, with an electric cooker, a sink, cupboards full of crockery, and a large fridge, from which Mrs. Martin brought out a bowl of ice cubes. They arranged their drinks, and then settled down with them in the big chairs by the fire.

"I think it's so clever of you to have all the kitchen doings separate from the living-room" Julia said, leaning back in her chair and looking round her appreciatively, as she lit a cigarette.

"I'm so glad you like it. I wanted to keep this room as plain as possible—though one must have comfortable chairs! —so I had the partition put up, and concentrated all the kitchen doings, as you call them, in there; and I built on some bedrooms and a bathroom out behind. They're pretty ugly," Mrs. Martin said regretfully; "but it would have taken so long to get them built of stone, as I'd have liked, and I wanted to settle in as soon as I could."

"Is this your headquarters in Ireland?" Julia asked.

"Oh no, I have a flat in Dublin; this is more a place for the holidays" Mrs. Martin said. "Ray and Annette go to school in England—I think England is tops for schools!—but Ireland is perfect the rest of the time." She paused, and seemed to hesitate; then, with the air of one who has taken a resolution, she said—"Look, I feel I have to tell you this, after the other day. My husband and I don't get on—he drinks too much, for one thing. And—well, there's always some other woman around, and I just can't take that sort of thing quietly. We were forever having rows, and I felt that was so bad for the children—so we just came apart. If Paddy had wanted me to put up with the American way of life for the children, he should never have brought me to Ireland!" she said with sudden energy.

"Oh, he brought you, did he?" Julia asked.

"Yes, for our honeymoon, and once after that—and I *adored* it." She broke off. "Let me fill you up" she said, and took Julia's glass, and her own, over to the drinks table; Julia raised no objection—she did not want to interrupt this flow of confidences. They continued while Mrs. Martin was busying herself with their drinks; speaking over her shoulder, she told of the overwhelming impression made on her by the gentle tempo of life in Ireland, the sweetness and simplicity and piety of the people; so utterly different from the hurry and uncertainty and anxiety of the rat-race in and around New York.

"Oh, I know the Irish are apt to be a bit light-fingered, and don't worry too much about speaking the truth if they think you'd sooner hear something else, or that it would suit

[71]

their book better to say something entirely different" she said, returning with the two glasses and reseating herself; "but there is peace here, faith and peace, and they're the important things to live with. So that's why I settled to make our home here. Does that sound crazy to you?"

"No, not a bit" Julia replied readily. "I think it's very understandable." She was both startled and slightly disconcerted by this unexpected out-pouring—it told her a great deal that was highly interesting in itself, but not in the least what she had come to find out; above all she felt the urgent need to make an adequate response. "You may prove to have been wise" she said. "Tell me, does he ever come over?"

"Paddy? Oh mercy, I hope he never takes that idea into his head!" Mrs. Martin said energetically.

"Do the children miss him at all?" Julia ventured.

"I don't think so. They were quite little when we came away, only three and five—and anyway, he never bothered with them." She paused, and looked earnestly at Julia. "Why? Do you think they might? I don't think they were all that fond of him; really they hardly knew him, you could say."

"I just feel it's more difficult for a woman to bring children up by herself" Julia said, thinking of her own problem, and how acute it was for her at the moment.

"Could you explain just why?"

"Oh, because then the masculine thing is lacking in their home life—it's something quite different from the feminine thing, and it's normal for children to have both" Julia said. "But I may be quite wrong about that" she added hastily.

"I think rows and quarrels in their home life, and seeing their father drunk half the time, are much worse" Mrs. Martin said firmly. "Anyway" she went on more hesitantly, "can't one bring in some of the masculine thing, as you call it, from outside? I mean, one generally has a man around quite a lot of the time."

Julia almost laughed, remembering the two men at the two railway-stations. "Yes, I suppose one does" she said smiling.

They had lunch; good to the point of extravagance, but labour-saving to the last degree—caviare out of the fridge, a raised game pie, which actually came piping hot out of the oven, but which Julia instantly recognized as having originated at Fortnums; ice-cream again from the fridge, and baked peaches from the oven, but both from the same source as the game pie—all her hostess had had to do was to dress the salad and cut the brown bread and butter for the caviare, Julia realised. Oh well, very nice if one could afford it, she thought a little uncharitably. She asked if Mrs. Martin had any help?

"Oh yes, old Mrs. O'Brien comes in and cleans, and does any wash-up we've left. She can't cook, except to do a roast, and make soda-bread; she makes lovely soda-bread. I do most of the cooking" Mrs. Martin said.

"Do you enjoy that? Some people love cooking" Julia said.

"I wouldn't say I love it, no; I don't mind it, only it takes up so much time, when one might be talking, or out in the air, or reading."

"How do you do for books here?" Julia asked; Lady Helen often moaned at the inadequacy of the library service in Mayo.

"Buy them—or borrow from Billy—Mr. O'Rahilly; he has stacks of books. Do you know him?"

"No, I've never met him—but then I'm not often here."

"He knows the O'Haras; but I don't think they see a lot

of him." Julia made no comment on this. "In fact, I have the idea that there's a sort of general anti-Billy feeling among a lot of the people around here" Mrs. Martin pursued. "That's a great mistake—he's so kind, and terribly clever. Even if his boat does have a pretty noisy engine, that's no reason for boycotting a nice kind person, who only wants to help people" she ended, almost indignantly. She got up. "Let's have coffee by the fire."

Julia picked up the coffee-tray, which stood ready at one end of the long table.

"Shall I put this on the hearth-stool?"

"Oh do—thank you." Mrs. Martin gathered up their plates and carried them out to the kitchen, from whence she returned with a metal coffee-pot; after filling their cups she set this down in the warm ashes on the hearth. But Julia in her turn had taken a resolution. It was senseless to miss such an opening as the fair woman had given her, just out of cowardice; and after lighting a cigarette she leaned forward and said—

"Mrs. Martin, do you *really* not know what the O'Haras, and a lot of other people, object to about Mr. O'Rahilly?"

"I know they dislike the row his boat makes."

"Yes, they do rather; but that isn't the main thing. It's this idea of his buying land along the coast for development—do you not know about that?"

"Well yes of course, vaguely—but what's wrong with that? It's to *help* the people: bring in more tourists, and more money, and give more employment. I don't see how anyone can object to that."

Julia sighed, almost in despair at such ignorance; she couldn't bring herself to believe it was perversity, in this pleasant person. She tried to explain how unsettling high wages for a short season, and unemployment the rest of the year, could be to the local population, and how such development would destroy the very character of the country-side, what the quiet and discerning visitors came to find and enjoy.

"I don't see why the season need be all that short—the swimming-pools will be heated anyway" Mrs. Martin objected.

"Yes, but the gales in winter!—the yacht-marina would have to pack up for seven months of the year. And the rain! —do you know that it rains 265 days out of the 365 in Mayo?"

"How do you know that?" Mrs. Martin asked sharply.

"Old Lord Oldport had a rain-gauge kept for over twenty years, and that was the steady average. You can't sit out and sun-bathe much in that sort of weather" Julia retorted vigorously. "And if people are only going to do indoor things, like in a discothèque or a casino, why plant it *here,* on this lovely unspoiled coast? Why not put it down in the suburbs of Dublin, which are spoiled anyway? No, I think it's all wrong, the whole idea."

Mrs. Martin shifted her ground.

"Then why wasn't there all this fuss about that German, who's doing a development scheme down a bit further south? He's put up a hotel and heaps of châlets, and no one seems to mind."

Julia pricked up her ears at this.

"Where is he doing it, do you know?" she asked.

"Somewhere beyond Galway—I didn't hear exactly. Oh, he's doing all sorts of things—he's started a tweed factory, and he's taken on the boatmen that go after crawfish on a regular basis, full-time, because he's built cement pens in the sea to keep the crawfish in alive, so he can sell them to the restaurateurs in France. I don't see why if this Weber is able to make packets of money, and no outcry, Billy shouldn't."

"I don't think there would be any outcry about the craw-fish industry," Julia said pacifically. "Nor about a tweed factory, so long as he doesn't try to pass the stuff off as hand-made. There's a mill, or whatever they call it, for machine-made tweeds up in Donegal; they make that soft fine stuff. But has this German started a casino? That's the sort of thing people think objectionable, here."

Mrs. Martin didn't know—or at least she didn't say; Julia steered the conversation into less uncomfortable channels, and presently took her leave. She had not learned much, and what she had learned was on the whole unsatisfactory.

As she reported to Gerald, when she went down to pay a second visit to Rossbeg at the week-end. This time Gerald took her straight to the house, and before lunch showed her all over it. It was more spacious than it looked from outside, with plenty of fair-sized rooms—Gerald showed her three, with a large bathroom adjoining them, which he had thought would do to accommodate Nannie Mack and The Peanut; two had the view over the lake.

"They're lovely" Julia said. "But where is the kitchen?"

"Do you want a separate kitchen for the nursery?" He sounded a little alarmed.

"No, no" Julia said laughing—"the house kitchen, I meant."

"Downstairs." Now he sounded puzzled.

"Yes, of course; but which side of the house?"

"The other side, next the haggard; that's nearer for carrying in the milk."

"Couldn't the nurseries be on that side? May we look?"

"Yes, but those rooms have no view," he said, leading the way towards them as he spoke. "Why do you want the nurseries over the kitchen? I assure you the whole house is quite warm, with the central heating."

Julia laughed again.

"It's not that. Oh Gerald darling, don't faint, but *the* key to peace in any household is a food-lift from the kitchen, or near it, to the nursery—no carrying trays upstairs, nor any fuss about nursery meals making crumbs and mess down." She told him about the food-lift at Glentoran, and what a boon it was—"It actually saves a whole extra domestic. And it need only be quite little—two or three shelves. In fact one shelf should be removable—then luggage can go up in it as well."

Gerald was somewhat reassured by this; they looked at spaces downstairs and rooms up, and eventually found three rooms upstairs perfectly situated—the lift could go up from a corner of that spacious scullery where the butter was made, and emerge into the largest of the three rooms, also in a corner.

"No trouble to anyone—perfect" Julia said happily.

"But it's got no view—only onto the haggard" Gerald said.

"Oh my dear man, children don't give tuppence for a view!—watching pigs and calves is much more fun. Let your guests enjoy the view! And these two rooms get a lot of sun."

Downstairs, over sherry, she told him about Mrs. Martin: how much she appeared to know about O'Rahilly's development plans, and how impermeable she seemed to the local objections, as put forward by her, Julia. "So you see it's no good trying to use *her* as a lever to stop Billy; and if the money behind him *is* her husband's, that's no good either, because she wants above all to avoid him—they're at daggers drawn. We seem to be properly stuck" Julia ended gloomily.

"Yes, it doesn't sound too good" Gerald agreed. "Tell me again *where* she said O'Rahilly was going to start next. I'm not clear on that."

"Because *she* wasn't clear. I don't know if her vagueness was deliberate or not, but all she said was something about 'beyond Galway.' No, that's wrong—that was the Hun who's already got a bit of development going. She branched off onto how unfair it was that he should be allowed to get away with it and not her precious Billy. She said there'd been no fuss about him, and his hotel and châlets."

"If she means Weber, that's all *she* knows! There was a lot of fuss."

"Weber is exactly whom she does mean—she mentioned his name. But Gerald, that's rather interesting in one way. It looks as though she really does know very little indeed."

"I don't see that that helps much, except to clear her character! She's obviously determined to support her precious Billy, as you call him, through thick and thin. I'd rather like to talk to Terence about this."

"Terence? Oh, you mean old Lady Browne's grandson. Why? I mean why not, of course!—but *why*, actually?"

"I'd like him to hear what you've told me, and learn anything more he may have sniffed out in the meantime."

"How horrid that sounds" Julia said.

"What?"

"Sniffed out. Still, I suppose that's exactly what I was doing."

"Terry sniffs much more vigorously than you did!" he said, patting her shoulder. "And you were perfectly open with her, I gather, about where you stood. So I don't think you need distress yourself." He got up, with a glance at his watch.

"I'll go and ring him up at once—I might just catch him before he leaves the office."

"That's all right" Gerald said, returning to the room a minute or two later. "He's coming over as soon as he's had a bite to eat. I just caught him, practically on the doorstep. Now come and have lunch."

Over the meal—"Where does Mr. White work?" Julia asked.

"In Martinstown, in a lawyer's office—like mine! I've sometimes thought I should try to tempt him to come into partnership. He'd be a great asset."

"In what way?" Julia asked.

"Oh, he's very bright, and he's a taking fellow; and he knows everyone here in the West. And he's young and active —he could take a lot off me, as time goes on."

Julia agreed that this might be a good idea, and when Terence arrived watched him with rather more attention than she had given when they met before. He came while they were still sitting over their dreary coffee; she had failed to find a percolator in Martinstown, and the one she had ordered from Dublin had not yet come. Bridgie had been told to bring a third cup, but "No, no coffee, thanks" Terence said—so wisely, Julia thought.

"Brandy?" Gerald asked.

"Oh yes, please."

Gerald went across the hall to the dining-room and returned with a bottle of brandy and, to Julia's infinite relief, three glasses. "Some for you?" he asked her.

"Yes, rather." She put her cup back on the tray.

"Well, sup some of that, and then tell Terence about Mrs. Martin."

The brandy was as good as the sherry had been; Julia enjoyed it, and presently rehearsed to White an abbreviated version of what she had already told Gerald, emphasising the fair woman's curious failure to understand the local point of view. At one point she mentioned Mrs. Martin's having said that one reason why the season need not be so short was that the swimming-pools would be heated.

"Goodness, you never told me she said that!" O'Brien exclaimed.

"Didn't I? Well she did. Is it important?"

"Only if Mrs. Martin knows that much detail, she must be pretty deeply in it, I'd say. What do you think?" he asked Terence.

"Up to her neck" White replied.

"Then why is she so vague about where Billy will try for a site next?" Julia asked.

"Because she didn't want you to know—or he didn't; it comes to the same thing! But that's no harm, because I've got a very fair idea myself of where he's after."

"And where is that, Terry?" Gerald asked.

"D'you know that tiny little stone-built quay and harbour at Lettersall?" O'Brien nodded. "Well, the fishermen there—there's six or seven boats fish out of that harbour—have seen (and heard!) a lot of Master Billy's boat lately, cruising up and down beyond Lettersall, right out to the headland. What's more they tell me they've even spotted him taking soundings, and going ashore and making measurements, both on the mainland and on those islands. D'you know the place I mean, Gerald?"

"I do indeed. You mean those two or three long bays of pure white sand; and the islands just opposite them have sandy beaches as well."

"That's the spot. There's a perfectly decent road, too, down to Lettersall, and actually it continues along the coast and then turns inland to join the road from Lough Sayle that goes down towards Galway. It's one of the most exquisite stretches of country in the whole of the West; on the other hand it's got practically everything that Billy wants, damn him!—easy access, sheltered water, marvellous beaches, glorious views."

"Yes, I can see that for his loathsome purposes it's ideal" Gerald said, thoughtfully. "All that strip of coast is on your grandmother's land, isn't it?"

"Unfortunately, it is."

"Did he approach her yet, do you know?"

"He'd hardly dare!—not in person. She'd set the dogs on him if she saw him coming up the path to the door!—if it was more than the two old pugs she had in it" Terence said, laughing.

"Why would she do that? Is she against his development scheme, then?" Julia asked hopefully.

"No, 'tis Billy she's against! She thinks he's an immoral character, and a bad influence."

"*Is* he an immoral character?" Julia asked, thinking of the fair woman's encomiums—"Kind, good, clever; always wanting to help people."

"*I* wouldn't know!" Terence White said. "And I'm certain Grandmother doesn't!—doesn't know definitely of anything that you or I would call immoral, anyhow. He writes poetry, with a leftish tinge, and spends a lot of time with the lefty crowd in Dublin; she's heard that much, and that's enough for her."

"If he were to put this scheme through she'd be right about his being a bad influence" Gerald observed.

"True for you! And he may lead the girls round Rostrunk astray, for anything I know. But I *don't* know, and nor does she."

"But if he can't approach her himself, how will he set about trying to buy her land?" Julia very reasonably asked.

"Ah, that's the 64,000-dollar question, Mrs. Jamieson! He'll have to use a go-between, but who will it be?"

"Her lawyers?" Julia suggested. Both the men laughed.

"Gerald here is her lawyer!" Terence said. "But I don't think she'd use him over this—I think she'd just take cash in notes and bank it. She's very secretive, is Grandmother."

"But will Mr. O'Rahilly, or his go-between—whoever that may turn out to be—hand over the cash before they know that they can get planning permission for the hotel and casino and what-have-you?" Julia objected. "One would hardly have thought that likely."

"Ah, there seem to be two 64,000-dollar questions in this business!" Terence said, laughing again. "In fact it bristles with them!"

"In view of what we know of who is probably behind Billy, money-wise, I should say it was most *un*likely" Gerald remarked.

"What *do* you know of 'Mr. X.'?" Terence asked, suddenly looking very alert.

"Ah, we didn't tell you that yet. According to Josie the husband of Julia's pretty friend, Mrs. Martin, is the Martin half of Sherwood Martin."

Terence White gave a long whistle.

"Good grief! No, *he'd* certainly never put up a single cent without being sure of the next five moves ahead! Do you suppose he's sent her over to supervise the deal?"

"No, that I'm sure he hasn't. They're separated—at least seven years ago" Julia stated roundly.

"How can you be so positive 'twas that long ago, Julia?" Gerald asked.

"By the children's ages—they must be at least ten and

twelve now, and she said they were only three and five when she came away."

"You seem to have got onto rather confidential terms with the lady" White remarked.

"In a way, yes" Julia answered, in rather a chilly tone. "But that is hardly relevant, is it?" she added repressively. "The important thing, surely, is to find out who is Mr. Martin's agent over here, besides Billy—if he has one."

"Wait now—I believe I have an idea," Terence said. "One day in the bar at Gresham's I overheard Peter Moran talking to a man I didn't know about 'a deal in the West,' and he mentioned the name Martin. *Yes!*—I'm sure he said something like 'You know you can rely on Martin.' Peter's very much tied up in deals and gambles of all kinds to do with property."

"I thought he was an architect" said Gerald.

"So he is—quite a good one, I believe—anyhow he belongs to that large firm of architects, half of whom are Morans. So he has all the technical qualifications for assessing what state a house is in, and what it's worth. But I'd say he spends far less time at the drawing-board, actually designing houses, than he does going round vetting properties, and in club and bars fixing up deals. Surely you know him, Gerald?—tall and dark, and quite unhealthily handsome?"

"Generally wearing a Charvet tie?" O'Brien asked, his sardonic grin appearing again.

"I should think so—he's always dressed up to the nines!"

Julia's thoughts, at this description, flew to the man she had watched seeing the fair woman off at Westland Row; it fitted him uncannily. Oh dear! But Terence was going on.

"Anyhow he'd be the ideal person for Martin to use, if he wanted to start a development racket over here. He often goes to the States, too."

"Do you think he would be the actual person who'd hand over the cash?" Gerald asked.

"He might, very well. Let Billy do the preliminary scouting round, and he be in charge of the business side. He'd probably be able to get some sort of assurance in advance from the planning permission people, too." He turned to Julia. "Don't you think you'd better go over and call on my grandmother and look at the famous fur coat? You might learn a bit about what goes on, so. You didn't go yet, did you?"

"No." If Julia had spoken what was in her mind she would have added "And I don't want to"—she was increasingly reluctant to become any more involved in uncovering O'Rahilly's activities, since they seemed to show the fair woman, whom she had so much liked, in an unfavourable light. But the flat monosyllable, to Gerald, showed her reluctance clearly enough.

"We do need to know, Julia, you know" he said.

"What I don't understand is what you can do if you *do* know" Julia objected, "unless Mr. White can think of some way of persuading his grandmother not to sell, which I gather is unlikely. We have no access to Mr. Martin, and no hold over him—nothing to persuade *him* with; and if this Moran person can really fix the planning permission people —with a quid pro quo in some shape or form, I suppose— there goes our last hope of stopping it. After all, Weber wasn't stopped."

"What do you know about Weber?" Terence White looked surprised. "And how did you hear of him?"

"Mrs. Martin just mentioned his name as someone who had done a bit of developing on the lines of what Billy wants to do, and had got away with it—only Gerald says he didn't really" Julia added, not very coherently.

"Well, he was stopped from putting up his ghastly casino; there was such a stink locally that his factory and hotel and his châlet village were all he did get planning permission for," Terence said, in a satisfied tone.

"Not his crawfish pens?" Julia asked.

"Oh, nobody minded them—they don't show, and in fact they're quite a help to the fishermen" Terence said. "He got permission for them all right. But he's an awkward customer; he'd be as sick as mud if he thought anyone else—such as Billy—was being allowed to do more than he had been. He'd lay him a stymie if he could."

"But how could he?" Julia was puzzled.

"Oh, in a dozen ways. Anyhow, will you go and look at Grandmother's—or rather, my mamma's—un-mink coat?"

"Oh, very well" said Julia resignedly.

5

AFTER TERENCE WHITE had left—he was going to play golf on Lord Oldport's course in the Park at Martinstown—Gerald said, "Now, darling, is there anything else you want to see, while you're here?"

Julia hesitated.

"Well, there might be, but I don't know if it exists" she said slowly.

"Dearest, what can you mean? Do explain."

"Well haven't you any *young* neighbours?" she asked, rather explosively. "All those people at the Fitzgeralds were about a thousand!—except Terence, and he's not married. Aren't there any people with young children?"

"Oh, for The Peanut—yes, I see. Well there are the Peter Herlihys; they've got two or three."

"What sort of age?"

"Oh, quite young, they must be—Peter only married Sonia seven or eight years ago."

"And where do they live?"

"The other side of the Lough, near Beltraveen."

"Oh dear, that's not much good."

"It's only about twenty minutes in the launch," Gerald said, a little dashed.

"Yes, but I don't suppose Nannie Mack can navigate the launch!—it would mean you, or a man. Better than nothing, for now and again" she added hastily, seeing his clouded face. "But I meant within walking distance, to play with quite often."

"I don't think there's anyone nearer than Ballibrigan" he said. "There are several couples with young families there."

"Is that the little town we came through last time?"

"Yes, where my office is. But that's all of three miles. Darling, I *am* sorry."

"Aren't any of your men married?" Julia asked.

"MacGarry is."

"Any children?"

"Dozens!" Gerald said, grinning.

"And how far off does he live?"

"Right here—the cottage is just beyond the haggard. I built it for them when he got married, to have him close by; his old cottage was two miles away, and it was falling to pieces anyhow."

"Well there you are, then," Julia said cheerfully. "What sort of ages?"

"Everything from zero to the lower teens, I'd say—and a new one every year!"

"Perfect—then there are bound to be two or three to fit the Philipino."

"What will Nannie Mack say? Will she approve?"

"Oh my dear, Nannie Mack is Highland! Who was it who said that the Scots don't have 'the personage system'? Anyhow they were quite right, though personally I don't see any need to use such an elegant euphemism to camouflage an unpleasant thing like snobbery!" Julia said vigorously.

"Would you like to come and see them?" Gerald asked; he looked more cheerful.

"Adore to" Julia said, getting up.

"Oh, you'd better put on a mack; it's coming on to rain" he said.

The MacGarrys' cottage was, as Gerald had said, just beyond the haggard; a gate gave onto a flagged path leading to a whitewashed two-storey building with a slate roof—a patch of ground in front was planted with shallots and potatoes, practically the only things the Irish country-people, left to themselves, ever grow. Mrs. MacGarry, a pleasant-faced young woman in the middle thirties, opened the door to Gerald's knock, and with the easy unembarrassed courtesy of the Irish country-side led them through a narrow lobby into a large kitchen, which to Julia's eyes seemed to be quite full of a flock of children of all ages: a girl who might have been as much as eleven was skilfully jigging a baby to and fro in a pram to stop it crying, some quite small ones were seated at a table in the window eating bread and jam, and to Julia's astonishment and dismay drinking watery *tea* from tin mugs; others, rather older, were scuffling on the cement floor—they were all perfectly clean and neat, with well-washed well-brushed hair, Julia noticed; when summoned to be introduced the older ones shook hands politely—the smaller fled to their mother's skirts and hid their faces. Full as the kitchen was of children, there was very little else in it—another table at which Mrs. MacGarry was in the middle of making soda-bread, a small range, a single ancient arm-chair before the open hearth, on which a turf fire burned, and one or two more kitchen chairs more or less completed the furnishings; a shelf on the wall held a couple of saucepans, and on another, a tiny oil-lamp burned before the inevitable statue of the Infant Jesus of Prague, in its brightly coloured, stiff mediaeval dress. Julia, as bidden, sat down in the armchair; Mrs. MacGarry, wiping her floury hands on her apron, drew up another for Gerald and one for herself— "Nana, do you take the Baba into the hall" she said.

O'Brien enquired whether the new lot of anthracite was doing all right in the range?

"Oh yes, thank you, Mr. O'Brien—'twas a bit slow at first, but Mac put some more draught on her with the register, and we get lovely hot water now."

"Good. Every lot of anthracite has its own tricks" he explained to Julia—"we never get two lots exactly alike."

Julia asked how many of the children went to school.

"All down to Elisabeth"—Mrs. MacGarry indicated a singularly beautiful little girl who was one of the tea-drinkers. "Come and speak to the lady, Elisabeth."

The child scrambled down from her chair and came and held out a tiny hand. "How old is she?" Julia asked.

"She's four last month."

"Goodness, do they have to go as young as that?" Julia said, surprised.

"No, the others didn't go till they were five; but the school-mistress wanted to get the numbers up, that way she'd qualify for an assistant, so she asked if Elisabeth could go."

"How far is the school?" Julia put this question to Gerald.

"The better part of two miles" he said, his grin appearing again.

"Gracious! How does she get there?"

"She walks it" said Elisabeth's mother cheerfully.

"And how does she get back?"

"She walks it" said Mrs. MacGarry again.

"No nonsense about school buses here!" Gerald said, laughing at Julia's aghast expression. "They're just starting them in one or two very 'with-it' places, but not here, thank Goodness! We walk it, and 'in our feet' at that—that's the way we get our constitutions."

A small boy, one size bigger than Elisabeth, with very dark hair and eyes, and bright-red cheeks, now came up to Julia, pushing the little girl roughly aside—"Want to shake hands with the lady," he pronounced truculently.

"Don't be bold, Shamus" his mother rebuked him.

"Jealous is what he is" Gerald said, drawing Shamus towards him and giving him a light slap on the cheek. "Say 'sorry' to Elisabeth, and then p'raps the lady will shake hands with you" he said.

"Sorry, Elisabeth" the child said perfunctorily, and again advanced on Julia, with outstretched hand.

"How do you do, Shamus?" she said formally, taking his hand. "How old are you?"

"I'm five last Patrick's Day. I can spell," he announced. "Elisabeth can't spell."

"She will when she's your age" Julia said. "I have a little boy of five" she added.

"Can he spell?" Shamus asked.

"A little" Julia said, smiling; she was thinking that this tough little creature would be an admirable companion for small Philip.

"Be off out with you now, the lot of you" Mrs. MacGarry told the children. "It doesn't rain any more." And with a good deal of noise they obediently trooped out. When they had gone—"Shamus is much darker than any of the others" Julia observed to his Mother. The rest had fair or mouse-brown hair.

"He is, well—Shamus is the blackest, and the crossest" Mrs. MacGarry said resignedly.

"Can he really spell, Agnes?" O'Brien asked.

"Yes, he's very quick, the schoolmistress says." She smiled to herself. "He says such funny things sometimes" she said, rather shyly, to Julia. "The other day the mistress was preparing them for their clerical"—she stumbled a little over the word—"examination; when the priest comes to see do they know their Catechism. She asked Shamus—'How many persons in God?' 'Three' says he. 'Can you name them?' says she. 'I can' says Shamus—'The Father, the Mother, and the Gossoon.' (Mrs. MacGarry pronounced it 'gossen.')

Gerald burst out laughing. "That's great, Agnes!" he said. He turned to Julia. "The gossen is the little boy" he explained.

"How sweet" Julia said to the proud mother, who was still smiling, shyly, and blushing a little. "It's a charming idea of the Trinity—and such a natural one, for a child."

"I wonder what Father Macarthy said" Gerald speculated.

"Oh, the mistress'd never tell him that!" Mrs. MacGarry said, looking horrified. "She put Shamus right at once. But I thought it was funny."

"It was, very funny" Gerald said, getting up and patting her shoulder. "Don't worry—I won't tell the Father. Come on, Julia; it's time I was taking you back." They made their farewells and left.

"What a sweet family" Julia observed, as they walked back to the house. "They'd be ideal for the Philipino."

"I'm glad" he said.

"But Gerald, why in the world does that dear, nice Mrs. MacGarry let the children drink *tea?* Even that tiny little Elisabeth was drinking tea."

"What would she drink?" he asked, surprised.

"Milk, I should have thought. Surely all young children drink milk, or ought to?"

"But if the children all drank it, there wouldn't be enough for the butter" the man said, looking rather worried.

"Do you mean she *makes* their butter? Couldn't she buy it?" asked ignorant Julia.

"*Buy* butter? Here, on a farm? What would be the point of that?"

"To let the children drink milk, at least until they're ten" Julia stated roundly.

"Oh, you'd never get them to do that" Gerald O'Brien said. "They'd think you were mad to suggest it. Why do they want to drink milk, anyhow?"

"To stop them getting rickets. That little Shamus has got slightly bandy legs, and so have one or two of the others."

"Oh my dear, all children here have bandy-legs, or bow-legs." He began to laugh. "The old people say their legs straighten out when they get the whiskey into them" he said.

"*Can* that be true?"

"Well, you don't see many bow-legged or bandy-legged men about, do you?"

"No" Julia admitted. She began to laugh herself, a little reluctantly. "And if the men aren't, I don't suppose the women are, though one can't see. But it seems fantastic to think that whiskey can have anything to do with it."

"I don't suppose it has. But it's what they say. Something straightens their legs, anyhow, when they grow up."

On the Monday Julia paid her visit to old Lady Browne—"to get it over," as she said. She knew the way to Lough Sayle: through Martinstown, and on westward by the inland road; Ponticum Cottage was not marked on the map, but

Lady Helen showed her where it was, close to the road at the north-east end of the Lough. It was a fine sunny day—Mayo was having a wonderful spring that year, Julia reflected, as she drove down the broad, grassy valley towards the mountains; she drove into them, drove through them, and emerged into more open country again, where Lough Sayle lies in a wide shallow trough, with low wooded hills on one side, and beyond, across the water, quite high mountains, rounded and pale, though blue with distance; one of them sparkled like crystal in the sun, and Julia remembered that Lady Helen had told her that it was full of mica, and so bore the name of "Diamond Mountain"—that must be it. A handing-post at a turning to the right indicated the road to Lettersall; it appeared, as Terence had said, to have quite a good surface.

Just beyond this turn Julia had to slow down because the road was occupied by a flock of donkeys, ten or a dozen of them, in the fairly incompetent charge of two small boys armed with long willow-rods; a large white American car, coming fast in the opposite direction, startled the asses, which began galloping about wildly. Julia pulled up, fearing lest the frightened animals should damage the wings of Helen's car; she tried to see who was driving so recklessly past livestock on the road, but the driver, a woman, was wearing dark glasses and a head-scarf, and anyhow Julia was trying, by waving out of the car window, to shoo the creatures away from her own vehicle—she couldn't pay much attention. Eventually the donkeys calmed down, and she was able to pass them, and drove on to pay her visit.

She had decided not to give any notice of her coming, on this occasion. Ponticum Cottage stood off the road, on a little promontory in the lake; a short drive, with abundant clumps of the hideous plant which gave it its name on either side, led out to it. Owing to the ponticums Julia couldn't see if there would be room to turn the car, so she left it on the road, and walked down the drive. It was a windy day; all down the lough little waves, white-capped, sparkled in the sun. Close to the cottage the rhododendrons ceased, and there was, she saw, ample turning-space in front of the low one-storey building; a window in a room on the right was open, and Julia was just thinking what a lovely view it must have when there came a sudden gust of wind, and out of the window poured a shower of pieces of paper, some coming right to her feet. Julia stooped to pick them up; short-sighted as she was, it was only when she had them in her hand that she realised what they were—£5 notes! At least a couple of dozen £5 notes! As she ran to and fro, picking them up—the wind, circling in front of the building, blew them this way and that—the window was slammed down; a moment later the door opened, followed by a fresh volley of currency, and storm of oaths in colloquial French, of which *Merde!* was the mildest. Julia, rather out of breath, began to laugh, while she continued to pick up the fivers; the door was slammed to again—when she had collected all she could see she went up and rang the bell.

It was opened by old Lady Browne. "Have you got them all?" she asked at once.

"Yes, I think so" Julia replied.

"Well come in, before they start blowing again" the old lady said; as Julia stepped into the passage she slammed the door after her, saying "This pernicious wind!" She led Julia into a room on the right, which went the whole depth of the house; another window on far side gave onto the mountains beyond the lough. This was open and had obviously caused the through draught which sent the notes flying; Lady Browne closed it with an angry slam, waved Julia to a chair, and seated herself at the desk in front of the other window, on which lay several bundles of £5 notes with elastic bands round them. Julia noticed this detail with slight surprise. She was familiar, in films, with the sight of notes in banks or stolen from banks, and they were always held together by narrow paper bands.

"Now, how many have you got there?" the old lady asked.

"I'll count them" Julia said, and did so. "Forty-three" she pronounced.

Lady Browne meanwhile had begun counting some notes in a loose pile on the desk. "And I've got fifty-seven here" she said. "Does that make a hundred?"

"Yes, exactly—seven and three are ten, forty and fifty are ninety" Julia said, childishly doing the sum aloud, "And the odd ten makes a hundred." She handed over her forty-three notes, and now at last the old lady said "Thank you; thank you very much." Then, with a sharp glance—"Who are you, and why have you come here?" she asked.

"I'm Julia Jamieson, whom you met at tea at the Fitzgeralds; you said you had a fur coat to sell, and kindly invited me to come and look at it—so here I am" Julia replied readily. But she was doing another sum in her head. Each of the bundles of one-hundred five-pound notes represented £500; beside the one round which Lady Browne, with gnarled and knobby hands, was trying to put an elastic band there were five bundles lying on the desk—£3,000 pounds!

"Oh yes—the mink coat. Well I'm not sure that I'll bother to sell it now" Lady Browne said.

"You said you wanted to buy a new pony" Julia remarked —"with the money from the coat."

"Yes, I did; but you see I sold something else instead. Some land I didn't really want, to someone who does really want it."

"Oh, how nice for you" Julia said politely.

"Yes, and nice for her, too. She said she wanted it terribly. She's going to pay much more than this"—Lady Browne waved her hand at the bundles of notes—"this is just a deposit. But she wanted to get the document today," the old woman went on, garrulously.

Today! The word knocked on Julia's mind, recalling the woman with dark glasses in the white American car, who had driven so recklessly past the donkeys, coming up the road from Lough Sayle, really only a few minutes ago. She made a guess, and chanced it.

"Oh, is your buyer pretty Mrs. Martin, from Achill?" she asked.

"Yes—isn't she pretty?" Lady Browne said. Then she caught herself up. "That is—I'm not sure that her name *is* Martin. Why do you want to know?" she asked sharply.

"I don't!" Julia said, with a laugh. "Only I met Mrs. Martin on the road just now, as I was coming down; she's one of the few people round here who have money to spend on this scale"—and she in her turn waved her hand at the notes. "Is she a friend of yours?"

"No, not really. I found her very pleasant. I thought she would make a nice neighbour" the old woman said rather wistfully.

Julia was touched by this in spite of herself.

"Oh dear Lady Browne, did she tell you she was going to build a house, and come and live here on the land she's bought?"

"Buying, you mean—she hasn't bought it yet. I told you this is only a deposit" the old lady said brusquely. "No, she didn't say that in so many words. But what else does one buy a piece of land for?"

Julia hesitated. She was wondering whether to say what

she guessed, and believed, to be Mrs. Martin's object, and possibly thus discourage Lady Browne from completing the sale?—she would certainly be very reluctant to sell if she knew that O'Rahilly had anything to gain from the purchase! She decided to wait, and try to learn more first.

"No, I suppose that is the usual reason" she said. "I wonder why she wanted the document in such a hurry, though? Land doesn't run away!"

"I think she wanted to have something signed to raise the rest of the price on" Lady Browne said, looking rather crafty. "She had the description of the land, and the acreage, all typed out ready—and the price, of course—and my agreement to sell; and I just wrote in the receipt for the deposit, and signed at the foot of the paper."

"Did she give you a copy of that paper?" Julia asked.

"No—what do I want that for? I've got the money!" Lady Browne looked craftier than ever as she said this.

"I hope you've got a safe to put it in" Julia said earnestly, "till you can get it to the Bank."

"Oh, I've got a safe place to put it in" the old lady said, with a complacent little smirk. "Not a safe—burglars blow safes open! Somewhere much safer." She gave a little dry cackle of laughter.

"I'm just a bit surprised that you don't mind making a big sale like this without a lawyer to advise you" Julia ventured to say.

"Oh, lawyers! What good do they do? Generally try to stop one from doing anything at all, and charge a big fee for being troublesome!" She looked rather sharply at Julia. "You know Gerald O'Brien, don't you? I remember Richard Fitzgerald saying 'twas he who brought you to Kilmichan. Well, he's my lawyer. Did he tell you to come and see me?"

"No, he didn't." Julia was thankful to be able to say this

with truth, since in fact the suggestion had come from Terence White. "And I don't believe he would ever charge you a fee he hadn't fully earned," she added stoutly.

"Nor do I" Lady Browne said. "He's a most honest, generous creature—I'll grant you that. Far too generous to make much of a living as a lawyer! But he might have tried to stop me" she added pugnaciously. "Now don't you tell him! Promise me you won't."

"I promise you he shan't hear it from me" Julia said readily—it was a promise she could give fairly honestly, for she had already settled on her next move.

"Good woman! It would only worry him for nothing, and make him waste time and petrol coming over here."

Julia got up. "I must be going" she said. "I'm sorry not to see the coat, though."

"You've wasted time and petrol, eh?" the surprising old party said, cackling with laughter again.

"Oh no—the drive was lovely, and it was nice to see you" Julia replied politely. "I wish I could drive you in to the Bank, but it's too late today," she added, with a glance at her watch.

"Oh, don't worry about me. I shall be all right," the old lady said. "Come again one day."

"I will" Julia said. "But do put that money in your safe place at once, won't you?"

"Yes, I will. You're a kind girl" she said, as she opened the front door. "Goodbye."

That last remark of Lady Browne's caused Julia some compunction as she drove back to Martinstown, but not enough to deflect her from her intention of seeing Terence White as soon as possible. She parked her car in the Mall outside one of the little town's two hotels, went in and ordered tea, and then rang up Gerald at his office and asked the name of the lawyers' firm where Terence worked.

"Walshe and Walshe, in the Mall" he said. "Are you in Martinstown?"

"Yes—in the Mall, at the pub."

"Oh well, that's easy—they're on the opposite side, about the middle. How did you get on?"

"Oh, so-so. Be seeing you." She rang off, determined not to get involved in any questioning which might jeopardise her keeping of her promise to old Lady Browne. The porter, from the hotel steps, showed her Walshe & Walshe's office —"That light grey house is the one"—and Julia nipped across one of the pretty bridges, went up to the dignified grey house, rang the bell, and asked to see Mr. White. An elderly man, who looked more like a clerk than a servant, led her up to the first floor, opened a door, and said—"A lady to see you, Mr. White."

Rather to Julia's dismay, Terence rose from one of four desks in the room, and came over to where she stood at the door.

"Hullo—come in" he said.

"Could you possibly come out for a minute?" she asked. "My business is rather private," she added, for the benefit of the occupants of the other three desks.

"Raftery, is there anyone in the waiting-room?" Terence asked the elderly man.

"Only three or four, Sir."

"Oh, let's go outside—there are seats under the trees" Julia said, distressfully. "Won't that be all right?" She put on her doves' eyes, and turned them first on Terence, then on the elderly man.

"Raftery, tell Mr. George I've been called out for a minute" Terence said, and went downstairs and out into the street with Julia.

"Sorry if I've come at a bad time, but I thought you ought to hear this at once" Julia said. "Actually I've got tea waiting at the hotel, and I could do with it! What about you?"

"Oh yes, I'll come across—what's the odds?"

There were not many people in the hall of the hotel, and Julia caused a waiter to move her tea to a table in an alcove, and to bring another cup and more cakes.

"Now what goes on?" Terence asked, as she poured out.

"Well, she's got what she called the 'deposit,' a first in-stalment, in cash—used fivers."

"She has, has she? How much?"

"Three thousand pounds."

"Golly! Did she tell you that?"

"No, I counted it." Julia went on to describe her arrival at the cottage, and the bank-notes blowing about the drive-way. "And when she let me in—she more or less had to, as my hands were full of her money!—there were five other bundles of five-pound notes lying on her desk, with elastic bands round them."

"Have you any idea who brought them?"

"A pretty fair idea—I think it was Mrs. Martin."

"Why do you think that?" he asked, looking at her keenly.

"Well, (a), I met a woman driving a big white Yank car, coming up from the direction of Lough Sayle, just a few minutes before I got to the cottage, and though I couldn't see her face properly behind her dark glasses, it was the right *size* for Mrs. Martin—and (b), Lady Browne admitted it was her, though she tried to be evasive afterwards. *I* think she'd just got the money, and was counting it, and that's why the notes blew out of the window. It would all fit."

"Yes, it would" he said thoughtfully. After a pause—"Oh,

bother Grandmother!" he burst out. "What a worry she is! She oughtn't to be alone in the house with all that money."

"No, she oughtn't. It was too late to get her to the Bank in time, and she said she'd got somewhere 'safer than a safe' to keep it in."

"The anthracite stove, among the cold ashes, I expect!" Terence said impatiently.

"Is she quite alone in the house? Doesn't she have a maid of any sort?"

"Oh, an old trout comes in the day-time, but at night she's entirely alone."

"Ought you to say a word to the police, so they could keep an eye on her?"

"The Gardai? No, I don't think that would do much good. If a Guard was seen hanging about the place it would only make people curious."

"Well look, there's something else I didn't tell you yet" Julia said. "She said Mrs. Martin brought a document giving a description of the site, and the number of acres, and the full price, all typed out, and got her to sign it, and a receipt for the deposit. She said she thought Mrs. Martin wanted something signed, to raise the balance on."

"She could be right, at that. She's a cunning old devil!" Terence said. "Had she got a copy of it?"

"No—I asked her that, she said she didn't need one, as she'd got the money."

"*We* could have done with it!" he said rather sourly. "Does Gerald know about this?"

"No, I came straight to you—you're on my way back to Rostrunk. And that's another thing" Julia said, leaning earnestly towards him across the tea-table. "You must be the one to tell him all this, what I've just told you."

"Why must I?"

"Because I promised her—she really forced me to—that he shouldn't hear it from me."

Terence White burst out laughing. "You are a one! Knowing you could let him know through me?"

"Yes, by then I'd decided to tell you today."

"How did Gerald come into it at all?"

"Oh, I said I was surprised that she would make a big sale like this without a lawyer to advise her; and she said lawyers only took huge fees for trying to stop you doing anything you wanted to!—and then suddenly she remembered that it was Gerald who had taken me to the Fitzgeralds, and she got all suspicious, and asked if he had sent me to see her?"

"What on earth did you say to that one?" he asked.

"I said No. That was true too—it was you who suggested it."

The young man laughed again.

"If the Jesuits ran colleges for women, I'd say you'd been trained at one!" he said.

"Well, will you be sure to tell him at once? Promise?"

"Yes, I think I'd better run down this evening—better than telephoning."

"Do that thing. It is important; he started asking me how I'd got on when I telephoned to him."

"Of course he would. Why did you telephone him?"

"To ask where to find you. I'd no idea."

"No—I see." He thought for a moment or two. "Of course she, my Grandmother—or more likely the other party—will have to get the Land Commission's approval before any change of ownership can go through."

"What's the Land Commission?" Julia asked.

"Oh, it's a department that was set up some time ago in connection with the Government's policy of giving more of the country-people holdings of their own, with security of tenure, instead of being, as they had been before, 'tenants-at-will' of the big land-owners—a tenant-at-will could have his rent put up arbitrarily, or even be turned out. This is a great improvement."

"Yes, I can see that," Julia said.

"So they are apt to take an interest, to say the least, when a large, or largish, area of land changes hands. I expect the famous 'document' Grandmother signed was an agreement to sell at a certain price 'subject to planning permission.' You have to have one of those, because it's usually the purchaser, not the seller, who applies for planning permission from the County Council, and it's quite a job to get it: you have not only to furnish details of acreage and a map reference, but to submit plans and drawings, and to show where your water will come from and your sewage go to, and so on—and of course, once planning permission is obtained, it adds enormously to the value of the land. If you hadn't got that preliminary agreement, you might go to all the bother of getting the permission, and then the owner of the land could turn round and say 'Oh, I don't think I'll sell to you after all.' Grandmother would do that like a shot!" Terence said, giggling, "if she thought there was something to be gained by it." He paused, and again he looked rather keenly at Julia. "Did you say anything to her about thinking putting up a hotel and a casino at Lettersall a bad plan?"

"No, and, after what you've just told me, I don't believe she can have looked very carefully at this precious document" Julia said. "She thinks Mrs. Martin is going to go and live there herself."

"Gracious! Did she actually tell you that?"

"No, but she said she thought she would be a nice person to have for a neighbour. I did ask her then if Mrs. Martin had said she was going to build herself a house down there, and her answer was 'Not in so many words, but what else does one buy land for?' So I do really think she has no idea, and I thought you or Gerald would be a better person than me to enlighten her" Julia ended firmly.

"Maybe" White said, rather abstractedly.

"You asked me to find out what goes on, remember—and I have found out, and told you. But I can't conceive what your next move is going to be."

"Nor can I. I must talk to Gerald" the young man said gloomily. He got up. "I must get back to the office."

"Yes. Sorry to have dragged you out."

"Not a bit. You've done a good job, and I'm very grateful. So will Gerald be. Goodbye."

"Just one thing" Julia said, putting a detaining hand on his arm. "Will it matter my talking to the O'Haras about this?"

"Oh, you'd better ask Gerald that. Meantime, if you feel like burgling Mrs. Martin's house for that document, it would be very handy!"

"Hold on a moment" Julia said. "No, I must ask you this" —as Terence glanced rather overtly at his watch. "Surely to goodness you or Gerald must know someone on the County Council who could tell you what the planning permission is given *for,* and to whom it is given—if—when—it is given? Then you wouldn't need the document."

"That sort of thing is supposed to be deadly confidential" the young man said.

"Oh, don't tell me that neither of you has ever breached the local 'confidentiality,' as I believe they now call it" Julia said impatiently.

"No" he said, grinning, "I wouldn't tell you that. In fact I think this is quite an idea."

"I expect your chum Moran would probably be the one

to get it" Julia speculated. "Mrs. M. wouldn't know how to go about it."

"She might, at that. Well, thank you very much indeed" Terence said, wringing her hand warmly. "I must flash—and I'll see Gerald this evening."

"Do—as early as you can" Julia said. "Goodbye."

When he had gone Julia sat down and had another cake, reflecting that she had better delay her return to Rostrunk as long as possible, to be out of Gerald's reach on the telephone until such time as Terence had had the chance to tell him her news. She also decided that she would talk it over with the O'Haras, Gerald or no Gerald; they knew old Lady Browne pretty well, and might be in a better position than most to make clear to her what she was really doing to the district in selling the strip of Lettersall coast to developers. And again, she wished that Mrs. Martin wasn't mixed up in it.

6

WHEN JULIA TOLD the O'Haras that Lady Browne was proposing to sell the strip of coast beyond Lettersall to O'Rahilly's developer associates, General O'Hara was every bit as indignant as she could have wished.

"Mary Browne going to sell that strip? And the islands too? The wicked old bitch! Are you sure, Julia? How do you know?"

"She was counting the deposit when I got there." Julia repeated the story of the five-pound notes blowing out of the open window—Lady Helen burst out laughing. Her husband rounded on her.

"It's no laughing matter, Helen. If she were to put this thing through, she'd not only wreck that exquisite bit of coast, but her infernal hotel and casino would suck in all the young people from Lettersall and from miles around for six months of the year, and corrupt them utterly, and then leave them idle for the rest of the twelve-month. It'd be ruination. I don't know how you can laugh."

"I know, Michael darling. I wasn't laughing at what the silly old monster is proposing to *do,* but at the picture of her and Julia chasing all those run-away fivers. Forgive?"

"Oh, all right." Slightly mollified where his wife was concerned, the General turned his wrath in Julia's direction.

"Can't think why your pal O'Brien let her do anything so monstrous. He's her lawyer, isn't he?"

"He didn't know—she kept it from him purposely; she told me so. Her grandson suspected, because the Lettersall people had seen O'Rahilly in that noisy great boat of his taking soundings, and measurings on the shore, and told him."

"Oh, the White boy, you mean? Has he got the sense to be against this odious plan?"

"Utterly against it—just as Gerald is. It was Terence White suggested I should blow in on her and see if I could learn how far the thing had gone."

"That's a pretty good cheek on his part! Why should you do their dirty work for them?"

"Oh Michael, there's no pleasing you!" his wife said. "Why *shouldn't* she? And anyhow, it wasn't dirty work— Julia just stumbled on the silly old thing counting her deposit. It seems to me that what everyone ought to be doing *now* is trying to stop her—and that goes for you, too, you cross old man!" she ended firmly.

"I shall go down and see Mary first thing tomorrow" O'Hara pronounced, "and tell her what I think of her."

"Do that thing—and tell her what we shall *all* think of her, if she doesn't give up the whole wicked idea. I wonder if Richard Fitzgerald knows about it? He might have a go at her too—she's rather fond of him."

"Mass assault!" the General said. "Not a bad idea, Helen —not a bad idea at all. I'll have a word with the priest down there, too; he's a good chap. What's his name?—Donnelly."

"You mean Father O'Donnell. Yes, do see him, by all means, Michael. He'll be appalled."

"Would Lady Browne pay any attention to him?" Julia asked of Helen; she was rather surprised at this suggestion, coming from General O'Hara.

"Everyone pays attention to Father O'Donnell" Lady Helen said. "He's a saint, and a scholar, and the world's charmer—when he chooses; and an angel with a flaming sword towards the wrong-doer, whoever he is!"

"We'd better get to bed—must make an early start" O'Hara said. This conversation took place in the library after dinner. "Will you come along, Helen?"

"What's tomorrow, Wednesday? Oh dear, I can't. The MacNeas are having their Station on Thursday, and I promised to take up flowers for them, and arrange the room."

"Having the Station" is a great feature of rural life in the West of Ireland. In rotation, the priest goes and celebrates Mass in every house in the parish in turn; in a fair-sized parish this means once every six or seven years. It is a tremendous occasion—the whole of the inside of the house is freshly white-washed, the main room is cleared and a table arranged as an altar, with flowers, candles, and a pure linen cloth (as the Church ordains for use under the Blessed Sacrament). But the Irish are not, like the English or the Scotch, a race of natural gardeners, and the brightly blooming cottage plots, almost universal in Britain, are a rarity in the Irish country-side; so flowers present a difficulty. So do a pair of candlesticks—a single flat-bottomed carry-candle is all most country-houses boast; even a white linen cloth is not usually to be found. So Lady Helen was wont to be applied to on these occasions, and it was her habit to cut flowers from her own garden, arrange them in a pair of her own vases, and, together with a plain linen sideboard-cloth and two candlesticks, take all up in the car to the house where the Station was impending; two children were generally sent down to sit in the car, and carry the vases upright to their destination. If the household was exceptionally poor, she often hid a bottle of whiskey and some glasses under the linen cloth in her big rush basket, for after Mass is over a terrific feast of cakes, sandwiches, and tea is customary, and it is proper to offer "a drop of the right stuff" to the priest; the cakes, the ham, the tea and sugar may already have strained the slender resources of, say, a pair of old-age pensioners.

Helen O'Hara always attended the Stations herself, a thing which was much appreciated; for her part, she found them very moving occasions: —the roomful of people, young and old, kneeling on the earth or stone floor fingering their rosaries; opening their mouths, like a flock of young birds, as the priest moved carefully among them to give them the Host; the simplicity and informality of the surroundings somehow enhanced the spontaneous and unforced reverence of their attitudes and expressions.

So now—"But why don't you take Julia along?" Lady Helen said. She greatly preferred that her elderly husband should not make long expeditions in his car alone, especially when they involved interviews liable to raise the blood-pressure, or even bring on a stroke. "She can drive the Rover, can't you, Julia? It's always nice to have a relief driver."

"Drive any make" Julia said—her invariable, and truthful, response to such a question.

The following morning, accordingly, Julia and the General set off on their punitive expedition against Lady Browne. He had decided to go and take a fresh look at the actual strip of coast, so as to be completely accurate in his arguments—"If that wicked old creature could trip one up on anything, she'd be overjoyed! Besides, if any of the inland part was arable, it would strengthen our hand." So short of Lough Sayle they took the turning to the right, up over the hill and down beside another lake, till they came to the small village of Lettersall, which culminated in its minute stone-built harbour, really a dolls'-house of a harbour, Julia thought. They drove straight through, the General waving as he passed to some of the villagers, who waved back; from his frequent fishing-trips he was a well-known figure in the district.

Out beyond the village they drove more slowly; in fact Julia drove while the General studied their surroundings through a pair of field-glasses. The road for the most part ran close to the sea, but to O'Hara's disappointment inland, between it and the mountains, there were no farms, and little arable—the land was mostly rough sandy grazing, with a few cattle on it, and plenty of sheep.

"Pity, that" he said. "The Land Commission doesn't worry so much about sheep."

Julia on the other hand was struck by the beauty of the long sandy beaches, broken into bays, some large, some small, their silvery sand gleaming in the sun beside the clear blue-green water. "It must be a marvellous place to bathe" she said.

"But who wants to bathe?" the General asked irritably.

Prudently, Julia made no reply; in any case at that moment she had to put on the brakes rather sharply to avoid a party of sheep which suddenly decided to cross the road.

"Sorry," she said. "Wretched animals!" She accelerated again. The road stretched ahead of them, whitely following the curves of the shore; presently they saw in front a tall black figure, thin and stooping, walking along it.

"Slow down" the General said—"I believe that's the

priest. Better have a word with him, if so. What's this Helen said his name was?"

"Father O'Donnell," replied Julia, who was blessed with a fly-paper memory.

Father O'Donnell it proved to be, when they overhauled him; in response to O'Hara's hail he came over to the car and leaned on the door. He had a lined intelligent face under dark hair turning grey, and a peculiarly sweet expression.

"Going far, Father? Have a lift?" O'Hara said.

"Oh, thank you, General, but it's barely a mile before I turn off. I'll not bother you. How is Lady Helen?" He looked rather questioningly at Julia.

"Quite O.K., thanks. This is Mrs. Jamieson, who's staying with us" O'Hara said. "And she's just brought some shocking bad news. You'd better get in and hear it as we go along." He got out as he spoke and held open the door at the back of the car; when the priest had got in he followed him.

"Not bad news about any of your family, I trust?" Father O'Donnell asked.

"No, about your flock! Do you know what old Lady Browne has been and done? Sold this strip of coast to be a Lido, and hotel, and casino, and God knows what else!" the General said indignantly.

"I knew that she was being approached about it, of course. But is Mrs. Jamieson certain that she has actually decided to sell?" O'Donnell asked quietly.

"She was counting three thousand pounds in five-pound notes yesterday, and she told me that that was just the deposit, Father" Julia said over her shoulder.

"Did she now? I wonder did she tell you who was after giving her the money?" the priest asked.

"She didn't tell me, but I have an idea it was Mrs. Martin from Achill who had actually brought it" Julia said.

"And what gave you that idea?" the priest enquired, but with perfect courtesy.

Julia described her encounter with the woman in the dark glasses in the white car—"So I can't be absolutely positive it was her, and then. But finding Lady Browne counting the notes immediately afterwards gave me that impression." Julia went on to mention that the old lady had first admitted that it was Mrs. Martin, and what she had said later about her being a nice neighbour.

"How pathetic!" Father O'Donnell said. "She obviously doesn't know in the least what she is doing."

"Pathetic my foot!" O'Hara exclaimed angrily. "She's a rich, greedy old woman, who has all the money she needs already, and just wants more for money's sake! Anyhow *we* know exactly what she's doing, and I'm on my way to tell her so! O'Rahilly tried to buy out some of the people on our bay, remember, so we know what *his* plans are."

"If you got them in detail directly from him, I should be grateful if you would repeat them to me, General" the priest said. "Such things are apt to get exaggerated in rumours, and rumour is all I have heard. I failed to get speech of Mr. O'Rahilly myself."

"You *would!*" O'Hara replied with energy. "Trust him to steer clear of you! He had to speak to me about the water-supply for that scheme of his, so I was able to get a fair idea. He was going to put up an hotel, with a restaurant attached, but open to non-residents, and a dance-hall ditto; and a casino for gambling; and he wanted to build a mole out into the bay to make an anchorage for yachts, where people could hire boats—what's this they call the things?"

"A marina?" the Father suggested.

"That's it. And there was to be a heated swimming-pool as well."

"You've forgotten the disgotax, General" Julia put in.

"The *what?*" Father O'Donnell not unnaturally asked.

"It was the local version for a discothèque" Julia explained. "One of the farmers' wives asked Lady Helen what a 'disgo-tax' might be?" The priest laughed.

"That item is innocent enough in itself" he said.

"Yes, Father, but it gives a sort of smell of the type of people Billy's hoping to attract" Julia said.

"I agree—and it's a bad smell. The casino is the worst, of course; but the whole thing rather reeks of idle pleasure-seeking in artificial surroundings; not in the least the same thing as healthful relaxation in beautiful scenery, which is what people used to come here for. The sort of person who would put up with the very modest degree of comfort afforded by the Lettersall Hotel was not normally a great menace to the innocence of my flock—let alone those who would take rooms in a farm!"

"Yes. And then look at the gross over-employment it would bring for half the year, tempting all the boys and girls off the farms, and almost total unemployment for the other half" the General said vigorously.

"Is that really definite? I wanted to ask about that," the Father said.

"O'Rahilly tried to beat me down over what he was to pay for his water, because he would only be using it at full blast for seven months of the year" O'Hara said drily. "And I hear that that Weber person down the coast shuts up his infernal outfit for a full six months."

Julia had been keeping an eye on the speedometer, and as they approached a lane leading off on the left she slowed down. "Would this be your turn, Father? It's just about a mile since we picked you up."

"Ah, it is. What an observant, practical young lady!" He

looked at his watch. "You wouldn't be coming back this same way, General? If so I should be rather inclined to come on with you, if you had no objection, and join my remonstrances to yours. It was only a sick call I had to pay: there's no great rush about it—it's a chronic case."

"Oh, I *wish* you would!" Julia exclaimed impulsively. "Couldn't we?" she said, leaning back and turning dove's eyes onto O'Hara.

"Don't see why not, if you can spare the time, Father." He too looked at his watch. "But we shall have to look sharp— it's a good bit longer round through Lettersall."

Julia trod on the accelerator, and they went on; she was careful however not to take the small by-road at a speed that would bounce the two men in the back—the great thing was to keep the General in a good temper. Her eagerness to have the priest's company for the coming interview was largely due to her fear that General O'Hara might use language that would provoke old Lady Browne, as stubborn as she was quick-tempered, to take up in argument a position from which she would find it impossible to retreat afterwards, however much later pleas might make her wish to do so— this, she already felt, was much less likely to happen in Father O'Donnell's presence. Once out on the main Galway road, however, with its good surface, she drove very fast indeed, and in a surprisingly short time they were turning in at the little lane that led down to the cottage.

The door was opened to them by an ancient domestic, whom the General greeted cheerfully with—"Hullo, Annie! I see you're keeping in great form. Is your Mistress in?"

"She is, well, General O'Hara, Sir. And how is yourself, and Lady?"

"Grand, grand! Well bring us in, Annie—we're a little short of time" O'Hara said impatiently.

"And his Reverence! Well isn't it great to see you!" Annie was not easily hurried. "And who's the young lady?"

At this point the door into the sitting-room was opened a crack.

"Now Annie, what's all this nattering and chattering? Who have you got there?" Lady Browne's voice asked sharply.

"May we come in, your Ladyship" Father O'Donnell asked, inserting his head into the crack.

"Of course, Father. Glad to see you." Now the old lady opened the door. "And Michael! Have you come to fish?"

"No, to read you the Riot Act, Mary" the General responded. "You know Mrs. Jamieson already, I think."

"Well come along in, all of you" Lady Browne said. "Annie, bring the sherry. Sit down—there's plenty of chairs. How d'ye do, Mrs. James. Now, Michael, what *are* you here for, if it's not fishing?"

"Lady Browne, may I begin?" the priest asked. "I've come to make an appeal to you on behalf of my flock?"

"Begging again! What does your flock need this time? They've got storage-heaters in the Church now, as well as the schools, haven't they?"

"They have indeed, and very grateful we are to you for them. When people get to Mass wet through after walking three miles, 'tis a great mercy not to have to sit in a cold damp church."

"Yes, yes—you've been telling me that all along!" the old lady said impatiently. "But what do they want now?"

"It's something they *don't* want this time, and that I greatly wish they may not have thrust upon them, that I am asking your help about" the Father said earnestly.

"Now you're talking in riddles! Speak out, man, and say what you mean!"

"He means he doesn't want you to sell that strip south of Lettersall, to be turned in a Pally de Danse and a gambling-hell!" the General broke in. "And nor do I, and nor would any decent person! It'd ruin the district. We've both come on the same errand, only we met the Father on the road, so we brought him along."

"Who says it's going to be turned into a gambling-hell?" the old lady asked—but she looked rather disconcerted.

"I do! And what's more I know it. That infernal chap O'Rahilly tried to buy land for the same scheme from some of my people, down the Bay, and of course had to come to me about the water, so I heard his plans in full detail. When I put a stop to him there he came on here."

"Mr. O'Rahilly! He's got nothing to do with it. I'd never sell a square foot to him!" the old lady protested vigorously, "as well you know, Michael."

"Ah, but that's just where you're wrong, Mary. He's behind the whole thing, and if you complete the deal he'll be living in Lettersall and running his hotel and casino and dance-hall. That'll be a nice neighbour for you!" O'Hara said bitterly.

"I don't believe a word of it" Lady Browne said. "He hasn't got the money, for one thing. You're just making this up to upset me." She did indeed look very upset, in spite of her stout words.

"Your Ladyship, Mr. O'Rahilly has spent a lot of time near Lettersall lately" Father O'Donnell put in, "measuring and prospecting the land down to the South—I've seen him there myself, several times. He would hardly do that unless he had some definite plan in mind."

"But the person who paid the deposit has nothing to do with Mr. O'Rahilly—it was someone quite different" the old lady said.

"Oh dear Lady Browne, she has, you know" Julia put in. "They see a lot of one another, and Mrs. Martin herself told me all about this development scheme. She didn't actually say that she was backing him, but she knew that he was going to heat his swimming-pools."

The General rounded sharply on Julia. "You never told us *that* Miss! When did she tell you that?"

"That time I went to see her in Achill."

"You ought to have told us at once" the General said, indignantly.

Julia was silent. But now she was assailed with equal vigour from another quarter.

"Oh, so it was Mrs. James who told you that I was selling my land! That's why you've come over to scold me, Michael." She turned to Julia. "I thought you'd come to spy on me yesterday, only I fancied it was Gerald O'Brien sent you. I never believed that nonsense about wanting to buy my fur coat!"

"Dear Lady Browne, I couldn't help it that I happened to come just when your deposit money was blowing all over the drive!" Julia protested. "Would you rather I hadn't picked it up, and let it blow into the Lough?"

"Don't you go dear Lady Browne-ing me! You're a bad, deceitful girl, pretending to want to take me to the Bank and all!—and then going and telling everyone about my affairs."

"Oh, so Helen and I are everyone now!" O'Hara broke out. "That's a nice thing to hear!" But the priest held up his hand with a gesture of such authority that the angry old soldier subsided.

"Lady Browne" Father O'Donnell said, speaking very gently, "if you think that what you are doing is perfectly right, why should you mind General O'Hara hearing about it?"

"Because one doesn't necessarily want one's private business discussed, even by one's friends" she said.

"No, I know that people have this curious shivering modesty, about their money-matters especially" the priest said with a smile of such amusement and sweetness combined that Julia was quite charmed. "It is almost as though they thought money was indecent! Perhaps it is—certainly some ways of making it are, like profiting out of prostitution."

"Are you suggesting that I would ever dream of doing anything like that?" the old lady asked angrily.

"No, I accept that you acted in ignorance and had no idea who the real purchaser was, nor what his plans were. But now that you *do* know, do you not realise that the end result, if you complete this deal, will come close to that very thing, under this scheme of Mr. O'Rahilly's? Who do you imagine will serve drinks in his casino and his dance-hall? Local girls, children whose souls are in my care! Do you seriously think that the kind of people who resort to that sort of place will not present any threat to their virtue, Lady Browne? You cannot know so little of the world as to believe that. And you will have made a profit on the sale of the land that made this possible! There isn't much difference."

"You can't do it, Mary!" the General said. "No one will ever want to speak to you again if you do."

"I won't be dictated to by you, or by anyone else, Michael!" the old lady said furiously. "What I do with my own property is *my* business, not yours. Or anyone else's, come to that!" she added, scowling at the priest. He smiled at her.

"I recognise your feelings, Lady Browne" he said quietly. "But you see you have been gravely misled as to the identity of the purchaser—through no fault of your own. You say yourself that you would not sell anything to Mr. O'Rahilly; nor, I imagine, to any associates of his."

"Certainly not."

"Quite so. But in these altered circumstances I am sure you see that you would do well to consider very carefully before completing this deal."

The poor old thing snatched at this.

"Yes, I must have time to think. You are quite right, Father," she said. "This has all been so sprung on me—first yesterday, and now today, with you all coming and harrying me!" she said rather plaintively.

"Indeed, I do see that it is all extremely trying for your Ladyship," Father O'Donnell said. "I wonder if you would mind my asking you one thing? It is not idle curiosity."

"Ask away—I shan't answer unless I choose!"

"Did you actually *sign* anything—any papers—when this person called yesterday to make the offer, bringing the money?"

"Yes, I signed the receipt for the deposit."

Julia felt she could not let this true, but very misleading, statement stand alone.

"Oh, but Lady Browne, surely you told me yesterday that there was a paper with details of the amount of land and so on, and that you signed that too?"

The old woman glared balefully at her. "What if I did?" she said. "What business is it of yours?"

"Well, *did* you, Mary?" O'Hara asked. "We want to know."

"If your Ladyship signed any sort of agreement to sell a definite piece of your property here, I am sure you realise that it is very *much* my business" the priest said quietly, "since there is a strong probability of its being used for a purpose highly injurious to the district and to my parishioners."

"Well, if I signed it, it's signed" Lady Browne said blusteringly.

"Oh no, not if your signature was obtained on false pretences" Father O'Donnell said—"and without legal advice."

"Come on, Mary—did you sign an agreement to sell or didn't you?" O'Hara asked. But it became clear, as they pressed her, that the poor old lady really didn't know *what* she had signed.

"Do you mean to say you signed something without reading it?" O'Hara eventually asked. "You must be mad!"

"I read the figures of the acreage, and saw a diagram showing where it was; I didn't read it all" Lady Browne said. "There was such masses of it."

"And you didn't get a copy?" he asked.

"No."

"Obviously, a signature obtained in such circumstances couldn't be held binding for a moment" the priest said.

"Oh, do you think not?" Lady Browne looked relieved.

"I should not have thought so. But I am sure you ought to get a lawyer's advice before you do anything else," Father O'Donnell said.

"I hate lawyers and their advice!" the old lady protested. "Couldn't you do it for me, Father? I could give you the money, and you could give it back to Mrs. Martin, and say I had changed my mind, and make her return that paper, and we could tear it up, and that would be the end of it."

"Oh don't be ridiculous, Mary! How can the Father do all that? He hasn't got a car, for one thing, to go chasing about in!"

"And I should very much doubt if Mrs. Martin still has the agreement about selling" Julia put in.

"Why should you say that?" Lady Browne asked angrily. "You've nothing to go on."

"I expect Mrs. Jamieson is right all the same. It's probably in O'Rahilly's hands by now" the General said.

"Or his chum Moran's" Julia added.

Lady Browne got up, a determined look on her harsh old face.

"Well, you all stay here. I won't be a minute!" She went out into the hall, shutting the door after her; a moment later they heard the sound of a key turning in a lock.

"Well I'm damned! I believe she's gone and locked us in!" the General said. The priest went and very softly tried the door-handle.

"Yes—but what does it matter?" he said, returning to his seat. "It will only be for a little while. The great thing is that she has decided to give up the sale, apparently."

"Apparently will probably turn out to be the operative word!" O'Hara said sarcastically. "She chops and changes from one minute to the next. She's really mad, you know!"

After a moment they heard the key turn in the lock again, and Lady Browne re-appeared carrying a bundle done up in newspaper; when she set it on the desk and began to undo it Julia noticed with amusement that a quantity of powdery white dust flew out—Terence White had obviously been right about the locality of the "safe place." However, ashy or not, out came the six bundles of five-pound notes—the two men stared at them in astonishment.

"Good Heavens!" the General exclaimed.

"You'd better count them" Lady Browne said, handing them to the priest—"but I'm sure there's a hundred in each; I counted them only yesterday."

"Then please let me have one packet at a time, your Ladyship," Father O'Donnell said; he drew his chair up to one end of the desk and began his task.

"Better look at them properly, to see if any are fakes" O'Hara suggested.

"Why should they be fakes?" the old lady asked indignantly.

"I couldn't possibly tell the difference, anyhow," the Father said and went quietly on with his counting. When he had finished he asked if he might borrow a sheet of writing-paper from the rack on the desk?—he wrote on it, and handed it to Lady Browne.

"What's this?" she asked, after putting on her spectacles and studying it.

"A receipt—I think from now on we had better have everything properly documented."

"But you haven't said £3,000!" She looked rather dissatisfied.

"Just keep it" the Father said gently. "Now, General, I really ought to be getting back, if you will be so good."

O'Hara glanced at his watch.

"Yes, by Jove! so ought we. Well goodbye, Mary. Try not to do anything else silly."

"Don't be so rude, Michael! Goodbye—give my love to Helen." She turned to the priest. "But you'll see to it all, Father?"

"I'll do my best, your Ladyship. Goodbye. Keep that receipt safely."

Julia also said Goodbye, and they went out to the car.

As they drove off—"If you don't mind my asking, what did you put on that receipt?" the General asked.

"Not at all. Thanks to you, I wrote a receipt for six bundles of used £5 notes, with a hundred notes in each bundle" Father O'Donnell said. "The bank will know if they are genuine or not."

"I can't believe they aren't" Julia said, startled at the idea.

"All the same, jolly sharp of you, Father! Much better to be on the safe side. By the way, how are you going to get them to the bank?"

"I was going to venture to ask you to add to your kindness and drop them in there for me on your way home. My account is in the Mayo and Leinster Bank, in the Mall," the priest said.

"Jolly good idea. That's a hell of a lot of money to have in the house" O'Hara said. He thought for a moment or two, and then said, in a more doubtful tone—"But the bank will think it pretty funny, me paying 3,000 quid into your account."

"I'll take it in" Julia volunteered. "They don't know me by sight. You needn't come into it at all, Michael."

"Pray don't take it, if it is in any way inconvenient" the Father said. "If you could wait exactly two-and-a-half minutes at the Presbytery, I will give Mrs. Jamieson a covering note to the manager, explaining that I am sending it by messenger."

This plan was duly carried out. Julia, carrying her rich parcel (still wrapped in newspaper) prudently asked to see the manager at the bank, and when asked gave her own name, adding that she was staying with Mr. Gerald O'Brien at Rossbeg. Gerald was sure to have to come into it sooner or later, and, as she had foreseen, his name opened all doors. It was close on lunch-time, but the manager was still in, and received her politely—always glad to do anything for a friend of Mr. O'Brien's, he said.

"It's not for me, or him," Julia said, handing over the priest's note. "Father O'Donnell asked me to bring this in, as I was passing"—and she put the parcel down on the manager's desk.

"Always happy to do anything for Father O'Donnell too"

the manager said cheerfully, opening the note. But when he also opened the parcel his jaw fairly dropped.

"Merciful Heavens! This must be three thousand pounds!" he exclaimed.

"Yes—if they're all genuine" Julia said calmly. "I think he wanted you to check on that. Could you?"

"I will of course." He looked at the note again. "But he doesn't say whether it's to go into his Current or his Deposit account."

"The Father was in rather a hurry" Julia said, "to take the chance of sending it in by a messenger at once, as I was coming. How long would it take to get it out if it was put on Deposit?"

"A week is the normal rule, but if the Father was in a hurry, he could have it in a cupla days."

"Then I should put it on Deposit," said money-minded Julia. It struck her that the interest on what seemed to her this enormous sum, even if it was only in for a week or two, would bring in at least a few shillings for candles or some other Church expense.

"I am afraid I must ask you to wait while I count the notes" the manager said.

"That's all right. May I smoke?"

"Yes, certainly." He pushed an ashtray towards her and began his counting. When he had finished he put the six bundles in a safe, and turned to her again. "Is there any reason to suppose that they are not genuine?" he asked. He was obviously seething with discreetly controlled curiosity.

"I have no idea" Julia said airily. "As I say, I'm only a messenger. No, I should do whatever you do, and write and let the Father know. Goodbye, and thank you." She hurried out, to avoid any further questions.

As they drove on up the Mall—"What did he say?" O'Hara asked.

"He wanted to know if it was to go on Current or Deposit —the Father hadn't said in his note. I told him on Deposit" Julia said.

"Don't suppose Mary will leave it in long enough to earn much interest!" the General said. "Still, it was a sound idea. Didn't he want to know anything else?"

"I think he *wanted* to know a whole lot more!" Julia said, laughing. "But I didn't tell him. I just gave my name and said I was staying with Gerald—I thought you would prefer that."

"Never prefer telling lies—that was a lie!" O'Hara said severely.

"Oh well!" Julia was quite unruffled. "At least if he thinks it all pretty screwy he'll connect it with Gerald and not with you." They were passing the premises of Messrs. Walshe & Walshe at that moment; Julia slowed down and pulled in to the kerb.

"What's up?" O'Hara asked.

"D'you mind going home alone?" Julia said. "I think I'd better go down and see Gerald right away, and tell him what goes on."

"How will you get down to Rossbeg?"

"I'll get Terry to take me in his lunch-hour, and Gerald can bring me back" Julia said. She got out as she spoke. "The priest said Lady Browne ought to get a lawyer onto this, and I'm sure he's right—and the sooner the better, I should say."

"Well, I agree with you there" the General said, squeezing across into the driving seat. "All right."

"Tell Helen I'm sorry" Julia called, as he drove away.

7

WHEN JULIA WALKED in to Walshe & Walshe's establishment, and as before asked for Mr. White, she was shown into the waiting-room—"Mr. White has a gentleman with him" she was told. She sent up her name, saying firmly—"It is rather urgent"—and a moment later there was a great clatter on the stairs, and not only Terence but Gerald came into the waiting room.

"Splendid!" Gerald said. "We were wondering how to get hold of you—Lady Helen said you were out with the old fella, when we rang up. Have you anything fresh for us?"

"Yes, lots. But I can't tell you here" Julia said, glancing at the three or four rather drab occupants of the rather drab room.

"No, of course not. Let's go to have lunch at the pub" Terence said. So they crossed the river by the nearest bridge and settled down in the dining-room of the hotel at a table near a window; over drinks, which he and Terence brought up with them from the bar—"Now, let's have it" Gerald said.

"Well, she's not going to sell that land after all" Julia pronounced.

"Merciful heaven!" and "Lawks" the two men exclaimed

simultaneously. "How on earth did you bring that off?" O'Brien asked.

"Oh, I had nothing to do with it" Julia disclaimed. "General O'Hara told her that O'Rahilly was the person she was selling it to, and the sort of thing he was proposing to build on it; she didn't much like that, but it was the priest who really did it, I'm sure."

"Father O'Donnell? How did he come into it?"

"We overtook him on the road, and the General made him get in and hear all about Billy's ghastly schemes—we'd gone round by Lettersall so as to be absolutely *au fait* with the present use of the land. And when the Father heard it all from Michael, and that he was actually on his way to remonstrate with Lady Browne, he suggested coming along."

"Poor Grandmother!" said Terence, laughing. "I must say that pair would make a formidable team to stand up to."

"What makes you think it was the priest who really made her change her mind? He's such a gentle creature" Gerald said.

"He wasn't gentle with her!" Julia said. "He told her that if she took money for land that was going to be used for purposes such as Billy's, she'd be living on immoral earnings, as good as. That really shook her; she'd been very stubborn before."

Terence was still incredulous.

"She may have *said* she wasn't going to complete the sale, but has she *done* anything about it?"

"Well, she went out and fetched the deposit money—you were quite right, the notes were in the stove in the hall, Terence; the desk was covered with ash when she undid them! —and gave them to the priest, and asked him to return them to Mrs. Martin, and to get 'the document' back and tear it up." She turned to O'Brien. "The Father told her she ought to get her lawyer to handle it, Gerald; but she begged him to see to it all for her, and in the end I think he thought he'd better go while the going was good."

"He was perfectly right" O'Brien said. "Where is the money now, do you know?"

"Yes, I've just paid it into his account in the Ulster and Mayo Bank. He asked us to bring it in, as we were coming, and it was so bulky."

Terence burst out laughing—he had been giggling softly ever since Julia mentioned the ashes on the desk.

"*That* must have given the tellers at the Ul. and M. a shock!" he said—"three thousand paid in in cash, and from the poorest priest in Mayo! They'll be talking about it for weeks."

"Don't be foolish" Julia said repressively. "Of course I took it to the manager—I used your name for that, Gerald; I knew you'd have to be dragged into it sooner or later."

"You did quite right. But wasn't Mr. O'Toole a little curious?"

"As curious as you like, I think; but he behaved very well. He counted it and put it in his safe. Only I thought I'd better come and tell you at once—well, I meant to get Terence to drive me down to you, but here you are—such luck!"

"What have you done with the General?"

"Oh, he's gone home."

There was a pause while the waiter brought their first course. Then Terence said—"Well, now what happens? Does the Father write a cheque for £3,000, made out to Mrs. Martin? Not even the manager will be able to hush that up; it'll be all over Mayo in no time."

"We must give it a little thought" O'Brien said. "We don't know for certain who the cheque ought to be made out to, for one thing; Mrs. Martin may only have been a messenger, as Julia has just been. I think I had better see O'Toole after lunch and ask him to hold on to the notes pro tem. I don't know that I think local gossip all that important, but notes are more anonymous than a cheque."

"And how do we recover the famous 'document'?" Terence asked.

"Ah, how indeed? I think I'd better nip over to Ballina and find out if the Land Commission has any news of it, as soon as I can."

"And if they haven't?" Julia enquired.

"Then it will mean tackling Mrs. Martin, I suppose—or O'Rahilly. It is all very complicated" O'Brien said, sighing a little.

"Grandmother is apt to be a perfect mine of complications" Terence observed, grinning.

"Oh well, don't let it spoil our lunch. Eat first, worry later. Julia, wouldn't you rather go on with sea-trout than switch to mutton? I would."

Before they parted—in the end it was Terence who drove Julia back to Rostrunk; Gerald had an appointment he couldn't break—she had promised to go down and spend another day at Rossbeg at the week-end. "You haven't seen the garden properly yet; only peeped at it" the man said. "There are all sorts of things I want to ask you about."

"I thought you knew all there was to know about gardening" Julia said thoughtlessly—this was while Terence was fetching his car.

"Even if I did, it wouldn't tell me what I want to know, which are *your* preferences" he said, pressing her arm.

That last remark made Julia rather *distraite* on the homeward drive and little disposed to respond to Terence's wise-cracking about his grandmother's activities. She had been wondering whether it would be fair to Gerald to agree to marry him if any element of securing a stepfather for the Philipino entered into her decision; now, in the face of his trustful acquiescence in her delays, she began to wonder if it would be fair *not* to marry him on any terms—or at least if she ought not to cease these visits to Rossbeg, with all the happy planning on his part that they involved.

So it was in rather a depressed and doubtful frame of mind that she set off, some days later, in Helen O'Hara's little car on the drive southwards. She drove rapidly to and through Martinstown, but, out on the road beyond, almost unconsciously she went more slowly, the uncertainty in her mind causing her to reduce her speed. Even so, she presently began to overhaul a vehicle in front of her, which caught her attention by its very peculiar appearance. It looked like a hearse, with glass sides and back; but she couldn't see what was in it, because inside the glass there were wooden boards. Certainly it was not performing the normal functions of a hearse, for it was rattling along at a fair pace; Julia was perfectly familiar with the desperate scurry of all motorists in Oldport to get out of the town when a funeral was seen descending the hill from the Church, to avoid the one and a half miles at a foot's pace, in bottom gear, behind the mourning procession, till the turning to the cemetery was reached —to overtake a funeral in the West of Ireland is so unheard-of as really to be impossible. But here were no mourners, either in vehicles or on foot, so she decided that it would be quite in order to pass the hearse, and accelerated a little in order to do so. It was a fairly straight stretch of road, with no incoming traffic; Julia hooted gently, to give warning of her intention. But just as she drew level with it the hearse, instead of maintaining its course on the left of the road, suddenly swung over to the right; Julia swerved too, but she couldn't avoid it altogether—the two vehicles scraped together with a nasty metallic crunch.

Both pulled up, and switched off their engines. Julia jumped out, and then saw what had caused the hearse to swerve—half a dozen cows emerging onto the road from a lane concealed between high hedges. But she cared less about the cause of the accident than about Helen's car—the front left wing was slightly dented, and the paint scratched. A young man with black hair, followed by a much older one, scrambled down off the hearse, and came to inspect the damage.

"Ye'd best back down a piece—nothing can pass, the way ye are," the older man said calmly. This made sense, and Julia acted on the suggestion—only she drove a few yards forward, and pulled in in front of the hearse; the two men came up to her again, and the young one rubbed the scratched paint with an enquiring finger.

"That will paint up all right, when it's hammered out" he said.

"Yes—but it isn't my car" Julia said distressfully. "Didn't you hear me hoot?"

"I did that—but I couldn't be ramming the cows."

"Whose car is it, then?" the older man asked, studying Julia with interest as he spoke.

"Lady Helen O'Hara's."

"Ah—I was thinking it had a look of Lady's car," he said. "I'd sooner damage any car in Mayo than that one."

"Well, it *is* damaged" said Julia bluntly. She opened her bag, took out a card, and handed it to the elderly man. "Now, could I have your name and address?"

" 'Tisn't my car—'tis Mrs. Keane's, his mother's" he said, indicating the black-haired young man.

"Then can I have your name?" Julia said, propping a note-book on the bonnet of the car; she stood, a silver pencil poised in her hand, while the young man stared at her card.

But all this was much too rapid and businesslike for the West of Ireland. Having established that it was "Lady's" car that had been dented and scratched—the hearse appeared quite undamaged—they wanted to know what relation she was of the O'Haras and seemed disappointed that she was only a friend; then, where she was bound for? On hearing that it was to Rossbeg, a chorus of praise for "Mr. O'Brien" —"there's no better lawyer in the West!" "Is it a law-case ye'll be seeing him about?" Julia laughed and said no, she was going to see his garden; all this interest and curiosity was somehow so gently and openly expressed as to be completely disarming. Eventually she felt it would be in order for her to enquire about the contents of the hearse, which still aroused her curiosity—she was fascinated to learn that Paddy Keane and the older man had been "after taking the sow to the boar" in it; it belonged to the undertaker in Martinstown. "We'd best be fetching her back, Paddy" said the older man. "Mr. Browne has a funeral this evening."

"No rush" Paddy responded, and insisted that Julia should come up to the farm and have "a droppeen"; it was only "a small piece" along the road. So, the hearse leading the way, they drove there; a narrow lane led up to a substantial white-washed house with farm buildings alongside and a neat garden with a couple of rose-bushes in it in front; two round stone-built gate-posts, washed a snowy white, supported the garden gate. Julia ran the car into a field gateway opposite the garden, whence she judged she could back out to return to the road, and get out; a flagged path led from those charming white gate-posts up to the door, which Paddy opened—however, to her surprise he walked through it in front of her, and announced—"Here's a lady to see ye, Mother."

Julia followed him into a large room. A dark-haired woman rose from a seat by the hearth—the usual open turf fire, with the usual large round metal pot hanging over it—and came forward to greet her. Mrs. Keane was not exactly handsome, though there was force and intelligence in her rather dark face, but—what instantly struck Julia—also an extraordinary expression of benevolence and sweetness. "You're heartily welcome" she said—and looked as though she meant it. "Will you not sit down and take a cup of tea?" —she drew forward a chair as she spoke.

"No, not tea, Mother—the lady'd be the better of some of the hard stuff" Paddy pronounced.

"Then ye must take the bucket to the spring-well" Mrs. Keane replied. "There's none fresh or cold in it." As she spoke she took up a bucket from the floor and emptied it into the huge pot hanging over the fire, before handing it to her son, who went out with it.

The elderly man now came in, seated himself on a settle beyond the fire, and lit a cigarette. He began to explain to the mistress of the house how "the lady" had been trying to pass the hearse when Paddy "shwung out, the way he wouldn't run into MacNally's cows," and they had collided. "But 'tis Lady's car she was driving—she does be staying in Rostrunk—and it's dunted."

"Oh, musha!" Mrs. Keane exclaimed distressfully. "Lady's car! Is it a bad dunt, Timmy?"

"Paddy thinks 'twill hammer out all right" Timmy replied.

While this was going on Julia was taking in the details of the room. At the far end opposite the fire, partly concealed by a screen, was a large double bed with a brass-knobbed bedstead; in the middle stood a plain deal table, and against the far wall were some shelves with crockery, and a small cupboard below them. But what particularly caught her attention was what appeared to be a bed built into the wall, up quite near the hearth—a pair of wooden doors, charmingly painted with flowers on a pale green ground, opened in the wall some three feet from the floor, to reveal blankets and pillows. It seemed obvious that this room was not only the living-room, but also the sleeping-place for the entire family.

Mrs. Keane now got up and went over to the shelves, from which she took several glasses, which she placed on the table; from the cupboard below she took out and set on the table a small bottle containing some colourless fluid. On her way back to her seat she drew the painted doors of that curious wall-bed together, so that the bedclothes were no longer visible.

A moment later Paddy returned with the bucket, which he set down on the floor; he unhooked a china jug from the shelves, dipped it into the bucket, and wiped it with his sleeve before setting it down—the bucket itself he carefully placed well in under the table. This small action suddenly made Julia realise that she was in a house which had no piped water at all—every drop had to be carried in from outside; and, since the roof was of thatch, that useful adjunct to so many English cottages, the rain-water butt by the door, did not exist either. One *would* be careful of water, living in such conditions! Paddy now opened the small bottle, poured some of the colourless contents into a glass, added a little water, and handed it to her. Julia was rather surprised—she had expected "the hard stuff" prescribed for her by Paddy to be whiskey. However, she drank a little—and sank back choking and gasping; it was so strong it took her breath away. Paddy, who was filling the other glasses, burst out laughing;

his mother got up, took the glass from Julia, and patted her on the back.

"Ye didn't put in enough water, son" she rebuked him. "The lady isn't accustomed to potheen." (She pronounced it *puccheen.*) She herself took the glass to the table, put in some more water, and tasted it carefully—"Try that, now, lady dear" she said, bringing it to Julia again.

Julia, while vexed by Paddy's unmannerliness, was also vexed with herself for having embarrassed this delightful woman—she took a more cautious sip this time, and then drank some more. "Yes, like that it's fine" she said, though in fact she thought it rather nasty—it had no particular flavour, it was just *strong.* Rather reluctantly, purely out of politeness, she emptied the glass, hoping it would leave her with a clear enough head to drive on to Rossbeg, and presently rose and took her leave.

"I wish I could stay longer Mrs. Keane, but Mr. O'Brien will be wondering what's become of me" she said. "Perhaps I might come and see you again sometime?"

This suggestion was enthusiastically welcomed. "And ye'll be sure to be telling Lady how sorry I am her car got dunted?" Mrs. Keane said earnestly.

"Certainly I will. Goodbye."

Paddy and Timmy came out with her, to go and retrieve the sow; as she started to back out into the lane she heard the hearse's engine start up. She put her head out of the car window. "Oh for God's sake let me get clear first, Paddy!" she called angrily.

"Sure we will, Miss—just you drive on" Timmy called back; Paddy merely gave more of his uncouth laughter.

Although she was aware of the after-effects of "the hard stuff," out on the road, Julia, driving slowly, managed to reach Rossbeg without further incident. Gerald was waiting for her in the drive.

"Did anything happen to you? I was expecting you earlier" he said.

"Yes, lots. I'm so sorry, Gerald. Let's come in, and I'll tell you" she said, getting out. In the library, when he offered her sherry—"Not on your life! I'm full up with that ghastly white potheen stuff" she said.

"Who on earth gave you that?" he asked, sitting down and beginning to sip the rejected sherry himself.

"That sweet Mrs. Keane at the farm. Wait, and I'll tell you the whole thing" Julia said, lighting a cigarette. And she told him the story. "I could see I was getting nowhere, there on the road, so when they pressed me to go up to the farm, I thought I'd better" she ended. "And I'm glad I did— I feel Mrs. Keane would be the nicest possible person to have living near one. I didn't think much of the son, though."

"Which son did you see?"

"Paddy. Why, is there another?"

"Yes, Tom. They're both completely useless creatures, and mannerless with it! Is Lady Helen's car much damaged?"

"No, mostly scratches, and one dent in the wing. I'm vexed that it happened, though."

"Of course. You poor darling!" He got up and kissed her. "Shall I go and look at it?"

"Oh, I wish you would! And tell me if you think it can be repaired locally—it'll be such a curse for Helen if it has to go to Dublin."

"Galway, more likely" Gerald said, and went out. When he returned a few minutes later—"No, Paddy Kelly in Martinstown will be able to fix that perfectly well" he pronounced. "And it won't cost anything that Helen will notice."

"Won't her insurance company pay for it?"

"I shouldn't think she'd bother with that for such a small amount. Anyhow, who's liable on the other side? The Keanes had the accident, but the hearse isn't theirs—it belongs to poor old Browne!"

Julia laughed.

"Yes, I see that makes it a bit complicated. Oh Gerald, do please tell me this—why on earth use a *hearse* to take a sow to the boar in?"

"What else would they use?" the man asked. "It's the right shape, and size, and has a back board that lets down to get her in and out."

Julia laughed again.

"Yes, I see—I mean I suppose so."

"Boarding it up is a bit of a chore, but Browne has all the boards now, so it doesn't take him long. I fancy the hearse brings him in quite as much from pigs' weddings as from humans' funerals!" Gerald observed, with his grin.

Over lunch Julia had another question arising out of her morning's adventures. They had been talking about the Keane family, Julia expressing surprise that such an ultra-nice woman should have such inferior sons—she was delighted that Gerald should usually refer to Paddy and his brother collectively as "the louts."

"I expect she spoiled them, and Timmy is there all the time to do most of the work—he's a cousin. If old Keane had lived he'd have put the fear of God into them with a strap!" Gerald observed, "but he died when they were quite small."

"Are they very poor?" Julia asked.

He stared at her. "Poor! Why on earth should you suppose they're poor? They're one of the richest families round here."

"The house is so bare" she said. "Those settles to sit at

table on, and not even a rug in front of the fire, to keep the old lady's feet warm! And no chest of drawers or wardrobe; I could see her cloak and shawl hanging on the wall, down at the far end of the room. The poorest peasant's house in Portugal has at least *one* piece of furniture!" Julia stated.

"I don't suppose the Portuguese peasants were tenants-at-will, under foreign landlords, for centuries on end" Gerald replied with vigour. "It's got into their blood here to have as little as possible of furniture, or anything else, for fear of having their rent put up."

"Oh yes, I remember your telling me about tenants-at-will the other day. But surely their rent wouldn't have been put up simply because they had a rug in their living-room?"

"My dear girl, if the land-agent happened to see a tenant's wife or daughter going to Mass on Sunday in a new bonnet, his rent would be likely to go up!" Gerald exploded.

"But that's nonsensical!" She was silent, frowning, pondering all this. After a moment—"And you said there'd been 'foreign' landlords for centuries—who were they?" she asked.

"The English, you blessed innocent! Who else?"

She stared at him.

"D'you mean people like the O'Haras?"

"No, no; Michael is what the country-people call 'one of the old lot.' People like Mary Browne, though; all the Brownes are English."

"But they've been here for *centuries!*" Julia protested.

"Only since Elizabethan days. That doesn't make them Irish."

"And Michael was a general in the British Army, anyhow" Julia pursued.

"That doesn't make him English!" Gerald said, laughing. "Do get it into your pretty head that the English and the

Irish are two utterly different races—don't be misled by the fact that they apparently talk the same language. That was force of circumstances, and in any case they don't, really— they use the same words and mean different things by them! That's why they have been trying to understand one another for nearly a thousand years and didn't really succeed yet!"

Julia sighed at this depressing pronouncement. She would have liked to ask why *now,* with their land their own, people as intelligent as Mrs. Keane, and by local standards as rich, should still not buy themselves a hearth-rug, but decided against it. Instead she enquired what "that ghastly 'hard stuff,' as Paddy calls it, is made of? It nearly blows your head off!"

"The potheen, you mean? Oats, as a rule; sometimes potatoes. I shall imagine the Keane's potheen was made from oats."

"It's odd that it has no colour at all, it's just like water, and it hasn't a nice taste, like whiskey—it hasn't any taste at all but fieriness."

"I imagine the difference in taste may partly be due to using oats or potatoes and not barley, and partly to do with malting; but I'm not a distiller, so I can't help you much there" O'Brien said, grinning. "The colour I do happen to have heard about; someone told me once that Scotch whiskey, when it's first made, is quite colourless, just like potheen; but the casks the makers used to put it in to mature were old sherry or Madeira casks—economy, see?—and after some years in those it came out the colour we're accustomed to. Whether they still do that I wouldn't know; people don't drink as much Madeira as they used to. But if there's a shortage of the right casks, there must be other ways of giving it the colour that has proved popular."

"How fascinating!" Julia said. Her mind went back to

Madeira, and the peasants carrying the loads of grapes down little hill-paths to the waiting lorries on the roads. Funny that those same grapes, years and years later, might passively impart some of their own colour to Scotch whiskey.

After lunch they went down to the kitchen garden, at which Julia had only taken a cursory look on her first visit. As before, she was struck with its extreme neatness, and said so.

"Yes, Mac and the boy do quite well, if you keep them at it. But is there anything we aren't growing that you think we ought to have?" Gerald asked earnestly, as they walked between the trim plots of vegetables and fruit-bushes.

"Well, where's your herb-bed?" Julia rather hesitantly enquired.

"Oh, we don't have an actual herb-*bed*. The sage is over there by the artichokes, and the thyme next to the cold frames, and parsley Mac sticks in wherever he has room for it. Ought there to be a regular herb-bed?"

"Well, if you could spare a small space in the border under the wall, up near the gate, it would save the cook's time when she comes down to get her herbs" Julia said.

"Right you are—can-do, and will-do! Anything else?" he asked.

Julia looked about her.

"Well, I see you've got glorious masses of raspberries" she said. "But I don't see any loganberries. They're not nearly as nice as rasps," she added hastily, "but they are rather useful for bottling, and they do come at a slightly different time, which is handy."

"Bridgie doesn't go in much for bottling, I don't think" he said doubtfully.

"Not with an Esse? Why it's *made* for bottling! You just fill the bottles and put them in the slow oven overnight, and take them out in the morning—there's nothing to it!" Julia said. "I wonder Helen didn't teach her that, while she was about it."

"She did try—she did one lot with her, of raspberries, and they were perfect; but when Bridgie tried alone, the bottles all broke. That rather upset her."

"Screwed the tops on tight, instead of leaving them loose, I expect" Julia said easily. "As I say, it's perfectly simple, and no trouble, but you must do all the little things exactly right, every time."

"Oh my dear child, you've put it in a sentence!" Gerald said on a long gusty sigh. "Doing all the little things *exactly* right, *every* time, is just the one thing this nation is practically incapable of! The English can't *not* do it; the Irish, I honestly believe, can't bear to do it."

"Have you any idea why not?" Julia asked, much interested.

"I think subconsciously they feel it ties them down to mechanical things" he answered slowly. "That's why ploughs and expensive mowers get left out in the fields to rust. They aren't like that with animals, or growing potatoes; over those, things with life in them, they'll usually pay immense attention to detail. Anyhow it's something you just have to recognise here, and live with."

The wrought-iron gate at the top of the garden whined on its hinges—O'Brien turned round.

"Oh good—it's Mr. MacIlroy!" he said; "come and meet him."

"Who's Mr. MacIlroy?" Julia asked, walking up the path beside him.

"The Horticultural Instructor from Castlebar—a most splendid person."

"Has he come to instruct you?" Julia asked, laughing.

"Oh, he likes to go round and keep an eye on everyone's gardens; he instructs those that want instruction, and helps everyone" Gerald replied. "Afternoon, Mr. MacIlroy; I'm delighted to see you." He shook hands with a middle-aged man in a well-worn burberry with bulging pockets and introduced him to Julia. "Mrs. Jamieson thinks we ought to grow loganberries" he said. "Now where will I get those, Mr. MacIlroy?"

"Loganberries? Well let me see—that's not just so easy, short of Dublin" the instructor replied. "Yes, ye could put them in over there by the glasshouse, if ye took out a few gooseberry-bushes; this garden is terrible full of gooseberries, and logans don't mind a bit of sun; they're not like rasps." He walked over towards the green-house, and indicated a couple of rows of gooseberry-bushes alongside it. "Just take those out—I know plenty of people would be glad of them, and the better of them too—our people don't eat enough fruit—and put in a few eight-foot stakes and run wires along them, and there ye are."

"And how long before they start bearing?" Gerald asked.

"Ah, that depends what age ye put them in at. Good, well-grown plants could give ye a small picking next year."

"And where will I get those?"

"I'll ask around and see who has some; the nearer the better, o' course. There's a place up in the Six Counties always has a good stock of bearing bushes, but that's a long journey, and would set them back a piece."

"I could go up and fetch them in the estate van; if your place is fairly near the Border they needn't be out of the ground more than twelve hours, if they lift them while I wait—I could have the holes ready" Gerald said.

"There's a proper gardener for you!" the instructor said to Julia. "I wish there were more like Mr. O'Brien—nothing's too much trouble for him!"

"It's the way to get results" Julia agreed.

"I didn't see ye since ye got back from Morocco" Mr. MacIlroy now said to Gerald. "What sort of a country is that for plants, Mr. O'Brien?"

"Well of course what catches a Northerner's eye is the palms, because we're so unused to them, and they are very striking—a big plantation of palm-trees, like the one outside Marrakesh, is a smashing sight" Gerald told him. "But I expect you were thinking more of the wild flowers."

"That's right, I was. What about those?"

"Well, there aren't all that many; the country is very densely cultivated, you see. I believe you find some nice things down in the Atlas Mountains, but I didn't get so far South. What strikes one up in the North is the Spanish irises, the blue ones—they grow in the fields as thick as moon-daisies in our hay, in fact the fields are blue with them. And along the banks of the streams are big clumps of paper-white narcissus."

"Wild?" MacIlroy asked eagerly.

"They must be, I think—this was in quite uncultivated country, where I saw them. What I found surprising" Gerald went on, "was that there was so much heathy country, especially near the coast, and it was full of little blue scillas."

"What sort of heaths? Mediterranea?"

"Yes, quite a lot of that, and some *vagans* and *cinerea,* but more ling than anything else."

"I was hearing that there's quite a bit of Mediterranea here in Mayo, but I didn't see it yet" the instructor said.

"Well next time you're going to Achill, look out for it just beyond Mulranny—it grows quite close to the road, on the right" Gerald told him. "Meantime, come to the toolshed for a moment." He walked to a large shed on the North side of the greenhouse, where it did not obstruct the sunlight;

inside, near the door, was a bench with the usual array of secateurs, tarred string, weed-killers and pesticides—tools leaned against the nearer walls, along with rolls of wire-netting. But at the far end, from floor to ceiling, the wall was covered with what looked like small square boxes, each with a label and a brass ring to pull it out by—Gerald peered at these for a moment, and then drew two a little way out, so that Julia saw that they were in fact over a foot long.

"That's a dodgy contraption of Mr. O'Brien's—I don't know another like it" Mr. MacIlroy observed to Julia.

"What's it for?" she asked.

"To keep his seeds and bulbs and all like that in."

From a larger drawer at one end Gerald now took out a couple of tough brown manila envelopes and wrote on them; then from each of the two extended boxes he took a handful of bulbs, which he placed in the envelopes.

"There" he said, handing them to Mr. MacIlroy—"I knew you'd be craving for some of those wild paper-whites, and the little scillas. See if you can flower them."

"That's terrible good of you, Mr. O'Brien" the man said. From each of the envelopes in turn he emptied a few of the bulbs into the palm of his hand and studied them, gloatingly. "Terrible good" he repeated, replacing them. Then—" 'Twas among heaths you say they were growing?" he said. "They should do in peat, so."

"The scillas, yes, peat with a good bit of sand—where they grow the sand off the shore blows a long way inland. Not the paper-whites—I should try them in a rather poor sandy loam, with plenty of stones. The soil of Morocco isn't at all rich, mostly, except where it's been tilled for centuries —the whole place is sand and stones."

"Well, I must be getting along" MacIlroy said, stuffing the envelopes into his already distended pockets. "Ye've got the place very nice" he added, walking out into the middle of the garden again; "and ye're making a good job of that lad"—he indicated a youth who was hand-weeding a bed of lettuce seedlings down at the bottom. "I'm awfully thankful to ye, Mr. O'Brien," he said again. "I'll ask about the logan-bushes, but there's no rush—early autumn's the best time to shift them." He touched his hat and went off.

"What a sweet man" Julia said, as the gate clanged behind the instructor.

"Yes, MacIlroy's a splendid fellow" Gerald agreed. He looked at her sideways a little quizzically. "But he came to get those bulbs, y'know."

"Do you always bring him back something from your trips abroad?" she asked.

"Well, mostly" he admitted.

"Then you can't blame him; it's your own fault" she said gaily. "I can see that you probably spoil everyone within miles of you!"

"Not children" he said, with sudden earnestness. "Never a child, Julia."

His emphasis made her blush.

"No, I'm sure you wouldn't, precious Gerald" she said.

8

JUST AS SHE was getting into the car to drive off, Julia suddenly remembered something.

"Oh, by the way, did you go and see the Land Commission people?" she asked. "And had the 'document' got to them?"

"I couldn't be sure" Gerald said, leaning on the car window as she seated herself. "By bad luck the man I know really well at Ballina was away—the Commission are as silent as *clams* about everything, but if he'd been there I think he would have told me, especially as old Mother B. is a client of mine. Even using that lever, all they would say was that they had no knowledge of any such application; but I wasn't at all sure that the men I saw were speaking the truth. I think, darling, it might'n't be a bad plan if you were to pop over to Achill again and call on your pretty friend, and see if she's got it."

"Would she tell me if she had?" Julia asked doubtfully.

"You can but try! At least you might be able to decide if she was lying, if she said she hadn't."

"Can I come completely clean with her? Tell her about finding the old lady counting the notes, and her giving them back to Michael?"

"No, I shouldn't tell her the last part; that might decide Billy and his pals to try to re-activate her. But about seeing her—Mrs. Martin—driving away, and finding the old lady counting the money just after, certainly."

"Right-oh" Julia said inelegantly. "I don't promise much in the way of results, though."

"Why not?"

"Oh, I feel sure Billy will have got hold of it by now, or his pal in Dublin."

"Well, if Billy's got it, we must think again. At least it would be a hard fact, which is what we're so short on. Oh" he said, as she switched on the engine—"don't on any account tell Mrs. M. that the old lady wants to cancel—just that she wants to check the acreage again before naming a final price."

"Right-oh" Julia repeated, and drove away.

As she passed back through Martinstown she stopped at Paddy Kelly's garage and showed him the damage to the car wing. Kelly, a tall and magnificently handsome man, examined the car carefully and thoroughly, but agreed that no harm had been done except to the wing, and gave what seemed to Julia an extremely modest estimate for repairing it. "But I'll not be able to do it for a week or two yet; I have a shocking lot of work waiting. Tell Lady I'll do it as soon as I can."

At Rostrunk Julia drove the car straight into the garage, and then went and sought out Helen—as she had hoped, her hostess was still in the garden.

"Helen, come and look at your car, there's an angel; I am most frightfully sorry, but I've dunted one wing."

"A bad dunt?" Lady Helen asked calmly, getting up from her kneeling-mat and wiping her little hand-fork on the palm of her glove.

"Not very, I don't think; Paddy Kelly looked at it, and said he could put it right for about three quid—which of course I'll pay."

"The insurance can do that—I lost my no-claims bonus last year" Lady Helen said. "Who was the other party, who hit you?"

"That's just it—it was two parties" Julia said. "The object I collided *with* was the Martinstown hearse, which belongs to a Mr. Browne, but it was being driven by a most uncouth creature called Paddy Keane."

"Oh, one of the Keane louts"—Julia was delighted to hear Gerald's so appropriate expression echoed by her friend. "Was the sow hurt?" Lady Helen asked.

"No, she was still visiting the boar. Here you are" Julia said, as they entered the garage.

Helen O'Hara switched on two or three electric lights and examined the car.

"No, that's nothing" she said easily. "In fact I shall cut a few bob off Paddy's price. You can't have hit the hearse, or the hearse hit you, at all hard."

"No, it was more a sort of graze." Julia explained what had happened. "I am most frightfully sorry" she said again.

"Not to worry. But there is one thing" she said, getting into the car and switching on the engine. "I'll take her out now, and come in and say I've coshed the wing—then we shan't have any trouble with Michael when you want to use her again."

"Helen, you're an angel!"

"Just put the kneeler and gloves, and the fork, in the tool-shed" Lady Helen said. "I shan't be any time."

"Just one minute—I may not be able to tell you later. That sweet Mrs. Keane at the farm sent you all sorts of messages, and said how sorry she was."

"Oh yes—she is a dear person."

"Wait" Julia said urgently. "If I see Michael, where shall I say you've gone?"

"Clever girl! Say up to the Post Office."

"Right."

Thanks to this sensible ruse of Lady Helen's, there was no trouble with the General when Julia borrowed the small car a couple of days later to go and see Mrs. Martin, though he spent a good deal of the intervening time scolding his wife for her carelessness in having the supposed accident, and cross-examining her about the other vehicle involved.

"Darling, I keep telling you it was a lorry, and it swerved because Affie King's cows ran out of the lane. He couldn't help it and nor could I."

"Can't think why you didn't take his number" O'Hara grumbled. Julia admired and pitied Helen sincerely, and felt very guilty; but she dared not confess, as she would have liked, because there was a job to be done, for which she had to have the car.

She decided this time not to give notice of her visit in advance, hoping to be able to "bounce" Mrs. Martin into giving her the document, or at least into an admission of its whereabouts, if she had passed it on to Billy. But this plan did not work out particularly well. When she reached the "shack" there was another car drawn up on the space in front of it, and, when Mrs. Martin opened the door to her knock and ushered her into the living-room, standing in front of the fire was the same thickset middle-aged man whom Julia had seen hugging Mrs. Martin so energetically at the station on the day of her arrival, whom Lady Helen had identified for her as "one of our poets." So she was not surprised when the fair woman said "I forget if you know Mr. O'Rahilly? Billy, this is Mrs. Jamieson."

"No, we've never met" Julia said, holding out her hand. "How do you do?"

"Billy, it's a quarter of twelve—isn't it time for drinks?" Mrs. Martin said. The man obediently went to the high shelf and fetched down several bottles, which he put on the table; then he went through to the kitchen and returned with the bowl of ice-cubes—he was evidently quite at home in the house, and accustomed to doing these chores. But he was not away long enough for Julia to put her question to Mrs. Martin without his hearing it, and she had to decide whether or not to ask it in front of him. She made up her mind to risk doing exactly that; and while the drinks were being organised, and she was refusing gin in any form—"Billy makes a marvellous dry Martini"—and accepting ice in her whiskey, she was planning in her head the most casual-sounding form of words in which to put it.

"Oh, Mrs. Martin," she said presently, "old Lady Browne wants you to let her have back that lease, or receipt, or whatever it was that she signed for you the other day—she wants to check the acreage, or something."

"How in all the earth do you know she signed a lease for me?" Mrs. Martin exclaimed, startled—Julia, watching O'Rahilly, saw him scowl at her. "Or rather, what makes you think I did?" she amended.

"Oh, she told me so. I got there just after you left—I'd gone to look at a fur coat she was talking of selling; she was counting the money, and she'd left both windows open, so the fivers were blowing all over the drive!—I picked a lot of them up for her" Julia said easily. "Anyway, I'm sure you won't mind letting her see it again, will you? You didn't give her a copy, did you?"

O'Rahilly, still looking rather cross, took over.

"Mrs. Jamieson, what did you say Lady Browne wants to see the lease again for? To check what acreage?"

"Of the strip of land below Lettersall that Mrs. Martin's buying from her. I *imagine*—I don't know—to decide the final price; the £3,000 was only a deposit, wasn't it?" Julia replied, still easily. "Anyway, I suppose 'lease' is the wrong word, as Mrs. Martin is buying it outright."

O'Rahilly looked more sour than ever when Julia came out so pat with the figure of three thousand pounds; clearly he hadn't expected her to be so well informed, and in such detail, and didn't much like it.

"She's a very old lady" Julia pursued, she hoped soothingly; "and old people don't take things in very quickly, and then they forget."

O'Rahilly didn't appear particularly soothed; he went on scowling. Julia turned to Mrs. Martin again.

"Anyhow you can't possibly have any objection to letting her see it again, surely? It's such a natural thing for her to want."

"I haven't got it any more—Billy has it" Mrs. Martin said, distressfully.

"Oh." Julia put on an air of surprise at this. "Well, Mr. O'Rahilly, then you can take it" she said smoothly. "Can't you?"

"Did she *ask* you to get it?" he enquired, rather inquisitorially, Julia thought.

"Not me personally—she asked the priest to get it. But Father O'Donnell has no car, so I said I would come over; Rostrunk is so near" Julia said, silkily. "But of course your house is nearer still."

"Well in fact I haven't got it any more; it's with my lawyers in Dublin," O'Rahilly said, but less disagreeably.

"Oh, well they can send it back to her, can't they? No trouble about that" Julia said, disliking him more and more every moment. She turned again to Mrs. Martin. "I wonder you didn't want Lady Browne to have a lawyer with her, over a deal like this" she said, still smoothly. "She is rather old to conduct business by herself, isn't she? I mean, she didn't even ask you for a copy of what she'd signed, which it would be the normal thing for her to have."

Mrs. Martin looked more distressed than ever.

"I was just taking the money for Billy" she blurted out. "I didn't really know exactly what was on the paper myself. He just said she was to read it, and sign it, and I . . ."

O'Rahilly interrupted her brusquely.

"Let's leave all that, Sally. I don't imagine Mrs. Jamieson is particularly interested in all those details. Indeed I'm not really quite clear as to how she comes into this business at all."

Oh aren't you, boy? And I daresay you'd a great deal rather I didn't! Julia thought to herself. But aloud what she said was—"Oh, didn't I make myself clear, Mr. O'Rahilly? I am carrying out a commission laid on me by Father O'Donnell of Lettersall, at Lady Browne's request. In fact her lawyer *was* present when she made that request; and he also heard me undertake to carry it out, as I have the use of a car, and the priest hasn't. I am in no doubt at all about *my* position." She paused, to see what response O'Rahilly would make to this; in fact he made none, but to get up and pour himself another drink, which he started to gulp down nervously, without offering to refill anyone else's glass. "But can I have your assurance that your lawyers will return the paper which Lady Browne signed to her forthwith, with a copy? If not, I shall have to tell Father O'Donnell so, and no doubt he will put the whole matter into the hands of Lady Browne's lawyers."

"Oh, do say yes, Billy" Mrs. Martin urged him. "We don't want a lot of legal bother, or any fuss."

"I am sure that would be your wisest course" Julia said, as the man still remained silent, continuing to drink whiskey.

"Very well—I'll tell the lawyers to send it back at once" O'Rahilly said at length. He emptied his glass. "Well, I'd better be getting along" he said. "Goodbye, Mrs. Jamieson—'bye, Sally. Thanks for the drink." He went off.

"I'm sorry I had to press Mr. O'Rahilly so," Julia said. "I wonder why he should even hesitate about letting the old lady check the acreage again—it seems the most natural thing in the world that she should."

"Billy's set his heart so terribly on getting that land—I think that's why" Mrs. Martin said. "And having that paper signed seemed to make it all certain—I think he's just simply nervous about it." She still looked rather distressed.

"All the same, I wonder he let you take over the money and get her to sign it. I mean, you're a stranger here and couldn't be expected to know how wrong it was to let an elderly person like Lady Browne sign such a document without her lawyer's advice, and without giving her a copy."

"Why wrong?" Mrs. Martin asked—but more curiously than anything else.

"Well, morally it was quite unfair; but legally, her lawyer says a document signed in such circumstances wouldn't hold up in a court of law for a moment. I don't suppose her signature was even witnessed, was it? *You* couldn't witness it, as an interested party; and I doubt if old Annie can sign her name!" Julia said briskly. She thought it just as well to make Mrs. Martin aware of the legal position, as no doubt it would get passed on to the horrid Billy, and make him less liable to run out on his undertaking to return the paper.

"No, of course I didn't understand all that" Sally Martin said. "I'm sorry if what I did was wrong, I was just trying to help Billy. But you and I can go on being friends, can't we?" she said, impulsively.

"Yes, we can and we will" Julia replied, warmly. She kissed the fair woman. "I must be off now, or I shall be late for lunch." She hastened out.

She stopped in Mulranny on her way back and put a call through to Gerald's office from the call-box in the hotel—he was in.

"What luck?" he asked at once.

"None. You-know-who was there too!"

"Was he, begob? So what did you do?"

"Asked her for it in front of him. She said he'd got it, so I asked him to take it back, or bring it to me to take back."

"And what did he say to that?"

"Said his lawyers in Dublin had got it. *Very* awkward, he was; he is a nasty bit of work, I must say."

"How did you end up?"

"Oh, I said if it wasn't sent back I should have to tell the Father, and he would put *her* lawyers on to it! He didn't relish that idea at all, and in the end he did promise that he would have it posted back to the old party, with a copy. Whether he will or not, you can probably guess better than I can."

"He will if he's sufficiently frightened. *Was* he frightened?"

"I think so—he kept on slugging down whiskey."

"Yes, that sounds like fright. Well, we must wait and see. I'm sorry you had such a disagreeable time, dearest."

"Oh, I didn't mind. I don't mind being tough with people as nasty as that" Julia said cheerfully.

"When do I see you again?" Gerald asked. "Can you come this week-end?"

"I should think so—I'll let you know." She was thinking of how she had been wondering, the previous week-end, of whether she ought not to curtail these visits to Rossbeg, until she had come to a decision about Gerald.

"Sunday better than Saturday, if it's equally good for you," he said.

"I'll let you know" Julia repeated. " 'Bye." She rang off.

But before the week-end a fresh development took place which rather pushed Julia's and Gerald's personal concerns into the background. Father O'Donnell rang up Rostrunk and asked for the General; both the O'Haras were out for the day—Julia took the call.

"Oh, Mrs. Jamieson, is it? Father O'Donnell here. Well, will you give the General a message as soon as he comes in?"

"Of course."

"I've had a letter from our old friend. I'm afraid she wants her money back—what he kindly banked for her."

"Oh Lord! What do you suppose that means?" Julia asked.

"I don't know—I've only just heard. I'm afraid it may mean that she's being got at again by someone. I'm going over to see her now and try to find out. But I thought I ought to let the General know at once. Our mutual legal friend told me about your efforts in Achill; I'm sorry they were only partly successful."

"I didn't think they were successful at all" Julia said bluntly.

"Oh *yes*. At least it gives us a pointer as to where the active parties are. I think that useful."

"Good. Oh, by the way, do *you* want the General to un-bank the cash?"

"Not at the moment. I shall try to stall—in any case I can invoke the seven-day rule. Goodbye—my regards to Lady Helen."

"Goodbye" Julia responded.

It occurred to her that, while her hosts were out and the telephone free, it might not be a bad plan to get hold of Terence White, and find out if he knew any reason for this *démarche* on his grandmother's part; she rang up Walshe and Walshe and got hold of him. When she reported, care-fully choosing her words, that "your aged relative wants her mon back" Terence burst out laughing down the telephone.

"What did I tell you?" he said. "I didn't think *that* change of heart would last very long!"

"No but Terence, have you any idea *why?*"

"Not a clue—I didn't see her these last ten days. More dirty work, I'll bet! Did you get the famous paper back?"

"No. I tried, but was told it was in Dublin."

"There you are! Well d'you want me to see her?"

"No, the Father's going over."

"Poor chap! I wish I thought she was going to spend some of the cash on buying him a car!—I hate the idea of his pedalling about on his old push-bike in all weathers. Well, let me know if there's anything I can do."

"I will" Julia replied.

The General, predictably, was greatly exasperated when, at tea-time, he got the priest's message.

"Mary's *mad!*" he exclaimed. "And utterly untrustworthy. I wonder what she's up to now?"

"More of the same, I expect" Lady Helen said calmly. "I don't imagine Mr. O'Rahilly gives up easily—money-grab-bers don't, as a rule."

"I shall go over tomorrow and see her—she's got to be stopped!" the old man thundered. Lady Helen let him rave himself out—when he had calmed down sufficiently to ask for a second cup of tea and start buttering a scone, she suggested that it might be a good plan to see the priest first, and find out if he had learned anything as to what lay behind this fresh move. "Did he say when he was going?" she asked Julia.

"Yes, he said 'now'—and that was about half-past eleven."

"Then he's sure to have gone today. I should certainly see him first, Michael" Lady Helen said—and eventually this plan was agreed on.

As before, Julia went too, as co-driver; Lady Helen rang up the Father to warn him of their advent. He was out, but his "house-keep" took the message, and said he should be back within the hour.

He was already at home when Julia and the General drove up to the Presbytery at Lettersall; he saw the car from the window, and came out into the hall to meet them. It was a small and rather comfortless-looking place, with no rugs on the dusty and ill-polished floor. "Come in to my study, I have a fire there—'tis quite chilly today" he said. It was—the weather had broken, and rain was borne on a north-west wind. The study however had a good turf fire going; the General stood in front of this, warming his hands, while Father O'Donnell bustled about, taking piles of books and journals off two chairs to make room for his guests to sit down—the whole room was smothered in books and papers, the desk piled high with them. "This is the most tossed room in Ireland!" the priest said apologetically. "But there—sit down now." After hunting about he produced a wooden box of rather withered-looking cigarettes—"Do you care to smoke?"

Julia took a cigarette—the General asked if he might smoke one of his own cheroots? "Mrs. Bassett" Father O'Donnell called down the passage, opening the door, "could you bring two saucers? For ash-trays" he explained to his guests; he piled up books by their chairs to serve as tables, and when Mrs. Bassett brought a couple of common kitchen saucers, he triumphantly placed these on them. "There—now we're all set" he said, sitting down behind his laden desk.

"Well, did you see that poor foolish old creature?" the General asked.

"I did. I'm afraid she has changed her mind, and does want to go on with the deal."

"Did you find out who's been after her this time?" O'Hara pursued.

"No. She was *very* unresponsive" Father O'Donnell said regretfully. "She didn't really want to talk about it at all. All she would vouchsafe was that 'a delightful gentleman' had been to see her, bringing the famous 'document,' and had convinced her that selling the land would be of great benefit to the district—and also that Mr. O'Rahilly had nothing to do with the purchase."

"As far as putting up the money goes, that's probably true enough" the General said, bitterly.

"Anyhow, all our efforts have been undone—she is determined to have her money back."

"And you couldn't get any idea who this 'delightful gentleman' was?" O'Hara asked.

"No. All I did manage to do was to get a description of him from old Annie—I left my gloves behind in the hall on purpose, and went back for them and saw Annie alone, and asked about the gentleman who had recently been to see her mistress. Annie has the usual clear peasant memory, and said he was 'middling young,' tall, dark and very good-looking; but what really impressed her, oddly enough, was his dress—'Ye never saw such an elegant gentleman!' Does that convey anything to you, General?"

"Not a thing!"

"Actually it does to me" Julia put in. The priest turned eagerly to her.

"It does, Mrs. Jamieson? And who might the 'elegant gentleman' be?"

"An architect called Moran, who's very much mixed up in property deals. Mr. O'Brien knows all about him."

"That is extremely useful—or might be" the Father said, eagerly. The General was less encouraging.

"How on earth can you know that, Julia, just from a description? Have you ever met this Moran?"

"No, but I've seen him—that's how I know what he looks like," Julia said firmly.

"Where have you seen him?" O'Hara asked.

"In Dublin." Julia hoped this bald statement would be enough; she would have preferred not to reveal Moran's connection with Mrs. Martin—but it wasn't.

"Where in Dublin?"

"At Westland Row Station, seeing someone off."

"And was he pointed out to you as Moran?" the General persisted.

"No—but the person he was seeing off travelled down in the same carriage with me. I was struck at the time by his being so frightfully over-dressed—that's why I remembered him" Julia said, again hoping that this hare might draw the General's interest away from Mrs. Martin; again she was disappointed.

"And did your fellow-traveller mention his name? Seems an odd thing to do, to a complete stranger."

"No. I heard it later from someone else."

"Oh ah—but the person you travelled down with was the Martin woman from Achill, O'Rahilly's pal!—I remember Helen telling me that. Yes, that would all fit in—it's likely enough it was him, so," O'Hara at last admitted. He turned to the priest. "But even if we know it's Moran who's after her, how can we stop him? Did he give her any more money, do you know?"

"I couldn't find that out. As I told you, Lady Browne was very reluctant to discuss the matter at all—she just insisted that she had entrusted a large sum of money to me, and that now she wanted it back."

"Wonder what she wants it back for, if she's proposing to get more by completing the deal," O'Hara speculated.

"I imagine to make sure I didn't complicate matters by returning the money to Mrs. Martin, as I had promised to do, *and* to tear up the document agreeing to sell. She was triumphant that this time she had been given a copy!" Father O'Donnell said wrily.

"Well, what do we do now? Put O'Brien onto this Moran man, and try to stop him?" the General asked.

"That will require some thought. I should like Mr. O'Brien's advice on that. I wish we could get hold of him—I tried, but he was neither at his office, nor at home."

Just then a car drew up in the drive, and a moment later Gerald O'Brien walked into the room.

"Talk of the devil, and let him appear!" O'Hara exclaimed.

"Oh, good Sir, you were never more welcome!" the priest said more agreeably, rising and wringing him by the hand. After further dislodging of papers and magazines another chair was freed, and the newcomer sat down.

"I came over because I heard that my old client has changed her mind again" he said. "I thought I would check, as I was somewhere in this direction. Is that really so?"

"Alas, yes" Father O'Donnell said ruefully.

"How on earth did *you* hear?" the General asked.

"Ill news travels fast" the lawyer said equably—at the same time he gave Julia a tiny, almost imperceptible wink, from which she deduced that Terence White had passed on the information. He turned to the priest. "Now, I take it that you have seen Lady Browne—may I hear what you have learned?"

Father O'Donnell repeated the rather scanty information he had already given the others, including Annie's description of the persuasive gentleman who had brought the copy of the document.

"And now Julia here fancies she knows who this person is" the General put in.

"Oh yes—quite certainly Moran" O'Brien said unhesitatingly, to Julia's secret pleasure.

"Ah, you are satisfied of that too—excellent" the priest said. "We were just discussing what should be done, on that assumption, and wishing that we might have had the benefit of your opinion—and now here you are to give it!"

"I'm afraid my opinion is that it is less a case of what should be done than of what *can* be done, where Master Moran is concerned" O'Brien said. "He's a tricky customer, and usually manages to get excellent technical advice, so that he can keep strictly within the law."

"But I thought you said before that the document Lady Browne originally signed couldn't stand up in a court of law, because of the circumstances in which it was obtained—a very old lady all alone, with no legal help, and not witnessed" Father O'Donnell objected.

"Quite true—which is probably why he's brought it back.

But you see it wasn't tricky Dicky Moran who got her to sign it, but poor ignorant Mrs. Martin, an alien! Next time, if the deal goes as he hopes, he'll come with a lawyer in his pocket—in every sense of the phrase!" Gerald said grinning. "It won't be me, and I shan't be told! And he has no moral sense to appeal to. No—I don't think one can do much with Moran. I'm sure for your best chance is to work on the old lady again; she *has* got some moral sense, though it's rather intermittent, let's face it! But you and the General succeeded with her once before, and I don't see why you shouldn't again."

Father O'Donnell looked doubtful.

"I repeated all the arguments I used before, yesterday, but they didn't seem to have any effect this time" he said.

"Did you tell her no decent person would speak to her again if she did this?" O'Hara demanded. "She didn't much like it when I told her so, you remember."

"Well, not in so many words," the Father admitted.

"Well, I think someone should reiterate that to her" the General persisted. "Someone she will listen to. If you ask me, her social sense—or sensibility—is a good deal stronger than her moral sense." He looked rather pleased with himself as he brought out this phrase.

"Who does she listen to, socially?" the priest asked, turning to O'Brien. "I mean, besides the General" he added hastily.

"I think probably Richard Fitzgerald of Kilmichan means a good deal more to her than I do—I mean his good opinion" O'Hara said unexpectedly. "For all her obtuseness, she is surprisingly conscious of the fact that the Brownes, locally, don't rate very high—only Elizabethans, of English origin. Whereas the Fitzgeralds *do* rate high—for all that they probably only came in with Strongbow. But the Irish have some-how annexed them as native, and their very own. Anyhow his mother was an O'Malley, and *they* were here when St. Patrick arrived, according to local belief!"

"Good grief!" Gerald exclaimed. "Can there be anything in that, General?"

"Oh, I'm no expert on pedigrees—but I once met a man who is, and he was firm that one Spanish family, quite obscure now, and the O'Malleys—ditto—could trace their ancestors back, Christian names and all, further than anyone else in Europe."

"Fascinating" Father O'Donnell said.

"Well, Father have you alerted the bank about releasing the money from your account yet?" Gerald now asked.

"No. I thought I had better hear what the General thought first. Was that wrong? I told Lady Browne it would take a week."

"Not wrong at all—normally it would take that time. Anyhow it will give us time to mobilise Richard Fitzgerald."

After further discussion it was agreed that O'Brien should ask "Mr. Richard" if he would undertake the task of making a second attempt to dissuade Lady Browne from her nefari-ous scheme. "He's near me—I can see him any time," the lawyer said. "But I should like to have Mrs. Jamieson with me when I do."

"Why on earth do you want her?" O'Hara asked.

"She was the first person on the spot after the deposit was given, and saw the old lady actually counting it, and was told about the 'document' then—and later also by Mrs. Mar-tin and O'Rahilly."

"Don't you think Fitzgerald will believe you, if you tell him the facts?" O'Hara asked incredulously.

"I think Mrs. Jamieson makes a good witness" O'Brien returned urbanely. "Would you mind?" he asked, turning to Julia.

"Not in the least—I'd love to meet him again" Julia said readily.

"Good—I'll fix a day and ring you up. We can meet in Martinstown."

"But what do I do about the money?" the priest asked.

"I was thinking about that. To put you in the clear I believe it would be a good plan to return it to the old lady, as she has asked for it. So I should like a chit from you to the bank manager asking him to hand it back to whoever you designate as messenger."

"And who do you suggest that should be?" O'Hara asked, rather impatiently.

"Richard Fitzgerald, if he agrees to. I think he would actually stand a better chance of succeeding in his main task if he came cash in hand, so to speak."

O'Hara thought this idea crazy. "Once that greedy old creature feels the actual money between her fingers again, she'll never let it go a second time! I know Mary."

But Father O'Donnell disagreed with him.

"No, General—I believe Mr. O'Brien is right about this. I think Fitzgerald would be more likely to persuade Lady Browne if he returned the money to her."

"But what's to be done with it then, if she were to give it back to him? Oh, and by the way, Father, did you manage to find out yesterday if Moran—if it *was* Moran—had brought her any more?"

"No. She didn't mention having received any, and I thought it more prudent not to ask her."

"Much wiser not" O'Brien said. "As to what to do with the original £3,000, if Richard gets it out of her, and the document, it can sit in his account till we find some means of returning the cash to Moran. Personally, I should greatly enjoy leaving the lot with the Land Commission, and telling Moran to collect it from them!"

Julia laughed at this, and Father O'Donnell looked amused, but O'Hara scowled at Julia, and said sharply— "Don't be frivolous, O'Brien. This has got to be dealt with properly."

"Well, I'm sure you can trust Richard Fitzgerald to do everything with the utmost propriety" the lawyer said. He got up. "I must be getting along. I'll ring you when I've made the appointment with him" he said to Julia. "Goodbye General; goodbye, Father." He went off, but a moment later came back again. "That chit for the bank, Father—I forgot it. We must have that."

"What do I say?" the priest asked, pulling a sheet of writing-paper out of a drawer in his desk. O'Brien dictated a brief simple formula. "We'll put in Fitzgerald's name— I'm sure he'll take it on. Be longing to get at her, when he hears what she's up to, if I know him!" He pocketed the note, and this time he really did drive away.

Julia looked forward to the interview with Richard Fitzgerald, and enjoyed it when it came off a couple of days later. She took the bus into Martinstown, where Gerald picked her up at the station. "Do we go to Kilmichan again?" she asked, as they drove off.

"No, he's coming down to my place. You can never be sure of not being interrupted with Norah in the house, so I asked him to lunch." In fact the Kilmichan car, a rather battered estate van, pulled up on the drive at Rossbeg only moments after they did, and they all went in to Gerald's study together. As before, Julia was struck by Richard's extreme neatness of appearance and precision of speech.

"Well, we want you to do a bit of a conservation job" O'Brien said, after drinks had been handed out.

"Of course, if I can. What, and where?"

"Well, it's quite a story already." He began by recounting O'Rahilly's so-called "development" plans, and his first abortive attempt to buy land for it near Rostrunk, thwarted by General O'Hara.

"How odious" Fitzgerald said.

"So when the General squashed that, he tried again—that strip running south from Lettersall. He got someone to take £3,000—in cash, old fivers—down to old Mary Browne, as a deposit, and got her to sign a typed agreement to sell. Julia here can tell you all about that—she came on her counting them."

Julia told about the fivers in the drive, and the full sum spread out on the desk.

"Poor, wicked old soul" Fitzgerald said with compassion in his voice. "She must be stopped, of course. But where do I come in?"

O'Brien told him the rest of the story, and how the General and Father O'Donnell between them had practically frightened the old woman into giving up the scheme; of the recent fresh approach to her by the "elegant gentleman"— ending up with "So the money is now in the bank, and she has asked the Father to give it back to her, so that she can start all over again."

"And has he done so?" Fitzgerald asked.

"Not yet—but I have advised him that it would be wiser to return it to her."

"I agree. And what do you wish me to do?"

"Take it to her!" O'Brien said laughing. "And use the occasion to make it very very clear to her that she will forfeit your respect, and that of all other reputable people, unless she abandons the whole idea."

"Poor Mary," Fitzgerald said, again compassionately. "But —yes, it must be done. We cannot allow the welfare of so many whole lives to be put at risk, just to spare her feelings. Yes, I will go. How do I get hold of the money?"

O'Brien pulled an envelope out of his pocket. "Here's a chit from the Father to Mr. O'Toole at the bank, instructing him to hand it over. But I'll see him beforehand and tell him to have it parcelled up ready, if you'll tell me when it will suit you to go. It mustn't be for another three days."

"Why not?"

"Because to gain time, and to ask the General's advice, Father O'Donnell told her that the money had been put on deposit—which in fact it was, by Julia here—and that it would take a week to get it out. The week will be up after three days."

"I see." Fitzgerald consulted a pocket diary. "That will be Thursday. Right—I will go over on Friday morning. The sooner one gets an unpleasant job done, the better."

"Splendid. It's very good of you to take it on."

"It is essential to take it on" Fitzgerald said decidedly. "Everyone must do all they can to prevent a thing like this. Oh, one point—suppose I succeed, and Lady Browne again says she doesn't want the cash, what do I do with it?"

"Put it in your account, till we find out who it belongs to" Gerald said, laughing again. "We don't know that yet, for certain, though we suspect Moran, or someone behind him." He got up. "Let's go and have lunch."

9

ON THE FOLLOWING Friday Richard Fitzgerald set out on his uncongenial errand to Ponticum Cottage. He had collected the bundle of notes from the bank the previous day, to allow himself more time, and also a case of whiskey from his wine-merchant; these, with his despatch-case, he loaded into his car. The weather was still broken and uncertain, heavy showers chasing patches of sunshine across the wide valley as he drove down it towards Lough Sayle; in fact it was teeming with rain when he pulled up at the cottage door. He got out, turning up his coat collar, and rang the bell; when Annie opened the door he first took in the case of whiskey, and then went back for his brief-case and the other bundle. By this time Lady Browne appeared, and greeted him warmly—"Richard! What a surprise! And what a pleasure to see you!"

"It may be the last time, Mary," he said taking off his burberry and shaking it out of the door before hanging it up.

"The last time! What can you mean? You're not leaving Kilmichan?"

"I'll tell you presently. Meanwhile here's a little present

for you—one form of comfort!" He indicated the case of spirits.

"Oh Richard, you're too good! Annie, put it in the dining-room. Come in to the fire, Richard—it's a most horrid day. And what is this?" she asked, as he put the parcel containing the notes down on the desk.

"I'll tell you that presently too" he said, warming his hands at the fire.

"You're full of mysteries today! Annie, bring in the decanter, and some glasses."

When the old servant had done this, and had left the room, and Lady Browne had poured out drinks for them both, she again enquired about the parcel.

"It is something of yours that you have no business to possess" he said, in a stern voice. "But you have asked for it to be returned to you, so to save Father O'Donnell trouble, I have brought it over."

"My money!" she exclaimed joyfully, a gleam of cupidity lighting up her old eyes; she started eagerly towards the desk.

"You would do better not to touch it, Mary" Richard said, still in that cold voice.

She stopped at that, and stood still, mid-way across the room, looking a little frightened at his tone.

"Why?" she asked.

"Because if you do, and don't empower me to return it to whoever sent it to you, you will never see me in this house again; and if I meet you outside this house, I will not speak to you. That is why I said this may be the last time" he said. "You have got to make up your mind, finally, Mary, whether you care more about dirty money, or your friends—you can't keep both."

Now she looked really frightened, and sank down into a chair.

"I don't understand you" she said, in rather a weak voice.

"Oh, yes you do. The General and the Father explained it all to you, so clearly that you agreed to return the money once—and then your greed got the better of you again! It is only that you won't face the facts. Well, now you must face them, once and for all."

She began to whimper. "Why are you being so horrid to me?" She dabbed at her eyes.

"I won't waste time arguing with you about what you already understand perfectly well, Mary" he said. "But tell me one thing—did the man who came to see you last week, and persuaded you to re-open the deal, give you any more money?"

"No. He promised me more, but he didn't actually hand any over" she said, in rather a quavering voice, which moved Richard to pity. But he had come to accomplish a task, and he must not let pity deflect him from it.

"Did he give you any promise in writing?"

"No, only a copy of the paper I signed before, with the details of what I was going to sell."

"I shall want you to give me that."

She got up and went to the desk, and took out an envelope; he opened it, and read the typed paper carefully.

"Yes, I see. Well, now you must make up your mind whether you want to ruin this lovely bit of country just to get a few thousands of pounds you don't in the least need, or keep your friends, and their respect and affection. The priest of course will have to visit you, it's his Christian duty; and O'Brien too, it's his legal obligation—but I think you can be sure that, except for the odd tinker who comes thieving or begging, they are the only people who will darken your door in future unless you give up all idea of this sale. Is that really what you want? Do you think it will bring you happiness in your declining years to be completely alone, always?"

"No, oh no" she almost sobbed. "Oh no. You can take the money away again, Richard. But what do I do about Mr. Moran?"

"I will tell you what to do, about him and everything else." He opened his brief-case and took out two letters, ready typed, and spread them on the desk, at the same time removing the parcel with the notes in it. "Read these, carefully, and then if you are prepared to sign them—we will get Annie in to witness your signature."

"Annie can't write her name" Lady Browne objected.

"No, but she can make an X—'Annie Kelly, her mark'— all right" Richard said, smiling. He drew out the chair for her. "Come and sit down, and read away."

She sat down, put on her spectacles, and read both the letters through. In one, to Gerald O'Brien, she solemnly undertook not to sell any land at all, to anyone; in the other, to Moran, she said that she had changed her mind, and was not going to sell any land, in any circumstances, and asked him to return the document agreeing to sell which he had taken away on his last visit—"I am assured that in any case it has no legal validity." As for the money which Mrs. Martin had brought here in cash on an earlier occasion, the letter went on, the owner could have it returned on application to her lawyers, after establishing suitable *bona fides* to his claim—and ended by giving Gerald's name and the address of his firm. Lady Browne read these slowly, occasionally muttering a sentence over to herself. At last—"Why do I have to sign these?" she asked.

"Because I don't trust you not to change your mind again

—and I imagine, my poor Mary, that you can't trust yourself" he said, smiling very gently at her. "These are a safeguard, a fence round your own weakness. Will you sign them?"

"Yes" she said, and reached for a pen.

"No, wait—we must get Annie; I want two witnesses, her as well as myself." He went to the fireplace and rang the bell. When the old servant appeared—"I want you to witness your mistress's signature to some papers, Annie" he told her.

"Sure, I can't write my name, Sir."

"You don't have to. Just watch her Ladyship write hers, here"—he indicated two pencil crosses with a space between them on the first letter, "and then make a cross down here" —he showed her another pencilled cross, below, after the words "First Witness."

"Now Mary, sign, please" he said, drawing the second letter out from under the first one. The old lady signed, Annie duly made her cross—a rather crooked one, as often happens with those who are unused to handling a pen— and Richard pulling the sheet to one side, signed his own name, and wrote in the necessary words after Annie's effort. The same process was gone through with the second letter, and then he told the old servant that that would be all; obviously relieved, she returned to her kitchen. Richard Fitzgerald put the two letters in his brief-case, and took out several carbon copies.

"No, don't get up, Mary—you'd better just initial these" he said, putting them down in front of her.

"What on earth are all these for?"

"One set is for you—you ought always to keep copies of any important papers—and Gerald O'Brien will want some for his files."

"Does Gerald know you're making me do this?"

"Goodness yes—we drafted the letters together. Have you got anywhere safe to keep them?"

"Yes, I've got a despatch-box for my papers. It's in here" she said, pushing back the chair and pointing to the knee-hole under the desk.

"That will do excellently" he said; he went round and drew the case out; Lady Browne, after some searching in her handbag, produced the key, and her copies were finally installed in the tin despatch-box, which Richard replaced under the desk.

"There! You've done the right thing, Mary" he said cheerfully. "Why not have a whiskey on it?"

"Yes, I think I will. I feel quite tired; you wouldn't think just signing your name could make you so tired," she said, going back to her own chair by the fire, and sitting down in it rather heavily. "But you must have one with me, Richard."

"Oh, I will." He poured out a large glass for her and carried it over. "You've taken an important decision this morning, dear Mary—and there is nothing more tiring than decision-making" he said, and stooped down and gave her a kiss. Then he poured out a smaller amount for himself, and raised his glass. "Here's to the right thing!" Richard Fitzgerald said, and drank.

"The right thing" she echoed rather weakly, and herself took a draught. She looked rather more cheerful at the idea of what she had just done being something to be drunk to.

"And here's to absent friends, who will now all remain your friends," he pursued. By the time he left the old lady was actually in quite good heart.

Before going home he reported to Father O'Donnell, who read the copies of the two letters with almost incredulous relief and pleasure. "You have done marvels, Mr. Fitzgerald!"

"I've got the cash too—I'll put that back in your account, till we know what to do with it."

"I have no sort of claim to it" the priest said.

"Well, it's got to be in someone's account" Richard pointed out, practically—"And 'twas to you she handed it over originally." And on his way back through Martinstown he saw the manager, and for the second time the £3,000 was placed on deposit in the priest's account. Mr. O'Toole was thoroughly intrigued, as well as rather amused, by these peculiar proceedings.

"I suppose ye couldn't give me a whiff of an idea why this bundle of money keeps dodging in and out of my safe, Mr. Richard?" he said wheedlingly. "Sure it can't really belong to the priest?"

"To tell you the truth, I don't know *who* it belongs to" Fitzgerald replied cheerfully. "But it has been entrusted to the Father for safe-keeping *pro tem,* so it's in his account it had better be."

O'Brien was as delighted as Father O'Donnell when he was handed the initialled copies of the two letters.

"Marvellous!" he said. "You've got her to tie herself up properly, poor old soul. Did she make a great fuss?"

"She wasn't absolutely enchanted at the idea" Richard said, with his sidelong smile. "But in the end she saw that it was the best thing to do. And the cash is safely back in the bank, earning deposit interest for Father O'Donnell! Oh, just let me have those carbons back for a moment—hadn't I better make a note on them that they were witnessed by myself and Annie Kelly—the signatures, I mean?"

"Yes, that would be as well" O'Brien agreed; Richard quickly made the notes, adding his own signature, and

O'Brien in his turn witnessed that. "You can't be too thorough, dealing with types like Moran" he said, putting the papers away.

"Yes—what *are* you going to do about Moran? It would be as well to keep him away from poor Mary, if it were at all possible—he'll only upset her."

"I don't really know what we *can* do" Gerald said worriedly. "I thought of getting someone in Dublin to go and see the head of his firm, in case they can put some sort of pressure on him. But it's not easy."

"Well, I must be getting along" Richard said, getting up.

"Thank you immensely for all you've done," Gerald said, rising too, and saw him out.

Late that evening Gerald rang up Julia. "I suppose you couldn't switch from Sunday to tomorrow? Lord Oldport has suddenly offered me a day's fishing on the Avonmor—it's one of the best salmon rivers in Mayo, and I'd love you to see a good day's salmon-fishing! He apologised for the short notice, and so do I!—but a tenant who'd rented it for three weeks has fallen ill, and had to cancel at the last minute, and he doesn't want to waste the good water, or the fish! Could you?"

"What time would we have to start?" Julia asked.

"Oh, the earlier the better—whatever you can manage."

"Well I know I can't have the little car tomorrow—Helen wants it, and Michael's going to a meeting in Ballina. Hold on, I'll go and look up the time of the early bus."

The early bus proved to be very early when it passed Rostrunk; 8:15. "I can be at the station at Martinstown by nine, or near after" Julia announced, returning to the telephone. "That do?"

"Yes, that will be all right. Right, see you there then.

Oh, and Julia, bring something to sit on—a mackintosh square or an oilskin."

"Will do."

In view of the early start Julia went out to the kitchen when Nonie and Attracta had gone to bed, and put herself up a lunch of meat pies and cold duck, and a flask of sherry, which she stowed in her haversack; she asked her host if he could lend her an old oilskin? "To sit on—Gerald's got a day's fishing from Lord Oldport, and he wants me to go along," she explained, in answer to his inevitable question.

"Which river, d'you know?" O'Hara enquired.

"It sounded like Avonmor."

"The Avonmor! Lucky devil!" The General exclaimed. "It ought to be fishing perfectly just now, too. Yes, come along"—and he presently routed out a rather elderly oilskin from among the welter which hung in the cloakroom passage. "If you fold that double, it'll keep you dry enough."

"Thank you, Michael."

"Better take plenty of gaspers—the midges can be pretty bad out there" he added.

Julia gratefully put an extra supply of cigarettes and a tube of midge-repellant cream into her haversack, took a thermos of coffee up to bed with her, and set her alarm-clock for 6:30. At ten to eight she was hurrying up the lane to catch the bus, and just after nine, descended from it at Martinstown station, where Gerald was waiting.

"Sorry I couldn't come and fetch you, and save you the early start" he said, as she got in, "but I had to get a lot of work polished off before I could get away. I was at my desk at 5:30!"

"You poor darling!"

The Avonmor proved to be the lower half of the river running down the wide valley by which one approached

Lough Sayle, on the right of the road and, except where a bridge crossed over, at some distance from it; Julia had never been down to the water. Gerald drove the car off the road, and they walked across the grass, grazed fairly short by sheep, which even so early in the summer had a yellowish tinge—indeed when the sun came out for a moment the whole valley looked golden. Julia commented on this.

"Yes, I don't know why it isn't more green—the sort of grass I suppose. We don't want too much of that sun, though."

On reaching the river-bank Gerald dumped his gear at the spot of his choice, pulled on his waders, set up his rod, and studied a book of flies carefully before selecting one and tying it to his cast. He handed Julia the landing-net—"If I'm lucky, you'll have to wield that."

"O.K." Julia said, spreading the General's oilskin, folded double, at the edge of a bank and seating herself; she knew how important it is, when sitting out of doors for hours on end, to have one's feet well below one's knees. The place Gerald had chosen was a long pool below a shallow fall, its further bank fringed with the tall dark-green fronds of Osmunda Regalis, Royal Fern, beautiful against the golden grass; behind her, the nearby mountains stood up with an extraordinary authority, grey and craggy, dominating the valley—a pair of ravens were tumbling and fooling about in the sky overhead, as ravens do—beyond the Osmunda, the ground fell away in gentle undulations towards a distant blue line—the Atlantic Ocean.

Immediately below the further bank ran a stream of bubbles from the fall, and into this Gerald threw his fly gently, and let it float downstream. Julia unslung her haversack and rubbed her face, neck and hands with her anti-midge mixture, lit a cigarette, and composed herself to watch. The solitude and isolation were complete; except for the nonsensical ravens she and her companion had this beautiful place entirely to themselves. But what soon struck her was that this man, her dear Gerald, who had been so insistent that she should come and share this wonderful thing, a day's salmon-fishing, had forgotten all about her—he was utterly absorbed in what he was doing. She for her part watched him more carefully than she had ever done before, for so long at a stretch: she was struck by his patience, his absolute concentration, the perfect co-ordination of his movements as he cast—hand, arm, and rod were like one beautiful piece of mechanism as, over and over again, he placed the fly so delicately on the water, in precisely the spot, she was sure, that he wished. A good angler at work is worth watching, on any showing; if the watcher happens to be intensely interested in the angler, something can be learned about him. Slowly, slowly, he moved down the pool, casting now on the far side, now in the centre, and letting the fly float gently down with the current.

At last, suddenly, she saw the rod bend—he was into a fish; Julia jumped at the scream of the reel as the line ran out. He got out onto the bank and stood there; slowly, steadily, carefully, he worked the head of the rod up; and then, still slowly and steadily, very gently, he began to reel in. The fish was a fair-sized one, and dashed wildly about the pool. Dumping all her belongings Julia took the landing-net and moved cautiously down towards her companion, and perched herself on a slab of rock. Gradually the fish's struggle grew less violent, its dashes about the pool more infrequent, till after some fifteen minutes it lay lax and passive at the end of the line.

"Julia, bring the landing-net!" Gerald shouted peremptorily.

"I've got it here" she said, coming up beside him.

"Well get the other side of me, put it in the water, and hold it still."

"Right." She moved round and a step or two downstream from him, and did as she was told; when the net was in the water Gerald floated the fish down into it. Using both hands, Julia managed to heave it out onto the grass behind her.

"Fine!" he said. "Gosh, he is a beauty!" He took the fish, still in the net, up onto the grass well away from the river, and laid it down—Julia herself was moved by its beauty, its strength and wildness.

"How will you kill it?" she asked. She had caught and killed plenty of trout in her time, up at Glentoran, but obviously one couldn't pick a salmon up in one hand and knock its head smartly against a rock—and the fish was still flapping its tail in the net, albeit rather feebly.

"So," Gerald said. He pulled a 9-inch bolt out of his pocket and hit the salmon on the nose with the heavy end —immediately it lay still.

"One ought to have a priest" he said, "but as I have no salmon water I've never bothered to get one. Anyhow this is every bit as good—the weight at the end is what matters." He wiped the bolt with a tuft of grass and put it back in his pocket. "You take the rod" he said, and carried the fish up to the head of the pool, where they had left their gear.

Julia followed with the rod, and managed to find a place on the uneven bank where she could lay it perfectly flat; having done this, she re-seated herself on the oilskin, and drew the haversack towards her.

"Lunch?" she asked.

"In a minute." He lit a cigarette, and for a few moments just stood looking at the salmon—Julia felt that he was still in the other world that he and the fish had shared during their long struggle. Then he came and perched beside her on the oilskin. "I can't hope that that has meant to you what it meant to me, but I hope you got something out of it, my dearest" he said gently, but with a sort of muted urgency, putting his arm round her.

She was moved by this.

"Indeed I did, dear Gerald" she said, and turned her face to his for a kiss; as she did so she realised that she was turning to him with her whole being, and that the answer to the question she had been asking herself for the past few weeks was an unhesitating Yes. She did love him, and always would; there was no question of marrying to secure a kind step-father for the Philipino, though that would undoubtedly be thrown in as a bonus. With a happy sigh she laid her head on his shoulder.

"It's so difficult to explain" he said. "When a salmon takes the fly it's like an earthquake—and afterwards its a mixture of a battle and a love-affair. Can you imagine that?"

"Yes, I can indeed. Oh Gerald, bless you for wanting me to understand."

"I want you to understand everything I do—that might seem to be only *my* thing" he said, slowly. He bent his head to kiss her again. "Why, you're crying!" he said—there were tears on her cheek.

"Only because I'm so happy" she said. "Oh Gerald, I do love you for being so kind!"

"I don't see what's kind about that" he said. "But darling —you say you love me—does that mean that you've made up your mind?"

"Yes."

"Oh my dearest!" He enveloped her in a tremendous embrace—then took her by the shoulder and held her a little away from him, and studied her face. "And you really think you can take it all—poor shabby old Rossbeg, and Bridgie, and everything?"

How like Gerald, she thought, to realise how daunting the prospect of Bridgie would be to any new mistress of his house. "Yes, precious Gerald" she repeated, nodding her head.

"I shouldn't like to fire Bridgie" he said thoughtfully, "she's been with me for such ages."

"No, you couldn't possibly. We'll make it work somehow. Are you fond of her?" she asked, with genuine curiosity.

"Oh no!—she's a maddening old creature, and lazy with it" he said frankly. "But if I'd been going to fire her, I ought to have done it years ago, and I was too lazy then."

"Well, now you can't, so that's settled" said Julia. "We'll make it work" she repeated.

They had a very peaceful, happy lunch after that; Julia observed with horror the sandwiches of meat paste and stale bread which the odious Bridgie had supplied for her master, and fed him copiously on the excellent provisions which she had brought from the Rostrunk larder.

"D'you think you could teach Bridgie to make meat pies like these?" he asked, munching.

"I doubt it. I'll make them myself when she's gone to bed. She goes up quite early."

"Does Helen make these herself?"

"I shouldn't think so—she's taught her girls to cook. They're younger—you can teach *young* Irish girls to be beautiful cooks, Helen says."

He drove her back to Rostrunk, but wouldn't come in— "There's more work I must finish at home tonight." They kissed goodbye in the lane, and Julia ran in over the cattle-stops. She went first to the garden; Helen as she had hoped, was there, just wiping her tools prior to bringing them in.

"Have a good day?" she asked.

"Yes, Gerald got a lovely salmon. Helen, I'm going to marry him."

"Oh, well *done!*" She dropped her tools and gave her friend a warm and unwonted kiss. "I *am* glad. You couldn't find a sweeter person if you combed Europe. And it will be lovely to have you within reach." She picked up her tools and started back towards the house. "What about Bridgie? Shall you be able to stand her? She's a ghastly old creature."

"Gerald asked that" Julia said, beginning to laugh.

"He *would!* And what did you say?"

"Oh, of course I said I could. What I'm secretly hoping is that she won't be able to stand me—*and* a nursery."

"Ah, I daresay you're right. Well, I couldn't be more glad, Julia." They stowed the tools in the shed; washing her hands in the adjoining cloak-room—"May I tell Michael?" Lady Helen asked.

"Yes, do."

"I'm not sure that he's back yet"—but when they went through into the library for drinks General O'Hara was there, pouring himself out a whiskey.

"Oh, hullo! Julia, how did O'Brien get on? Get some fish?"

"One—a beauty."

"What weight?"

"I've no idea, but it was *that* long" Julia said, holding her hands some thirty inches apart. "And it was all I could do to lift it out of the water in the landing-net."

"H'm—nine or ten-pounder, I expect. Which pool did he kill it in?"

But Julia wasn't able to describe the pool and its location in such a way as to satisfy O'Hara as to its identity, nor could she say what fly had been used; however she was able to state firmly that Gerald had played the fish for just over a quarter of an hour before it was landed—it so happened that she had looked at her watch with the idea of suggesting lunch just before that unforgettable moment when the scream of the reel made her jump. Lady Helen wisely waited till her husband had finished his inquisition before coming out with the news which she was burning to impart, but as he poured himself a second small whiskey she said—

"Michael, Julia's going to marry Gerald O'Brien."

"That so, Julia? Oh, good show! Fix it up today? no wonder you're pretty vague about the fishing! Well, I congratulate you—he's a first-class chap. Bit retiring, but I daresay you'll be able to alter that—bring him out, and so on." He came over and wrung her by the hand. Julia was very much startled and touched by this expansiveness on her host's part, and his unexpected percipience; she was still more touched when he looked at his watch and saying—"Yes, there's just time to chill it"—hurried out to the cellar to get out a bottle of champagne, in which her and Gerald's health was formally drunk at dinner.

This pleasant business over, the husband and wife each began to recount their doings, as middle-aged, and still more elderly, married people are wont to do when they have spent the day apart. Lady Helen's activities were soon dealt with, they were customary and dull, but the General had plenty to say. After the Committee in Ballina he had had lunch with some fellas, and they had started talking about the fella Moran and his development schemes—"He *is* behind O'Rahilly, so I daresay you were right about him being the man who went to see Mary Browne, Julia" O'Hara said—very handsomely, Julia thought. "And they say there's some big American interest behind Moran. Of course I told them how I'd given O'Rahilly the brush-off."

"Well, have they got any plans for stopping horrible Moran? That seems to be the important thing" Lady Helen asked.

"Ah, the less said about that the better" the General said darkly. "There are a lot of riding men in Dublin."

"I don't like that idea much" said his wife. "But if it's the only way . . ."

"Gerald thought it might be worth while if someone went to see the head of Moran's firm, and got them to tell him to lay off" Julia put in.

"Ah, one of the fellas at Ballina had that idea too" O'Hara said. "Seems he knows them all. Did O'Brien say anything else, Julia?"

"Yes. He told me that Mr. Fitzgerald had been to see Lady Browne, and had got her to sign two letters, which they had drafted together—one to him, Gerald, undertaking not to sell any land at all, to anyone; and the other to Moran, saying that she had changed her mind and wasn't going to sell, ever, and that he could have his £3,000 deposit back on application to her lawyers. He's got copies of them, initialled by Mr. Fitzgerald; they were witnessed by 'Mr. Richard,' as they call him, and old Annie."

"Well, I suppose that gives a certain measure of security" Lady Helen said.

"Mr. Fitzgerald gave the priest copies of both, so that he could keep an eye on her" Julia went on.

"Smart fella, Richard!" O'Hara said. "But I should like to see those letters. Did you say O'Brien's got copies of them, Julia?"

"Yes, he said so today. Mr. Fitzgerald brought them to him yesterday evening, I think."

"I should like to see what young Richard got Mary to put

her name to, I must say" the General repeated. "I don't suppose O'Brien would mind, eh?"

"I've no idea" Julia replied prudently.

"You could ring him up and ask him, dear" Lady Helen said.

"No, better not telephone about it."

"Then send a note."

"Don't want that sort of thing in writing, either." O'Hara hummed and hemmed, in obvious embarrassment; at last—"I don't suppose you'd mind taking a message to him, Julia, verbally?" he said, with unwonted hesitation. "Then, if he didn't mind, you could bring them over."

"I don't mind doing that in the least" Julia said readily. "Only I shan't be able to catch him at home unless I go tomorrow. Would I be able to have the car, Helen? What about Mass?"

"Have the big car. You'd better ring him up and fix a time. Has everyone finished? If so, let's go" the General said, getting up, regardless of the slice of pineapple half-finished on his wife's plate.

This plan was soon settled on the telephone. Gerald expressed a wish only to go to late Mass, as he had been up so early that morning, so Julia's visit was arranged for the afternoon; Lady Helen did up two sections of honey for Mrs. Keane—"You won't mind dropping them, Julia, as you're passing the gate? She adores honey in the comb." Julia again said that she would not mind in the least; she would like to see Mrs. Keane again. So the following afternoon found her backing the car into the field-road opposite the two pretty whitewashed stone gate-posts, ready to drive straight out again; the car was heard, and as she walked up the path between the rose bushes Mrs. Keane opened the door to her.

"Well well, if it isn't Mrs. Jamieson! You're heartily welcome. Come in to the fire."

"I've brought you a little present from Lady," Julia said, sitting down by the glowing turfs—to her relief "the louts" appeared to be absent. Mrs. Keane took the honey joyfully— "Well now, isn't Lady too kind altogether!"—and put it in the cupboard below the shelves, from which she reached down glasses and the bottle of the detested "hard stuff"; but Julia begged off this, and asked if she couldn't have a cup of tea?—the metal teapot was sitting snugly in the ashes on the hearth.

" 'Tis only a minyit since I wet it, but I'll make fresh" Mrs. Keane said; this Julia wouldn't allow, and presently they were sitting sipping cups of fine strong tea. After enquiries for "Lady" and "the Gineral" Mrs. Keane asked anxiously about the well-being of "Lady's" car—"Didn't it get mended yet? I see 'tis the big car ye have today."

"Oh that's only because Lady wanted the little car for visits, and the General wasn't going out this afternoon" Julia explained.

"Ah, I heard he was in Ballina yesterday" Mrs. Keane said, surprising Julia—now how on earth did this pleasant woman know that? Oh well, something might have taken the louts to Ballina, she supposed, or a neighbour might have been there. But she was more surprised still when, after refilling her cup with tea now the colour of stewed prunes, Mrs. Keane asked—"And did Billy O'Rahilly get poor old Lady Browne to sell him the land he was wanting for his hotel? I'm after hearing he was going to have a swimming-pool with *hot* water in it!"

"I don't think anything has been settled yet" Julia replied cautiously.

"The General soon stopped him back the Bay at Rostrunk!" Mrs. Keane pronounced with evident satisfaction in her tone. "Sure and why wouldn't he? What do he and Lady want with a great hotel right at the end of their garden?"

"I don't think they were worrying so much about themselves, and the hotel, though it would have disturbed their privacy, of course" Julia was moved to say—since Mrs. Keane knew so much already, she might as well hear of the more objectionable features of Billy's plans. "It was the casino they thought would be so bad for the neighbourhood."

"And what might that be, Mrs. Jamieson, dear?"

"Oh, a casino is a place for all sorts of gambling—with cards, and gambling machines, and of course lots of drinks. But more for gambling than anything else. That's putting a terrible and perfectly needless temptation in the way of all the young people for miles around, the General felt."

"He was in the right of it" Mrs. Keane said. "Will Billy put one of them things up on Lady Browne's land, if he gets it?"

"Yes—he seems to have a casino along with the hotel, wherever he puts it—you can be sure of that" Julia stated roundly.

"The Lord have mercy on us! That's a wicked thing altogether. Well, well! 'Tis to be hoped Mr. O'Brien will argue her out of it, the creature! He and that priest at Lettersall—he's a most holy man, they say. And Mr. O'Brien's a good Cat'lic himself." She eyed Julia rather craftily. "Is Mrs. Jamieson a Cat'lic?"

"No" Julia said smiling. She got up. "I must be getting along" she said.

"Ye'll be looking in at Rossbeg?"

"Yes, I've got to fetch something for the General. Goodbye." She rather hastened out—Mrs. Keane might be a sweet person, but her all-knowingness and interest could be a little embarrassing.

Gerald was perfectly ready to let General O'Hara see the copies of Lady Browne's two letters. "After all, he laid the ground work, and persuaded her to give up the money the first time" he said. "He has every right to see them. But I shall want them back. Maybe you could bring them?"

"Yes, next week-end."

"Oh my darling, do let's get married soon! I hate being rationed to seeing you once a week!" the man burst out. "When can we get married?"

"Well, how long does it take in your Church? Do you have to have banns called once a week for three weeks?"

"Not called, no—the notice of the marriage is put up in writing in the Church porch on three successive Sundays. But darling, don't say *your Church*, like that! Couldn't you become a Catholic? Should you mind very much?"

She laid her hand on his distressed face.

"I don't think I should mind at all" she said. "Nearly all the nicest people I've known have been Catholics. It's more a question of whether the Church would mind a rather un-religious person becoming a Catholic just to please somebody else."

"I think the Church holds that a good action is a good action, even if the motive could be improved upon" Gerald said smiling, "and she certainly regards becoming a Catholic as a good action! And I don't think your motive is too bad either—to please someone else is an act of charity, surely?"

"I should never have thought of it like that—it seems to me just a perfectly natural thing to do."

"I don't imagine you have ever thought about it at all" he said, still smiling. "You have loving impulses, and act on them. The trouble with the Church is that she does think, and tries to make her children think too. That's why she insists on people—if they're adults, at least—receiving thorough instruction before they can be welcomed into the Church."

"How long does thorough instruction take?" Julia asked.

"I don't really know—most of my friends are cradle Catholics. Anyhow, they would know at Farm Street, or the Oratory; and you'd do better to receive instruction in London."

"Why?"

"Oh, most of our priests here are pretty fundamentalist still!" O'Brien said smiling. "You'd much better get your instruction in London. And there's no great rush; I'm sure the dear old Archbishop would get me a dispensation for a mixed marriage."

"You mean marry first and become a Catholic later?"

"Yes—on the assumption that you were thinking of getting married rather quickly. Were you?" He took her hand and looked eagerly into her face.

"I just thought it mightn't be a bad plan to get married while I'm over here anyhow, without any fuss or anything, and then go back and fetch the Philipino. It was just an idea" Julia said.

He got up and walked about the room.

"You don't realise how much I long to agree" he said, sitting down and taking her hand again. "But—no, my dearest heart, it isn't a good idea. All those dear people at Glentoran, who are devoted to you, would be disappointed, and even hurt, and justly so—especially that quite darling old Mrs. Hathaway."

"She doesn't live up there—she lives in London" Julia said, foolishly—she was so startled that he should feel so strongly about this that she spoke without thinking.

"Well, then she can come up again and stay for the wedding—and you can stay with her in London first and let her help to choose your trousseau, which she'll adore doing," he said, smiling at her very tenderly.

"I don't really need a trousseau—I've got heaps of things."

"Well, only buy as little as she will allow!" he said, still smiling. "But do be married from Glentoran—it's been your home for so long. There's a Catholic Church within reach, isn't there?"

"Oh Lord yes—the Macdonalds' Chapel is quite close."

"There you are then. That's settled."

10

IN FACT there was a great deal more to be settled, as Gerald and Julia found out even before she left that afternoon—in fact as soon as they sat down and began to make plans. Gerald raised the question of the lift from the kitchen to the nursery, which Julia had suggested on an earlier visit—"If we're going to have alterations done, I'd better put them in hand at once; we don't work all that fast in the West. You'd better come and show me exactly where you want it"—and he took a pad from his desk and made her come out and decide on the exact place there and then, and afterwards go round the house with him to see if she wanted anything else done? That was really all that was needed in the way of structural alterations, except for the addition of a hot rail for airing in the nursery bathroom; but in the course of this peregrination Julia was painfully struck by the extreme ugliness of a great deal of the furniture. This reminded her, inevitably, of all the beautiful pieces from Gray's Inn, now in store, and of her and Philip Jamieson's pictures, some very good, as she looked at the sad and rather faded watercolours in the drawing room—all-too-obviously amateur family productions. She sank down into a chair and looked about her, discouraged.

"I've tired you, marching you about like that" he said, looking at her with concern.

"Not really. Gerald, do you *like* these pictures?"

"I've never really noticed them—yes, I suppose I do. I don't mind them; they've always been there. Why? Are they very bad?"

"Yes, frightful!" she said, smiling. "Who painted them?"

"Oh, various grandmothers and great-aunts, I think—I don't really know. But if you don't like them, we'll take them down. What would you put in their place? I mean, it's nice to have *some* pictures in a room, isn't it?"

"Over the mantel-piece I'd like to put a rather lovely Seurat I've got. But what about the wallpaper? I expect it's faded."

"We'll soon see." He lifted one or two pictures down off the walls. In fact in the West of Ireland, with little strong sunshine, wallpaper doesn't fade as much as in England, but where the pictures had been the difference in tone was fairly marked. "Well, it's time this room was re-papered, anyhow" Gerald said cheerfully.

"Yes—or perhaps just colour-washed; ever so much cheaper" Julia said, feeling remorseful. "There must be firms in Galway who do colour-washing."

"Oh yes, I'm sure there are—Helen will know. Then you can scrap these and hang others wherever you like. Have you got a lot of pictures?"

"Quite a number, yes. But we won't put up any you don't like, dearest" she said. "You may think mine frightful!"

"I don't notice pictures much" he said, cheerfully. "What about furniture—have you got a lot of that too? If so, I expect you'd like to have your own stuff about you."

"How good you are!" But Julia didn't feel equal to tackling the question of furniture in depth just then—she approached it from a slant.

"Can I have a morning-room?" she asked.

"I'm sure you can—but what is a morning-room?"

"Oh, a little room of my own, preferably downstairs, where I can keep my books and papers, and write letters and do accounts. There's one I saw just now, near the front door, that would do beautifully."

"Show me" he said. "No, not if you're tired."

"Not in the least tired." She got up, and led him down the hall—on the opposite side to the drawing-room she opened a door into a small room with a large window looking onto the drive and the pastures beyond it; there were several rows of coat-hooks on the walls, but very little else.

"But this is part of the gents!" Gerald objected.

"Well, need it be? Isn't there room enough to hang coats in the hall?"

"But it *is*" he said; he opened a door on one side of the room which did indeed, as Julia saw, lead into the men's lavatory, wash-basin and all.

"Well, wall that door up. This would be perfect; my desk in the window, so that I can watch your pretty horses while I lick my stamps, and plenty of room for books on the other walls."

"Shall you want book-shelves put up?" he asked, getting out his pad. "How many?"

"None, bless you! I've got plenty of book-cases, and removable shelves too—they can all come over with the nursery stuff."

"Why, does the nursery have to have special furniture?" he asked, surprised, as they walked back to the drawing-room.

"Nothing much—children do have cots and play-pens,

you know, and their own little tables and chairs; and as I've got all that, why buy new? Oh, and fenders round the fires, of course; and I daresay Nannine Mack would like her old armchair—make her feel at home. That lot will really mean a lift-van anyhow, so we might just as well fill it up with my pictures and book-shelves and desk."

"Then what about the furniture that's in those rooms now?"

Julia repressed a strong impulse to say "Burn it!" and substituted "Give it away! I'm sure there are nuns in Galway who could find a use for it—nuns find a use for everything!"

But Gerald was as sharp as a razor, especially where Julia was concerned, and read her unspoken thought. "Is it frightful, like these pictures?" he enquired.

"Well actually, *yes*" Julia stated frankly—now they were at it.

"Is the furniture in this room frightful too? I daresay it is; one doesn't notice things one's grown up with. Do say" he said earnestly.

"Not the upholstered stuff, with the pretty cretonnes Helen got for you; that's perfectly all right," Julia said remorsefully. "But I don't honestly like all those black painted Victorian tables and shelves and what-nots, very much. I've got some rather lovely Queen Anne things we could replace them with, if you didn't mind."

"I don't mind anything, so long as you have the place the way you want it," he said, kissing her. "Surely you know that by now?"

"Oh Gerald, you are a love! Very well, we'll have *two* lift-vans, and enrich the nuns with all the horrors! And I can have all my pretty things, and everyone will be happy. I've got enough for several bedrooms, too." At the mention of bedrooms a thought struck her—probably the beds at Rossbeg were as ghastly to sleep on as the furniture was to look at. She got up. "May we go and see?"

Her foreboding proved to be perfectly correct. Gerald—they began with his room—slept in a smallish double bed with quantities of brass knobs at its head and foot; Julia at once got onto it, and bounced up and down; it sagged in the middle, and the mattress was lumpy.

"Goodness! Can you sleep on this? I shouldn't get a wink."

"Don't you like sleeping in a double-bed?"

"Yes, very much, darling—only a really *big* one, six feet wide, with a box-spring mattress, and a proper over-lay. Actually that's one thing I haven't got, but I'm sure you can get them in Dublin; Helen has a beauty."

"Well, you order whatever you like in Dublin as you go through, and have it sent down."

"Oh, bless you"—but before she could say any more Bridgie burst into the room, her greying red hair wilder than ever, her face distraught.

"Oh, may the Lord have mercy on us! Timmie Keane is dead!"

Gerald crossed himself. "When? And what of?"

"They found him in the field by the tractor, Jamesy Halloran said. I can't know what of. Oh, may the Lord have mercy on us!" Bridgie repeated, and burst into loud sobs.

"I'd better see Halloran—the bran will have come, so. Can you see to her, Julia? I'll not be long" Gerald said, and hurried out. Julia led the sobbing Bridgie back to the kitchen, sat her down at the table, and gave her a glass of water, wondering a little what connection there might be between these ill tidings and the advent of the bran? Bridgie, after a taste of the water, asked if she could have a "suppeen" of whiskey —"There's some in the dining-room, Mrs. Jamieson." Julia fetched it, and presently Bridgie began to mop her eyes, and took the glasses over to the sink; when Julia judged that she could be left she went through to the drawing-room, prudently taking the whiskey-bottle with her. After a few moments she heard Gerald's step in the hall—she went out, and found him at the telephone.

"Is Dr. Fergus in? Oh, where did he go, d'you know? To Keane's, did he? Is it true that Timmie Kelly had an accident? Oh, that's very bad!—I'm awful sorry. Thanks." He rang off.

"What did they say?" Julia asked.

"Yes, I'm afraid he is dead."

"Oh dear! He was so nice."

"Come in and sit down" Gerald said, leading her back to the drawing-room. As they sat—"Why are you carrying that whiskey-bottle round with you?" he asked in surprise.

"Oh, I gave Bridgie some—she was upset. I didn't want to leave the bottle in the kitchen."

"Quite right!"

"I *am* sorry for Mrs. Keane" Julia said. "Shall you go over?"

"Presently. I think I'll just ring up Father MacCarthy and see if he knows what happened."

"Gerald, tell me one thing—I know Timmie was a cousin, but is his name really Kelly?"

"Yes, certainly."

"Then why did Bridgie call him Timmie *Keane?*"

"Oh, they always do that here—refer to a person by the surname of whoever employs them—it's one means of identification. I bet you anything you like that Bridgie is always spoken of as Bridgie O'Brien, locally, and Mac as Mac O'Brien."

"I should have thought that made things rather confusing."

"No, not really. In Gaelic there would probably be an inflexion of the surname implying the genitive, so that they would be saying 'Keane's Timmie' or 'O'Brien's Bridgie'— but these shades of meaning get obliterated in English." He got up. "Now I'll go and ring Father MacCarthy."

Julia sat on, pondering this information, and thinking sadly of Mrs. Keane's distress and loss, left with no support but that of the louts;—absent-mindedly she was still nursing the bottle of whiskey; when she heard Gerald saying goodbye she went through and put it back on the dining-room sideboard.

"Yes, he was dead when the Father got there" Gerald said, returning. "He seems to have fallen off the tractor; Dr. Fergus told the priest he thought it might have been a heart attack—it seems he'd had heart trouble for a goodish time. I think I'll just go and get a few roses, and take them over."

"Yes, and I'll be getting back. Oh dear, I am so sorry." She kissed him and went.

Lady Helen was greatly distressed when Julia brought her the tidings of Timmie's death.

"Oh, *poor* Mrs. Keane! How terrible for her—he managed everything after Keane died. Did you hear when the funeral was to be?"

"No, Gerald didn't say. He was going to take her some flowers after I left."

"Oh well, I'll ring Father MacCarthy. Day after tomorrow, I expect; and he's sure to be buried from the Chapel at Kilmichan."

Both these surmises proved to be correct, and Gerald provided the further information that the "wake," which in Ireland always immediately precedes the funeral, would take place at three P.M.

"Yes, of course I shall go" Lady Helen said, in reply to

her husband's enquiry. "But I don't think you need trouble, Michael."

"Certainly I shall come" the General said. "Keane was a very decent fellow, and she's a good woman."

"Would you care to come, Julia?"

"Yes, I'd love to."

"Anyhow you know her, and you're going to be neighbours. I expect she'd appreciate it if you went."

So the Rostrunk party all drove down together. Julia had been wondering where on earth they would be able to leave the car, at the top of that narrow road; but a stretch of the dry-stone wall just short of the farm had been pulled down, giving access to a field which was already in use as a car-park —they left the car there and went to the house on foot. Mrs. Keane, all in black, met them at the door and greeted them with sad dignity; she at once led them to the far end of the room, where all that was mortal of Timmie lay in his open coffin—the large bed and the screen had been removed, and the table pushed to one side. Timmie lay looking exceedingly peaceful, but with that strange remoteness which death confers; Julia was a little startled to see that he was neatly dressed in, obviously, his best suit, his tie fastened with a handsome gold tie-pin. Lady Helen crossed herself, dropped to her knees and said a prayer; when she got up Mrs. Keane said—"I knew he'd like to be buried wearing your tie-pin, Lady."

"Oh, bless you, Agnes" Helen said, a tear or two falling as she spoke.

"Ah" said an elderly woman, who was standing at the far side of the coffin, "I never saw a finer corpse above board."

One of the Keane sons now came up with a glass of whiskey for the General, who was accommodated on a settle; the room was crowded with people, among whom Julia noticed the Fitzgeralds as well as O'Brien. There was a general murmur of conversation, but in lowered tones; the men were all drinking whiskey, not the colourless home-brewed "hard stuff," but normal John Jamieson out of bottles, got in for the occasion. Lady Helen moved about, talking to this one and that, she obviously knew everyone—Julia, rather at a loss, remained close to the General; Mrs. Keane continued to greet any new arrivals at the door.

After about half an hour the men, as by some common impulse, all went out and stood in the garden and the road outside, the General among them, where they began to smoke; Mrs. Keane and two or three younger women took up a couple of tea-pots from by the fire and poured out cups of tea which they handed round to the women; they were followed by three little girls who did the same with plates of sandwiches and cakes. While this was going on two or three men came in and began, unobtrusively, to place the lid on the coffin; Mrs. Keane, her tears now flowing freely, took a last sad glance at Timmie's calm face, and then went on re-filling tea-cups. Julia wondered if she was about to renew her acquaintance with her old adversary, the Martinstown hearse, but when the coffin was carried out it was placed on a farm-cart; the men, putting out their cigarettes, formed up behind it, and the long, sad procession wound down the road towards Kilmichan. Lady Helen managed to intercept her husband before he could join it—"Michael, *please* don't try to walk it; *please*. Come in the car with us. It's over a mile and a half."

"I often walk more than that on the river" he grumbled, nevertheless coming with her.

"Yes, but then you can sit for a minute whenever you want to—this is a steady plug, and so *slow*."

Julia had managed to snatch a word with Gerald before

he, like Richard Fitzgerald, started to walk with the other men behind the coffin; when she went back to the car the General was urging his wife to start the engine.

"Darling, we must let Mrs. Keane get away first; she's got Kelly's hire-car—I don't think she drives herself, and anyhow she wouldn't today. The engine will get quite hot enough with over a mile in bottom gear."

"Oh—ah" O'Hara grunted, in reluctant assent.

"Helen, may I ask you something while we wait?" Julia asked.

"Of course."

"That old woman who was standing near the coffin when Mrs. Keane took us over said something so extraordinary. I want to know what she can have meant."

"What did she say?" Lady Helen asked.

"She said she'd never seen a finer corpse 'above board.' What *did* she mean?"

"Oh, when the corpse is washed and dressed, and before rigor sets in, it's placed on a board while the women who are laying it out put the finishing touches—like doing a woman's hair, or brushing a man's; that's all 'above board' means— it's quite a common expression for a corpse after it's been laid out."

"Thank you. I wonder if it has any connection with the ordinary use of 'above board' in English" Julia speculated.

"What extraordinary things you want to know!" the General commented.

"I've no idea—it's an interesting notion" Lady Helen said, starting the engine; Mrs. Keane's hire-car had moved down the road. The long procession of cars crept after it; several were emitting steam, their radiators obviously boiling, by the time they pulled up outside the Chapel at Kilmichan. The coffin had been carried in for the Requiem Mass; Julia and

Lady Helen attended this, but O'Hara, on his wife's advice, remained outside in the car—"You'll be much more comfortable; it's sure to get terribly stuffy and airless in there, with all this crowd" she told him. The Mass over, the coffin was carried on men's shoulders to the graveyard, which here was next door to the Church; the General made to rejoin his wife, but stood back when he saw that Mrs. Keane was leaning on her arm—both women looked rather white. Julia joined him, and they followed to the graveside, where Mrs. Keane stood, still with her arm through Helen O'Hara's. When, at the words "ashes to ashes, dust to dust," the ritual handful of soil was thrown onto the coffin—"Oh, Lady, they're throwing the clay on him!" the poor woman burst out, in uncontrollable grief.

When the funeral was over, Lady Helen slipped across to where her husband stood with Julia.

"You two go on home—I'm going back with Agnes for a little while."

"How will you get home?" O'Hara asked.

"Keep the hire-car, and come back in that."

"It'll cost the earth" the General objected.

"Well, I'll pay." She went back to Mrs. Keane and got into the car with her, and they drove off.

The wake and the funeral together had made a strong impression on Julia—the simplicity and dignity of the proceedings, the devoutness and reverence of the participants. She had told Gerald that she had no objection to becoming a Catholic in a rather neutral frame of mind—today, suddenly, it was as if she saw a door opening, that she was presently going to walk through. And during all the conversation that ensued when Gerald O'Brien came across to speak to them, her thoughts were not on what was being said, but on the vista through that partly open door. After an exchange of greetings—"That was a good job, getting Mary Browne to sign those letters about not selling any land. But what are you doing to make that fellow Moran shut up? I don't want him going on coming down and pestering her," the General said.

"I have something in mind," O'Brien replied.

"Well, I wish you could keep him out of Mayo altogether —that would be the best; nobody wants him here," O'Hara pursued.

"Short of getting him imprisoned, I should have thought that might not be so easy" Julia put in.

"I may be on to something that might have the desired effect" O'Brien said. But he was rather mysterious about it, and though the General pressed him, he wouldn't say any more.

Lady Helen only got back just in time to change for dinner; over the meal she passed on various items of gossip which she had learned from the car-hire driver, who like most of his kind was a fountain of local information. Eventually—

"And the *poor* nuns at Roskeen! Their school was growing so fast, they needed a much larger house; and when old Sir Thomas O'Kelly died they sold the convent—to some German, of course—and bought White Place. And now they find it's full of dry-rot, and the roof has got to come off, and I don't know what else—anyhow it will cost more than they paid for it originally to have the place put right, and they had to get a bank loan for that!—and they have nowhere to go meantime."

"More fools them not to have it vetted before they bought it" was the General's unsympathetic response.

"Oh but they did!—they paid someone to examine the house, only he didn't spot the dry-rot."

"They can't have employed anyone very competent."

"He was a professional architect, or surveyor, or whatever you call it" Lady Helen said stoutly, holding her ground in the nuns' defence.

"Then he can't have been very honest."

As sometimes happened with her, an idea suddenly clicked into Julia's mind like a bolt into a socket or a penny into a slot.

"Helen, who actually *sold* White Place to the nuns? Did your man know?"

"Oh, the O'Kelly boy—I forget his Christian name; he hates the country and spends all his time in Dublin with 'the young rowdy set,' according to my driver."

Hm! It was more than likely that Moran, whose headquarters were in Dublin, was well acquainted with "the young rowdy set" too, Julia thought to herself; and it ought not to be too difficult to ascertain from the Reverend Mother of the Roskeen Convent whether he had been employed to "vet" White Place. If he had, probably Gerald knew it already. Of course it would be much more difficult to get firm evidence, or any evidence at all, of some "consideration" having passed from young O'Kelly to Moran to ensure the giving of a false report—but if such evidence, or even the hint of it, were forthcoming, there was something that would certainly be capable of producing what Gerald had called "the desired effect." At the time—"Helen, what on earth are the nuns doing now, poor creatures?" she asked.

"Oh, parked here and there; one or two other convents have taken in a good many, and some have been given shelter in various houses round about—it isn't an enclosed order, mercifully. But the great worry is the money for the roof."

"Nuns always get whatever money they want" O'Hara stated.

"Well, the people in Martinstown are going to take up a collection for them, my driver said; everyone is very angry about it."

"I don't wonder" Julia said. "What a mean trick."

Julia felt that she must make sure that Gerald heard this latest news item, and next morning she borrowed the little car and drove to Mulranny to ring him up from the Hotel call-box; there were so many calls from there, from total strangers, that they were less likely to attract, let alone hold the attention of the girl in the Post Office who handled local calls than those from private numbers. Even so she chose her words carefully, avoiding the use of any names.

"Gerald, have you heard about the nuns and the dry-rot? I expect you have, but I wanted to be certain."

He gave a startled exclamation. "Good Lord! How on earth did *you* hear about that?"

"Oh, Helen's car-hire man was full of it yesterday, bringing her back from the farm."

She heard him chuckle. "Well that's all to the good! But we can't talk about it on the telephone. Could you possibly come into Martinstown?"

"Yes, I expect so. Tea-time-ish?"

"Yes, that's all right. I should be free by then."

"Right—pick me up at the Station."

As before, Julia went in by bus, and had only waited a short time before Gerald appeared in his car—once again, he drove into the Mall and pulled up under the trees by the river, where Julia reported what Lady Helen had been told by her hire-car man, including his phrase about the "young rowdy set" in Dublin. Gerald was particularly pleased with the item that the good people of Martinstown were so angry about how the nuns had been treated that they were going to take up a collection on their behalf.

"That's absolutely first *class!*" he said. "Public feeling must be really strong if people are willing to put their hands in their pockets to back it—and strong public feeling is just what we need."

"I suppose you've seen Reverend Mother, and know that it really was Moran who was sent to vet old Sir Thomas's house?"

"Yes, and I know what she paid him!—he signed the receipt. *And* I know what young O'Kelly paid to induce Master Moran to give a false report."

"How much?" Julia was genuinely curious to know how large a bribe would be necessary to make even an unscrupulous person do such a monstrous thing.

"Wait for it! Three thousand pounds in used fivers!" Gerald pronounced.

"No! But—good Heavens! Then it really *was* Moran's money that Mrs. Martin took to old Lady Browne!" she exclaimed.

"Yes. Ill-gotten gains, if ever the phrase was applicable!"

"But have you . . ." Julia was beginning—he guessed what her question would be, and interrupted her.

"*Yes!*—I have got the necessary evidence; but I can't and won't tell you precisely how I got it—not even you, my dearest heart" he added, seeing her dashed face. "What I can say is that what Lady Helen's well-informed driver calls 'the young rowdy set' drink rather a lot, and when people are no longer sober they give away all manner of things, even about their close friends."

And if one has a contact in that set, one can get the evidence one needs, Julia thought to herself. Aloud—"I see" she said meditatively. "I'm surprised you didn't have to up to Dublin yourself, though."

"Good contacts!—and a bit of luck," Gerald said easily.

"But I am going up to Dublin, to settle everything."

"Settle exactly what? Or can't you tell me that either?" Julia asked.

"Settle what's to happen to Moran, primarily. I'm not sure that he knows how much we know; he may guess, but not be certain—but it is a weapon, and it's got to be wielded."

"Prosecute him, do you mean?"

"Oh Lord no! Get rid of him for good. The General was asking me at the funeral if I couldn't keep him out of Mayo—you heard him; I hope to get him out of Ireland altogether."

"Where to?"

"Probably America; he has business contacts there. I'll see him myself; if he won't do it on what I say, I shall see the heads of his firm, who can, and will, insist on his going. They won't want to be involved a moment longer than they can help with a man who has this sort of scandal attached to him."

"And what about the money?" Julia asked.

"He'll have to sign a paper formally making it over to someone—me, or good kind Richard Fitzgerald, preferably."

"And what will you or Mr. Fitzgerald do with it?"

"Give it to the nuns!—£3,000 should go a long way towards putting a new roof on White Place," Gerald said, grinning. Julia laughed.

"When do you go to Dublin?" she asked.

"Tomorrow."

"How much may I tell Sally?"

"Who's Sally?"

"Sally Martin. I do think she ought to be warned about Moran—the sort of person he is, I mean; they seemed to be rather close, and it's so easy to flip over to the States from Shannon."

"Well, I see no harm in telling her what he's done. Don't say what I'm doing about him."

"And what about the O'Haras?"

"Oh, by all means tell them that the villain of her driver's story is Moran—the more people who know that the better, and the General sees a lot of people. But, again, don't say what I'm trying to do till I get back from Dublin."

"When will that be?"

"I don't know. You be getting on with getting our banns put up, and telling the Glentoran people and Mrs. Hathaway —you'll have plenty to do arranging our wedding!" he said happily. "Now I'd better run you back."

"That would be lovely—if you've got time."

Gerald made time; he drove very fast, and dropped her at the top of the lane. She ran down, and turned into the library, where her host and hostess were still having drinks.

"Where've you been?" the General asked, brusquely.

"Martinstown, to see Gerald." She decided to blurt out the news. "Helen, the architect who was supposed to vet White Place for the nuns was that horrible Moran, and young O'Kelly bribed him not to tell them about the dry-rot."

"How wicked!" Lady Helen said, shocked. The General, like Julia, wanted to know how large the bribe had been?

"Three thousand pounds. And to be less traceable than a cheque O'Kelly gave it him in used £5 notes—the very notes that were sent to try to buy Lady Browne's land with, that I saw her counting, and that *you* persuaded her to give back!" Julia said, turning to O'Hara.

"But I thought it was O'Rahilly that sent them to Mary by your precious friend the Martin woman" O'Hara objected.

"Oh, he was only the front-man; Moran was behind the whole thing, all along."

The General, very naturally, expressed strong reprobation

of this fraudulent behaviour, and voiced the hope that in future Julia would choose her friends more carefully.

"Dearest, Mr. O'Rahilly isn't a friend of Julia's" Lady Helen put in—"and we don't know that poor Mrs. Martin knew anything about where the money came from."

"Well, what's O'Brien doing about Moran?" The General wanted to know. "If he can't get him put in quod for this, I shan't think much of him as a lawyer!"

But Julia would only admit to knowing that her fiancé was going up to Dublin "to see about it." Later, when she got Lady Helen alone, she asked, as so often before, for the loan of the little car. "I do feel Sally Martin ought to be warned about that man; I'm afraid they're on rather friendly terms, to put it mildly, and she has no means of knowing what he's really like." Lady Helen quite agreed. "I imagine she needs friends—after all, this isn't her own country," she said. "Yes, do go, Julia."

Julia decided to undertake the warning of Mrs. Martin even before she embarked on the much pleasanter task of announcing her engagement to Mrs. Hathaway, and the Reeders, and asking them to have her banns put up, and generally organising her wedding. She drove over the following morning, full of disrelish for the job; usually when driving to an interview she spent the time on the way planning out in her mind what to say to put over her point most effectively, but on this occasion every approach seemed equally difficult. Mrs. Martin was in, and greeted her with evident pleasure; she went through to the kitchen to put on some coffee, and then returned to where her guest sat by the fire.

"It's good to see you again" she said.

"I've come to tell you a long, rather horrid story" Julia said.

"What about?" Sally Martin asked gaily.

"Some nuns."

"I like nuns; stories about them are usually rather sweet." Mrs. Martin was still gay. Julia had suddenly decided, in those moments while her hostess was out in the kitchen, to tell the story as it were anonymously, and only to pin it onto Moran when it had been thoroughly taken in—otherwise she feared that Mrs. Martin might refuse to listen.

"This one isn't very sweet" she said, and proceeded to relate it—the need for a large building for the convent school, the suitable house suddenly falling vacant, the precautions prudently taken; the bribe offered, the false report duly given, the consequent distress and loss.

"But that's just plain wicked!" Sally Martin exclaimed, at the end, "I never heard of anything so bad. And to do it to nuns, of all people, who are always so good and kind! I can't imagine the kind of person who could go and do a cruel thing like that."

"You don't have to imagine him—you know him" Julia said bluntly. "The architect who took that bribe and lied to the nuns was Peter Moran."

Mrs. Martin stared at her.

"What makes you say a thing like that?" she said at last, slowly.

"Because it's true." Julia stared back at her, steadily, holding the hazel eyes with her own.

"How can you know?"

"There's one way *you* can know it's true, too, Sally," Julia said. "To be less traceable than a cheque, the bribe was given in old five-pound notes, six bundles each of one hundred five-pound notes—the parcel of notes that you took over to Lady Browne, and that I saw her counting just afterwards."

Sally Martin's square face, always rather pale, turned white at the mention of the notes.

"But—but I took that money over for Billy, not Peter" she said at length, defensively.

"Yes, but they didn't belong to Billy; he was acting for Moran, who very naturally wanted to keep in the background. Mr. O'Rahilly hasn't got that sort of money" Julia affirmed. "I don't say that he even knew how Moran came by the notes, though he had been acting for him in checking on the land, and would have had a hand in building the hotel and casino, if he got it."

Mrs. Martin suddenly burst into tears.

"Oh, I hope he didn't! I can't bear *everyone* to be so horrible!" she sobbed out. Presently she dabbed at her eyes, blew her nose, and turned to Julia with a rather pathetic air of resolution.

"How do *you* know all this? And why do I have to believe it's true?" she asked.

"You asked me, after I'd met Mr. O'Rahilly here, if we couldn't go on being friends" Julia said slowly. "I said we would. And it's because I want to be your friend that I've come over today to tell you this. The way the nuns were swindled over the dry-rot is all over the country—Helen O'Hara's hire-car man told her about it coming back from that funeral we went to at Kilmichan. Only you're a stranger, and would be the last person in Mayo to hear it! And"—she paused—"I only heard yesterday *who* had perpetrated the swindle" she went on. "But the very day we met I saw you saying goodbye to Mr. Moran at Westland Row, and you seemed on very affectionate terms. What would you expect a friend to do, in such circumstances? Keep quiet?"

Sally Martin began to cry again. Presently—"Yes, I guess you had to tell me to put me straight about it" she said. Suddenly—"Oh mercy! The coffee!" she exclaimed, and ran out to the kitchen, whence she returned with two steaming cups. Stirring hers—"But you don't think Billy necessarily knew anything about that part?" she asked.

"I've no means of knowing, one way or the other" Julia said. "But I don't see how he *could* know unless Moran told him, and I should hardly expect even Peter Moran to broadcast something so discreditable about himself."

"You still haven't told me how *you* know" Sally Martin said.

"No, and I'm not going to! But it's not much good being friends if you don't believe what I say" Julia said roundly.

"Oh, I will! I'm sorry—it's all so awful—I don't know what I'm doing."

"Don't start crying again! Look, Sally, I know all this is very horrid for you" Julia said, "but the only thing to do is to face the facts."

"Will it matter if I talk to Billy about it?"

"No, of course not. He'll be the next last person in Mayo, after you, to hear the talk!" Julia said, smiling. She got up. "I must be off." She kissed her friend. "Keep your heart up. Bless you."

11

As Julia drove back towards The Sound she began to wonder if she had been very wise to tell Mrs. Martin that she might talk to Mr. O'Rahilly about Moran's behaviour. Sally would inevitably mention that she had learned this unpalatable news from her, Julia; and this, almost equally inevitably, would make him guess that Gerald O'Brien was the source of Julia's information. She stopped at The Sound and rang up the shack from the call-box there; Sally was in, and she asked her not to mention the business to Billy "for the present"—as before, she used no names.

"Well, when can I?"

"When I say you can—not before."

"But I must tell Bi——."

"No names!" Julia shut her up. "Have some sense! I'll let you know as soon as ever I can, when you can talk to him. Bye." She cut off.

Back in Rostrunk, she got off a letter to Mrs. Hathaway, giving the news of her engagement and imminent marriage, by the afternoon post; the old lady was apt to be fussed by long-distance calls about anything important. Not so the

Reeders, and after 6 P.M. she put in a personal call to Edina Reeder, giving the same tidings, and asking her good offices in the matter of the Macdonald's chapel and getting the banns posted. Edina expressed herself as delighted—"He's the *nicest* person—" and promised to set everything in train. When Julia had ascertained the vast price of the call, and took the money in to Lady Helen in the library, the General, *more suo*, scolded her for her extravagance.

"What on earth did you want to telephone for, and spend all that money? Why wouldn't a letter do?"

"Save time—we want to get married *quickly*, Michael. And give the Reeders as much notice as possible. Glentoran's awfully out of the way, and to get things up by steamer from Glasgow takes ages—it only goes once a month."

"What on earth would they have to get up from Glasgow?" O'Hara wanted to know.

"Darling, Julia *is* their cousin—they'll want to give her the nicest wedding they can. A proper cake, and flowers for the chapel, and extra eats—all sorts of things" Lady Helen said pacifically.

"Waste of money" was the General's sympathetic comment.

After dinner the telephone rang—O'Hara answered it. "Who's that? Speak up, I can't hear you. Father *who?* Oh yes, at Lettersall. Bad news?—well, cough it up, man. Oh, good God! When? *Who* found her? Oh, old Annie. What of? I see. Stupid creature! Well, I'll be over in the morning first thing of course. O'Brien?—wait, I'll ask Mrs. Jamieson; she'll know." He put his hand over the mouth-piece. "Julia, when does O'Brien get back from Dublin? You don't know? Well, where can he be reached in Dublin? You don't know that either!" He spoke into the telephone again. "Sorry,

Father, she doesn't know anything! His office should know where he can be reached, but that won't be open till tomorrow, of course. So sorry. Thanks for letting us know."

He put down the receiver. "Poor old Mary's gone" he said, coming back to the fire with a look of stricken astonishment on his face. "Some time last night—that old servant found her when she came in this morning, but of course she was too stupid to tell anyone, or get the Doctor—she just pulled down the blinds and left it at that! The Father only heard when the postman got back to Lettersall this afternoon—he *did* give him a ring—he saw the blinds down and asked Annie. Of course the post doesn't get to Mary's till after midday." He sat down, rather heavily. "Poor Mary, all alone! I wish I'd been there." He looked at his watch. "I've a good mind to go over tonight—there's another couple of hours of daylight, or nearly."

"Oh, please don't, dearest" Lady Helen said. "You'll be much more useful if you get a good quiet night here first. We'll have breakfast very early, and you can get off in good time, and pick the priest up on the way, after he's said early Mass."

"What do I want the priest for?"

"Oh, he'll get much more out of Annie than anyone else will. Do you know who poor Mary's Doctor was?"

"There's no Doctor at Lettersall, so I suppose it was Dr. Fergus. I'll give him a ring."

But Dr. Fergus was out, and his household had no idea when he would be in again. So finally the General accepted, reluctantly, his wife's suggestion that he should go to bed and get an early night, since he was to make such an early start next day.

Lady Helen was a thoroughly practical person, and when her husband, with Julia as usual as co-driver, were setting off she put a picnic-hamper in the car. "You've no idea when you'll get back, and I don't suppose Annie has thought to prepare any food, even supposing she's got any in the house" she said in reply to O'Hara's customary protests. Julia had taken upon herself, at Lady Helen's suggestion, to ring up Father O'Donnell the previous night to say that they would call for him—"Poor man, he oughtn't to go peddling all the way over to Mary's *again*" Helen O'Hara said. So he was waiting on the Presbytery steps, a bunch of white roses in his hand, when they drew up.

"This is most good of you, General," he said, getting in. "I'm hoping Dr. Fergus will get over this morning—of course I telephoned to him as soon as I heard, but he had *three* confinements yesterday afternoon and evening, one a very difficult one, and he couldn't come. It was nearly midnight when he got home, and got the message I had left. He telephoned to me then—but I told him to leave it till the morning."

Indeed when they got to the cottage the Doctor's car was already drawn up in the little drive. Old Annie ushered them into the sitting-room, but there was no sign of the doctor. "He's within in the bedroom, with the corp" Annie said, in reply to O'Hara's brusque enquiry. "Oh, the Lord have mercy on us!" She burst into noisy weeping, and retired to her kitchen.

"I should leave him for a little while, General" Father O'Donnell said, as O'Hara moved towards the door. "We may embarrass him if he's still making an examination." Reluctantly, O'Hara sat down and indeed in a couple of minutes Dr. Fergus came in, wiping his hands on a towel.

"Yes, it was her heart—she's had a heart condition for some time" he said. "I should say it was very sudden; I don't imagine Lady Browne knew what was happening, or suffered at all. Miss Kelly found her sitting in her chair, looking perfectly peaceful, with her eyes closed—she may even have died in her sleep. I shall be quite happy to sign a death certificate, so that the funeral can be arranged at once. Death probably took place at least thirty-six hours ago. I presume her lawyer will see to the funeral."

"O'Brien's away in Dublin, and no one knows when he'll be back" the General said discontentedly.

"Surely Terence White can arrange that" Julia put in. She was getting rather tired of these complaints about Gerald's absence. "After all, he is her grandson, and he's a lawyer too."

"Oh—ah—I'd forgotten young White" Dr. Fergus said. "He'll know where to get hold of the daughter, too; they're abroad somewhere, aren't they?"

"Africa" from Julia.

"Then they can't very well get back in time. Well, I'll just sign that certificate and be getting along—I have my hands rather full with the rising generation at the moment" the doctor said cheerfully, seating himself at the desk.

"That is an excellent thought of yours" Father O'Donnell said to Julia. "Do you know where young Mr. White can be got hold of?"

"Yes, he works in Walshe & Walshe's office in Martinstown—we could look in and tell him on the way back, after we've dropped you" Julia said.

"There!" Dr. Fergus said, getting up. "Who do I give this to?"—brandishing the death certificate.

"Mr. White had better have it, if you're going to see him" the priest said. "Doctor, are you by any chance going to look up your patients in Lettersall, as you're so near?"

"Yes, I might as well. Can I give you a lift?"

"I should be most grateful—and that will save you an

extra journey, and delay," the priest said to O'Hara. "And get the news more quickly to Mr. White." He handed over the white roses, and the death certificate, and he and the doctor left together.

When they had gone Julia went out to the kitchen and asked Annie Kelly to take them to see Lady Browne. The old servant led them through into a room at the back of the house, looking out onto the lough; evidently the late owner's bedroom, for a dressing-table with a big swing mirror stood at the further end, next to a tall wardrobe. But it had been beautifully arranged; all the toilet things had been removed from the dressing-table, and the furniture pushed together, leaving a clear space round the bed, on which, on a brilliant paisley shawl, all that was mortal of Mary Browne lay, calm and composed, her hands folded on her breast, holding a small plain wooden cross; candles in silver candle-sticks burned at the four corners of the bed, and vases of flowers stood on the mantel-piece and the empty dressing-table. Julia felt pretty sure that this was mainly the priest's handiwork—a faint smell of incense hung on the air. She dropped to her knees and said a prayer, as Lady Helen had done beside Timmie's open coffin; rather to her surprise the General knelt down too—Annie Kelly crossed herself, and stood fingering her rosary. When they got up O'Hara stood looking round him for a moment.

"Well, it's all very nice" he said. "That priest's a decent chap." He laid Father O'Donnell's bunch of white roses gently beside the calm face on the pillow. "Now we'd better find young What's-his-name as soon as we can" he said, and left the room; Julia, with a word of thanks to Annie, followed.

In the Mall at Martinstown Julia ran in to Walshe & Walshe's office; it was lunch-time, and clerks were pouring out—she could see no sign of old Raftery, and hurried up to the room where she had found Terence last time—he was there, alone, putting his papers together.

"Oh, thank goodness!" she said and dropped into a chair, panting a little.

"Hul*lo!* What goes on?" the young man asked, in surprise.

"Lady Browne is dead" Julia blurted out. "We've just come from there."

"No! When?" Terence asked, also sitting down.

"Day before yesterday—no, night before last, so far as anyone knows."

"What of? What happened?" He looked very disturbed.

"Dr. Fergus says it was her heart, and that very likely she died in her sleep." Julia went on to relate the whole story, as they had heard it from the priest.

"I can't think why we never thought to ring you up last night, but anyhow by the time we heard the office would have been shut, and I don't know your home number."

"I haven't got one—there's no telephone at my digs. But Doctor Fergus is sure she didn't suffer?" he asked, with an anxiety which touched and pleased Julia.

"I don't think she can have. Father O'Donnell saw her as Annie found her, sitting in her chair with her eyes shut, looking absolutely peaceful, as if she had just dozed off."

"She oughtn't to be left sitting in a chair" Terence said, looking worried.

"She hasn't been. She's on the bed in her room, all arranged beautifully, with a cross in her hands, and flowers, and candles burning—I bet you the Father did all that. But look, can you see to the funeral and everything? Here's the death-certificate" Julia said, handing it to him. "Dr. Fergus signed it, so that there need be no delay."

"Yes, of course. I must cable my parents before I do any-

thing else—it will upset my Mother terribly, especially if
she can't get home in time. Perhaps if they flew . . ."

"Well, I'll leave you to it. Let us know when the funeral
is, and if there's anything we can do. Just now I want to get
Michael home—it's been a goodish shock to him."

"Yes, of course. I believe he really was rather attached to
her, and I know she counted on him tremendously. Goodbye"
—as Julia got up. "Thank you for coming to let me know."

"Goodbye. So sorry" Julia said, and hastened downstairs.

As they drove away, "When do we eat?" O'Hara asked
Julia. "It's after half-past one, and I'm getting peckish.
Where's that hamper of Helen's?"

"In the back. Why don't we go into the park and find a
quiet place?"

"Good idea." So they drove through Lord Oldport's big
black-and-gold wrought-iron gates, and pulled up under a
group of trees, which commanded a view of a small lake with
water fowl on it, and there partook of Lady Helen's excellent
picnic lunch.

The funeral was two days later. In Martinstown, as in
many other places in the West, where people of differing
faiths live and work harmoniously together, Catholics and
Protestants share the same graveyard; the Catholics are in
the majority of course, but a good third, if not more, of the
large burial-ground is allocated to the graves of Protestants—
in smaller places, with less spacious graveyards, the last rest-
ing-places of both denominations are mixed up indiscrim-
inately. The funeral service took place in the Protestant
Church; it was sparsely attended, the congregation consisting
mainly of the O'Haras and the Fitzgeralds, and of course
Terence White; but Julia was touched and pleased to see the
tall figure of Father O'Donnell, in a plain dark suit, among
the little group that seemed so sparse in the large ugly build-

ing. Sally Martin was there too, escorted by Billy O'Rahilly —"She won't know, so she won't mind, and he wanted to come" Sally whispered to Julia. Lord Oldport had taken the trouble to come, which greatly pleased the General.

"No, Sir, my Mother is ill, and my Father didn't like to leave her" Julia overheard Terence explaining to Lord Oldport, in reply to courteous condolences and enquiries as they left the graveside.

"I shall write to him, if you will send me his address."

"Of course, Sir—he will like that" Terence said, warmly.

Gerald O'Brien only got back three days later. He rang up General O'Hara to express his regret at Lady Browne's death, and at not having been able to get to the funeral.

"Ah well, we thought it a bit odd, I must say" the General said bluntly. "What have you done about Moran?" he asked then.

"He's in New York—I saw him off from Shannon yesterday."

These tidings pleased O'Hara so much that he promptly invited O'Brien to lunch the following day, and he and Julia listened with interest, over drinks in the library, to Gerald's account of the business—Lady Helen, as so often before a meal, was still getting her hands clean after gardening.

"No, he wouldn't go for me—I had to tell his firm about it; that's why it all took so long" Gerald said. "He is an unpleasant customer, I must say."

"What did his firm say?"

"Oh, they were appalled, of course. I don't know what means they used—I gather they had to threaten him with the police, practically—but in the end he signed a document making the £3,000 over to Richard Fitzgerald, and handed back the agreement to sell that he'd twisted out of the poor old lady. That was before we heard she was dead. Then there was no end of cabling and even telephoning to the branch of their firm in New York, and they agreed to give him a berth for six months on trial, and to keep an eye on him. It was all about as disagreeable as anything could be" O'Brien said with an expression of disgust. "And even when they had booked the flight, they didn't trust him actually to go—so I agreed to drive him down and put him on the plane."

"Why was the £3,000 to be made over to Fitzgerald?" the General asked.

"He happened to be in Dublin, and he knew all about it already, of course—he took the notes back to Lady Browne at one point, you remember, when she wanted them. No, that's wrong; it was when he went to her to sign those letters. But with him there it was easy to settle it all on the spot. He will pay it to the nuns at Roskeen, or wherever they are, poor dears. All that is rather complicated; it has to be done through the Mother House of the Order, and that's in Belgium. But we'll get round that somehow."

"And what architect will see to putting the new roof on White Place?" O'Hara asked.

"Oh, we'll find someone—there are plenty of good architects about, and *honest* ones, too."

Lady Helen appeared at this point, and they went in to lunch; Gerald left immediately afterwards. "Sorry, but there's rather a lot to see to; we haven't found Lady Browne's will yet."

"Didn't she keep it in your office? That's the normal place for a will, the lawyer's office" the General affirmed.

"It is usually with us, but she asked for it back, not long ago."

"Wonder what she's been up to now? Be just like Mary to spring some surprise on us from beyond the grave!" O'Hara said, chuckling at his own macabre jest.

Julia went out to see Gerald off. "If the will isn't in the despatch box under the desk, I should look in the stove in the hall" she said. "That was where she kept the notes."

"Good idea!—We'll try that. 'Bye, my darling. When do I see you again?"

"I'll ring you. Goodbye, and bless you. I'm *sorry* you're having all this bother!" She kissed him.

When he had gone Julia decided that her next job was to see Sally Martin and tell her that she might now tell Mr. O'Rahilly about Moran and the nuns. Lady Helen was already back in the garden, and willingly lent her car, and Julia drove straight up to Achill. Mrs. Martin was in, helping the children with their homework, but she told them to put up their books and go and play outside.

"Well, can I tell Billy now?" she asked as soon as they had gone off. "He keeps coming over and asking and asking about Peter, and when he's coming down again?—it's quite awkward."

"Yes, you can tell him the whole horrible story now" Julia said. "And that it's no use his trying to see Moran in Dublin, because he's in New York. He flew there day before yesterday."

"Do you know that for a fact?"

"Yes, positive. His firm sent him, and he won't be coming back for some time."

Sally Martin sat down in a chair, and put her face in her hands.

"Oh, it is wretched" she said after a moment, looking up —Julia was relieved to see that she wasn't crying. "I was terribly fond of him."

"Yes, it is miserable to find one has been totally mistaken about a person one likes" Julia agreed, with real sympathy for this pretty creature, who for all her appearance of sophistication was such an innocent. She accepted a cup of tea, early as it was, and sat for twenty minutes or more—it was borne in on her that Mrs. Martin was really very lonely. As she drove back towards The Sound she was quite relieved to meet O'Rahilly's car driving towards the shack. Billy might not be the ideal companion, but he was *some* one.

Gerald was rather surprised that Terence had not found Lady Browne's will during his own so inconvenient absence —"The will is usually read out after the funeral" he said, a little reprovingly.

"Well, the funeral was in Martinstown, so unless we'd read it in the Church, I don't know when we could have" Terry said, with a brief giggle. "Anyhow, I didn't like to make a thing about getting it read—I'm not her lawyer, and I thought it might look greedy. I expect she'll have left most of whatever there was to the parents."

"Yes, I see. Well, now we'll go over and see if it really is in the stove" O'Brien said.

It was. Both men laughed a little when they came on the large envelope among the cold ashes. They dusted it on the doorstep, and took it into the sitting-room; Annie Kelly appeared to ask if they would be wanting a fire?

"No thank you, Annie; we shan't be very long."

When the maid had gone—"Has Annie been given notice?" O'Brien asked.

"No. Should she be?"

"It is usual to give all employees notice when a death occurs," Gerald said.

"Obviously I'm not much good at death" Terence said, gloomily. "I wonder when she was last paid any wages?"

"We'll ask her presently—that's something she *will* know, and remember. Now let's open this will—you're the nearest thing to a next of kin available for it to be read to."

At this point Annie appeared with a tray of glasses and a bottle of whiskey. "I thought ye'd be the better of this" she remarked, setting it down on the table. " 'Tis some of what Mr. Richard brought."

"Thank you, Annie—that's an excellent idea."

"All the letters that come since I put together in the basket" Annie pursued, indicating a wicker tray on the desk; it was piled with envelopes.

"Oh lawks!" Terence said.

"Well, you can take those home to go through them, and answer any that need answering—all this is a very useful part of your legal training!" Gerald said, grinning. "Really much more to the point than reading law books in Walshe & Walshe's. Now give me some of the family whiskey."

Terence poured out glasses for them both, while O'Brien opened the envelope containing the will. He turned the typed sheets over rapidly—"Ah, here we are!" he said, when he came to a manuscript appendix on a sheet which had been clipped on at the end. "This may be the bomb the General was expecting."

In fact it wasn't much of a bomb; it was quite sensible, and very efficiently made out. Lady Browne instructed her executors—who were Gerald O'Brien and General O'Hara— to arrange for an annuity of £150 a year to be paid to Annie Kelly, and for the sum of £1,000 to be given to Father O'Donnell "for the benefit of his Church at Lettersall." The O'Haras and a few other friends were to be invited to come and choose a piece of furniture "as a keepsake"; £500 apiece was left to her executors "for their trouble." It had been witnessed by two individuals called Greene and Browne, who had, most correctly, given their addresses and occupations as well as their names—they were the postman and the local plumber.

"Ah, she was very practical in some ways, was Lady Browne" O'Brien remarked, having read out this information.

"But who does the cottage go to, and such money as she had left after all her muddles over near Rossbeg?" Terence asked. "My mother?"

"No—to you, my boy!—every penny of it! Congratulations."

"Good Lord!" Terence sat down in a chair, quite overcome. "What on earth would Grandmother want to do that for?"

"She *says*, because your Mother has married a man of means, who is in a career which brings him in a comfortable livelihood and a good pension. And also because, so far as she has been able to judge, she thinks you are a steady young man, who will put it to some sensible use. I'm inclined to agree with her there!" Gerald said, smiling very pleasantly at the sensible young man, who still sat, staring in front of him.

"Have you any idea how much there is?" Terence asked at length.

"That will depend a good deal on how much the cottage goes for, if you decide to sell it—and the land. And of course the fishing rights are worth quite a lot."

"I don't want the cottage—I should like to keep some of the fishing."

"Well, you can sell some of the fishing with the cottage, to put up its price, and keep enough to enjoy and to pleasure your friends with" Gerald said. "There's no hurry—think it over. I'll have a look at her investments, too, they're over at the office, and give you a rough idea. Now we ought to draft a notice to put in *The Times,* and the *Irish Times,* and the *Mayo News.*"

They did this, and then O'Brien began to go through the

tin deed-box under the desk, while Terence, on his instructions, looked through the drawers. These contained quantities of old letters, many as much as half a century old, but the top left-hand drawer was devoted to bills, of which there were quite a quantity. "Better find where she put her receipts" Gerald said; "then you can check these over, and pay any that are outstanding. I'll advance you whatever you need from her ready cash, without waiting for probate. Better come over and do it from here—save carting a lot of papers about, and then you can use her writing-paper. Keep a list of what you pay, and put down the price of your cheque-books; you'll need one or two extra ones for all this."

The deed-box contained some £160 in notes and silver. Annie was summoned, and asked when she had last received any wages?

"Lady paid me up to Whit, because I wanted to get me a new dress—I be's always accustomed to a new dress for Whit," Annie said.

"Quite right. Well"—he glanced at his diary—"that was five weeks ago. Were you paid by the week or the month, Annie?"

"By the week, Sir, when Lady remembered. Fifteen-and-six a week I got."

"Right. Well, here's your pay from Whitsun up to this week, and here's another month's wages in lieu of notice. I'm afraid you'll have to take a month's notice, Annie, but I should like you to stay on here for at least the month, to show people over who come to look at it with a view to buying it."

"Then I'll want me board as well as me wages" Annie affirmed. " 'Tis to be sold, so?"

"Yes, is to be sold. And you shall have your board, of course. But Lady Browne has left you some money, Annie."

Annie began to look very animated.

"How much, Mr. O'Brien, Sir?"

"Do you know what an annuity is?"

"No, I can't know what that is—I never heard of it."

"It's so much money to be paid to you every week, or every month, whichever you prefer; yours will be £3 a week, or £12 a month, roughly. You'll get that as long as you live."

Annie looked still more animated.

"Who will be paying it to me? Will it be you, Sir?"

"No. You will collect it from the Post Office, or the bank —again, whichever you prefer."

"Oh, I'd rather the bank. At the Post Office every soul knows what you're getting!"

"Could you get to the bank in Martinstown once a month?"

"I could that, Sir." Annie paused; O'Brien guessed that she was doing sums in her head; the least literate Irish peasant can always do that! His guess was confirmed when she asked —"Could I have the—whatever you call it—all at once?"

"No, Annie; I'm afraid it has to be paid weekly or monthly. And Mr. Richard will pay you your board weekly in advance; he will be here a great deal, clearing up papers, the next week or two."

Annie didn't look best pleased at this information, and presently took herself off to her kitchen.

"I wonder what she's got in her head?" Terence speculated.

"Wanted to buy the cottage herself, I expect" Gerald replied. He was amused, but not in the least surprised, when Terence reported less than a week later, after a visit to go on dealing with Lady Browne's papers and bills, that there was now a small notice-board on the main road beside the drive leading down to the cottage, bearing the words FISHING AND

MEALS. MODERATE PRICES. PARKING FREE—and that he had later seen three young Englishmen having lunch in the dining-room, when he went to get himself a glass of "Mr. Richard's" whiskey.

"Did you say anything to them?" O'Brien asked.

"Not really. One of them had the *toupet* to ask me what I was up to, so I just said I was the owner of the house. He didn't half look embarrassed" Terence said cheerfully.

In fact the cottage sold very quickly—Gerald put it in the hands of an agent with offices in London and Dublin, and an American made a handsome offer within a few days. Gerald asked Terence to come down and discuss the details of exactly what fishing rights were to go with the cottage, and they plotted them on a large-scale map. "I'll have smaller-scale photo-stats made of that, to go with the deed of sale, and one for the cottage, and keep one here—then there will be less argument" O'Brien said. "Fishing-limits are the devil, unless everyone has a map."

"You'd better have an extra one made for General O'Hara, so" Terence said, grinning. "I'd like him to go on fishing the water I keep while he's up to it, poor old boy."

"Good idea" O'Brien agreed.

"D'you know anything about this Yank who's bought the cottage?" Terence asked.

"Practically nothing, except that his money's good. He's deposited it with the Bank of Ireland."

"Oh well, so long as it's not another German!" Terence said. "Too many Huns have moved in on us lately, for my liking."

O'Brien ignored this expression of political opinion; he was rummaging in the drawers of his desk.

"Ah, here we are! I've totted up the old lady's securities,

and there's a bit more than I expected—with the price of the cottage it's practically £16,000."

"Lawks!" Terence said—a favourite expression of his when startled. He sat silent for some time, staring in front of him— O'Brien was rather puzzled. There was no expression of satisfaction, such as might have been expected from the recipient of such news; he began to wonder if Terence had hoped the sum to be larger, and was disappointed. At last—"Did you hope it would be more?" he asked.

"Goodness no!" Terence jerked himself out of his abstraction. "No, it was just an idea I had." He fell silent again. O'Brien waited a little, but he was busy, and really wanted to get on with his work, so at last he said—"Do you want to talk about it?"

"Well yes, in a way."

"Then fire ahead."

"Well"—Terence said, very hesitantly, and stuck again.

"Yes, go on."

"Well, I know I'm very young, and all that—I say, don't hesitate to slap me down; I should quite understand" Terence said, urgently.

"My dear chap, do for goodness sake come out with your idea, whatever it is" O'Brien said, but not impatiently. "Of course I'll slap you down if I think it's silly."

But when he heard the idea O'Brien didn't think it silly at all. Terence's notion was that with this amount of capital they might go into partnership: "We could buy a place in Martinstown and have an office there as well as yours here— save no end of traipsing to and fro. I know I'm very young" he repeated.

"Not as young as all that" O'Brien said. He was both touched and pleased. "I think it might be an excellent plan, and work very well" he said. "But you don't want to rush at it. Better think it over for a bit, and make sure that this is *really* what you want to do with this lump of capital."

"What else would I do with it?"

"Well, you could re-invest it, or leave it in the present investments—I myself should only want to change one or two, at the most—and give yourself a larger income."

"What do I want a larger income for?" Terence asked.

"The steady young man" O'Brien said, beginning to laugh. "Your grandmother wasn't so far out! No, think it over. I should like to have you as a partner very much, but you oughtn't to do a thing like this on an impulse, and without advice. Why don't you talk to Father O'Donnell about it?"

"I will, if it will make you any happier, though I've never thought of him as a financial wizard, I must say. I'm quite sure myself what I want to do."

"Right—do that" O'Brien said, getting up. "And thank you for thinking of it." He more or less pushed the young man out.

But when Terence had gone he didn't at once settle down to work; he sat at his desk, thinking there was plenty of work for two partners in two offices, and the money would run to an extra desk and typist—the whole plan was most attractive. And, as Terence had said, it would save the constant dodging over to Martinstown, where his business was increasing rather fast. But he didn't want the boy to go into it without reflection, and other advice than his. At last he put through a call to Richard Fitzgerald, and asked him to see Terence and advise him about what to do with a rather sizeable legacy that had come to him from Lady Browne.

"Oh, she's left it to him, has she? Has he no idea what to do with it?"

"Yes, he has an idea, but he ought to have advice."

"Well, can't you advise him?" Richard asked.

"Not about this" Gerald said firmly.

"All right—I'll get hold of him" Richard promised.

But as it turned out, the person whom Terence saw before either the priest or Richard Fitzgerald, and who finally clinched his decision, was Julia. He ran into her in Martinstown, whither she had driven Lady Helen to see her dressmaker; she had parked the car in the Mall and was sauntering up the main street, looking idly into the not very enticing shop-windows, as he was coming down it, and he coaxed her into a pub to have a drink. Now O'Brien had already notified the General that he was an executor, and of the bequest of £500; and since O'Hara was to be an executor he readily told him, in reply to his questions, that the bulk of Lady Browne's property was left to Terence White; naturally the General passed this on to his wife and Julia, and the latter, now meeting Terence, equally naturally congratulated him.

"Yes, it is nice" the young man said. "And I am in hopes that it may make possible something I've had in mind for a long time."

"What's that?"

"To go into partnership with Gerald O'Brien—this little whack of capital would make a second office possible, here in Martinstown. Of course I should be very much the junior partner, but with an experienced clerk I think I could manage."

"Oh, Gerald *would* like that!" Julia exclaimed.

"What on earth makes you say so?" Terence asked in surprise.

"Because he said so to me ages ago, only about the second time I was at Rossbeg—the day he rang you up and got you to come down to hear what I'd learned from Sally Martin about O'Rahilly's plans—don't you remember?"

"I remember coming down perfectly well," Terence admitted. "But what did Gerald say about a partnership?"

"Oh, what a help you could be to him, because you knew everyone and got on with everyone, and people talked to you about everything—that sort of thing" Julia said readily.

"You're sure he used the word partnership?"

"Yes, positive—partnership or having you as a partner."

"That settles it, then" Terence said firmly. "I'll talk to Richard, if he wants me to, but I won't change my mind."

"Oh, I *am* glad. It will help Gerald, and save him getting so tired. How nice this is, Terence."

12

THE THREE THOUSAND pounds in used fivers, to the bank manager's great amusement, found their way back into Richard Fitzgerald's account, and eventually were returned to the Bank of Ireland; in exchange he was given £25 notes, which the head of the Mother House in Belgium had said she would prefer to any other denomination—to Gerald's great relief Richard volunteered to take the money over to Belgium. For some reason which, he told Julia, he didn't pretend to understand, this large donation had to get to the nuns at Roskeen by this roundabout method.

"What about the roof on White Place? Surely they ought to be getting on with that?" Julia asked.

"They *are,* darling—they've got a new, decent architect, and the roof is being seen to already; as soon as that is done, and the place is water-tight, they'll start on the interior alterations. In fact, with this extra money they'll be able to do more than they'd ever expected, just with what they got from selling the old convent at Roskeen. So Moran's wickedness in taking that bribe has turned out all for the best!"

"What an extraordinary business it all is!" Julia said. "I wonder what O'Rahilly will do now?"

"Why should he do anything? I'm not sure that I am with you" Gerald said, looking puzzled.

"Well, he'll want to put up his hotel and have his yacht-marina somewhere, if he can get the money, won't he?"

"Oh-ah! Well, it's all sure he won't be able to put them up anywhere near Lettersall, and ruin that lovely bit of coast, now that it belongs to Terry" Gerald observed, with great satisfaction. "I'm not terribly concerned about Master O'Rahilly and his troubles. Are you?"

"Only because of Sally."

"Who's Sally?"

"Sally Martin, at Achill. She and O'Rahilly are rather friends, and now that Moran's out of the picture, I think they might become more than friends."

"She'd do better to keep clear of him, I'd say."

"Oh, why? Is there *really* anything definite wrong with him, that you know of for a fact?"

"Only his being mixed up with Moran, and never taking a job and doing an honest day's work—just writing these lefty poems" Gerald said, a little taken aback by the firmness of her questions.

"Oh, well that sounds to me uncomfortably like the sort of thing the General says about him! If there was anything *real* against him, you'd be sure to know, wouldn't you?"

"I expect I should" Gerald said. He too was uncomfortable at his attitude being compared to that of General O'Hara. "It's probably just prejudice. I admit to being prejudiced in favour of young men who do a regular job of work—like Terry. He need never do another hand's turn, but he's determined to go on working like a Trojan at being a lawyer."

"Yes, he's a nice creature—and intelligent. I do like him so much."

"Do you?" he asked earnestly.

"Yes, indeed I do."

"I'm glad, because he and I are going to be partners—so we shall be seeing a lot of him, I expect."

Julia just managed to refrain from a reply that would have revealed that she already knew this, which would not have been tactful—feeling rather guilty at even this tiny deception of her dear Gerald, she merely said how nice that would be, and rather hastily expressed the hope that the American purchaser of Ponticum Cottage was someone nice.

"Martin? I know nothing whatever about him, except that he's given a very good price, and paid, on the nail—and that he's keen on fishing."

Julia pricked up her ears at the name Martin, but again refrained from questions. And when she got back from Martinstown, where she and Gerald had met for lunch, she found a letter from Edina Reeder which so much disconcerted her that for the time being it put everything else out of her head.

Edina wrote that Father Kennedy, the local priest who served the Macdonalds' Chapel, had said that he could not celebrate the marriage of a non-Catholic to a Catholic without a dispensation; also that the Catholic bridegroom's parish priest must send him, Father Kennedy, a written delegation of authority to arrange the marriage. Julia's heart quailed at the thought of wrestling with Father Murphy over all this; and, though Edina had thoughtfully sent Fr. Kennedy's address, she did not say who was to apply for the dispensation, nor from whom it could be obtained. In her distress and concern she decided to go and consult Father O'Donnell at Lettersall—he would be more likely to know and, if he didn't know, would be more energetic about finding out, she felt sure. She telephoned for an appointment—the priest said he could see her at 3:30 the following afternoon, and she drove over in Helen O'Hara's little car.

She was slightly fussed to see another car standing in the drive outside the presbytery—could the Father have an unexpected visitor? But he heard her and came out before she had time to ring the bell.

"You *did* say today, didn't you?" Julia asked rather nervously, with a glance at the other car.

"Yes, indeed. What do you think of my new means of locomotion?" Father O'Donnell said, patting the new Ford affectionately as he passed it.

"Oh, is it yours? How *good!*" Julia responded warmly.

"Yes. Lady Mary left me £1,000 'for the good of my Church,' by which I judged it reasonable to assume that she meant for the benefit of my parish and parishioners—and the extra amount of time and strength I shall have for them and their needs as a result of driving rather than bicycling I felt warranted the purchase of a car" the Father said, smiling finely, as he led her into his study. "Come and sit down" he went on, as before clearing a chair for her. "Now how do you think I can help you?"

"Father, I'm going to marry Gerald O'Brien" Julia began.

"So I heard. I congratulate you *both* most warmly."

"And I've promised Gerald that I would become a Catholic" Julia went on.

"Then I congratulate you both more warmly still. This is splendid news" the priest said.

"But we wanted to get married rather quickly" Julia pursued "And it seems that in Scotland"—she pulled out Edina's letter—"if a Catholic wants to marry a non-Catholic, they must get a dispensation." She paused again; she was unwontedly hesitant about this enquiry.

"That rule doesn't only apply 'in Scotland'—the need for a dispensation for a mixed marriage is *absolute, everywhere*" Father O'Donnell said, but quite kindly.

"But who gives the dispensation?"

"The Bishop of the diocese in which the bridegroom lives."

"Even if he's going to get married somewhere else?"

"Yes. And his own parish priest must make the application to his Bishop for it. That is the first step. If the dispensation is granted, the Scottish parish priest must also get what is called an exequatur from the Bishop of his diocese, enabling him to celebrate the marriage. But the essential thing is that the bridegroom's (if, as in this case, he is the Catholic partner) local parish priest must delegate authority to arrange the marriage to the priest of the parish where it will take place."

Julia sighed. "It all seems very complicated."

"Why do you want to be married in Scotland?" the priest asked.

"It was Gerald's idea. He knows that Glentoran has always been my second home, and he thought all my relations there would be hurt if we got married here, as I had suggested."

"I think he is right. It was a very considerate and charitable thought. Well, the first thing is for Mr. O'Brien to ask Father Murphy to apply to Bishop Browne for a dispensation."

But Julia had been thinking rather fast.

"Father, how long would it take for me to be instructed and received into the Church? It seems to me, as I want to become a Catholic anyhow, that it would all be very much simpler if I were to be received first. Then there need be no worry about a dispensation, at least."

Father O'Donnell looked at her thoughtfully.

"Do you know anything about the Catholic faith?" he asked after a moment.

"Not a great deal—of the theology part, I mean. I know what goes *on,* because I've lived a lot in Portugal, in a very devout family—I was governess to the daughter."

"What do you mean by very devout?" Father O'Donnell asked, smiling.

"Oh, Mass every day in their own Chapel—my pupil and I always went."

"By your own choice?"

"Well, it wouldn't have been very courteous not to, and anyhow I liked going—it's a nice beginning to the day" Julia said.

"How right you are! Have you been baptised?" he asked.

"Oh yes, into the C. of E., as a baby."

"Are you *sure?* People always assume they have been baptised, when obviously they cannot know it of their own knowledge."

"Well, I've got a godmother still living, and *compos mentis;* she would remember. She said it was in that Church in The Boltons, so it should be in the parish register there," Julia said. "How long does instruction take?"

"Ten sessions is usually regarded as the minimum; for an educated adult it is usually longer."

"Why?" She was surprised.

"They know more, and therefore require fuller information."

"Could *you* instruct me?"

"If that was your and your fiancé's wish. My own view is that it is generally more helpful if a person is instructed by a priest in their own country; then accidental elements of race and outlook and tradition are less likely to enter and interfere. Becoming a Catholic is a very big step, Mrs. Jamieson," he said, with great kindness in his voice, "and a very precious thing."

Julia's mind flashed back to those moments after Timmie's funeral Mass, and the strange sense she had had of a door opening before her, and the vista beyond through which she would presently walk.

"Yes, I know, Father; at least I'm beginning to get some idea" she said. Then—"Could *you* receive me?" she asked.

"With the Bishop's permission, Yes." He saw a doubtful look come into her face, and added, "That need not involve more delay—there is a formula for the request: 'May I receive X, when she has completed her instruction?' which would avoid that."

"Thank you, Father. May I talk to Gerald about it? I feel it would be rather a *corvée* for you, anyhow."

"Don't even *think* of that. But do discuss it with Mr. O'Brien. And then you or he will let me know what you decide." He made as if to rise. "Just one minute, Father, if you can spare it" Julia said. She must find out about the "Martin" who had taken Ponticum Cottage. He relapsed into his chair again.

"Yes—what now?"

"Have you met the American who has bought Lady Browne's house?"

"Yes, I have. Why? Do you know him?"

"No, but I heard that his name was Martin, and I wondered if by any chance he was a relation of the Mrs. Martin who lives in Achill."

Father O'Donnell suddenly looked very alert.

"Do you know her?" he asked, briskly.

"Yes—she and I have made friends."

"Oh, excellent! I wanted to contact someone who knew her."

"Then *is* he the husband?"

"Yes, he is."

"Oh, goodness!" Julia said. "Poor Sally."

"Why do you say that?" the priest asked.

"She was so hoping he wouldn't come over here."

"Do you know that for a fact, or are you speaking from a general impression?"

"She said it in so many words, when she was telling me about the separation, and her troubles with him. I can remember her very words—when I asked if he ever came over to Ireland, she said 'Oh mercy, I hope Paddy doesn't ever take that idea into his head.' "

"Poor soul." He got up and rang the bell, saying "Excuse me a moment." When his housekeeper came Julia heard him instructing her to show his next visitor into the dining-room; then he came back and sat down again.

"This will take a little time" he said. "I feel sure you had better know it, though you will realise that except where Mrs. Martin is concerned, it is confidential. In her case you must use your discretion."

"Of course" Julia said. She was rather puzzled as to what Father O'Donnell could tell her about Paddy Martin that she didn't already know—what she was to hear was completely unexpected.

"You know, of course, that he was a terrible drinker" the Father began. "In fact, a regular alcoholic—quite impossible to live with. And he took up with other women too. His wife must have suffered appallingly. And in the end she brought the children away, and came and settled down over here—would you say happily?"

"Yes. I think she is rather lonely, but on the whole I think she has settled in happily."

"That is a mercy. Well, about five years ago Martin was

taken by a friend to a meeting of Alcoholics Anonymous."

"What is that?" Julia asked.

"A society of people who have decided to give up drinking, and meet regularly to reinforce one another in their resolve —and to help others to come to the same decision. It was started in America, but now it has spread all over the world —more in Europe and the Anglo-Saxon parts of the New World, because alcohol is not such a problem among Asiatics and Africans."

"Really?" Julia asked in surprise.

"Yes. This tendency to excess in alcohol is the real White Man's Burden" Father O'Donnell said, with a wry smile. "However, to return to Alcoholics Anonymous. It is non-denominational, but definitely in the Christian mood. Martin joined it, and has not touched a drop of drink for five years."

"But how amazing!" Julia was very much startled.

"Oh, I know of many such cases. And he has entirely given up the other women he used to consort with; for the last four-and-a-half years, at least, he has led a perfectly chaste and orderly life. And now, if she would agree, he would like to rejoin his wife and resume their marriage."

Julia was silent. She was thinking of Peter Moran—well, he was out of it now—and of Billy O'Rahilly. Neither of them was good enough for Sally; she would not have been happy with either. But was Paddy Martin any better? Certainly he must have character, to have given up both drinking and his women.

"Now you see why I was anxious to get in touch with someone who knew Mrs. Martin" the Father said. "He didn't want to rush things, and he wanted to do what is most fair by his wife—she might well be involved with someone else by this time. So when he heard of Lady Browne's little cottage being for sale, he bought it at once, and has settled down here to find out how the land lies. Also he wanted someone here in Mayo to be able to vouch for the fact of his reformation, so when he had told me his story he insisted that I send a cable, reply paid, at *his* expense, to his priest in Philadelphia, asking him if he could verify Martin's statements. Actually I only signed it—I think Martin telephoned it to a friend in Dublin and had it cabled from there."

"Much wiser" Julia commented.

"Yes, an obvious precaution—especially when money is no object!" said Father O'Donnell, again with his wry smile. "And an honest and sensible action all round—otherwise I should only have had his word for it. I think he is an honest and sensible person."

"I'm very glad. Did the reply come yet?"

"Yes, it came this morning. It confirms everything he told me, and speaks of Mr. Martin most warmly, as a good influence in the parish."

"Well, what shall you do now? Send her a copy of the priest's cable?" Julia asked practically.

"It requires a little thinking about" Father O'Donnell said. "One wants to handle it in the wisest way."

"I shouldn't leave it too long" Julia said.

"You mean there are other people about? Men, I mean?"

"Oh Father, are there bees round a honey-pot? Mrs. Martin is a very attractive woman—of course people are after her. She's had one lucky escape from a real bad hat—Gerald managed to get him out of the country—but it shouldn't be left too long."

"I should like to consult your fiancé about this" the priest said slowly. "He is a very wise man."

At that moment a car drew up before the presbytery, and a tall, strikingly good-looking red-haired man sprang out, ran up the steps, and hammered on the door.

"Here he *is*!" Father O'Donnell exclaimed, getting up.

"I'd better be off" Julia said, also getting up.

But before she had time to do more than take a few steps towards the door it opened, and the red-haired man appeared at it.

"Hullo, Father—may I come in?" He checked on seeing Julia. "Oh, sorry—you've got a visitor. I only came to ask did that cable come yet? I'll come back presently."

"No, come in and meet Mrs. Jamieson," the Father said. "She is a friend of your wife's."

At that the new-comer blushed, the ready blush of a red-haired person; he came forward and wrung Julia by the hand with an eagerness that she found rather touching.

"Is that so? Did you see her recently? How is she?"

"I saw her four days ago. She is very well." She turned to Father O'Donnell, "I'll be off now, Father."

Just then Mrs. Bassett appeared with a tray of tea-things, which she dumped on the floor while she fetched a small table from the passage.

"Oh we don't need tea yet, Mrs. Bassett" the priest said.

"There's a sponge-cake just out of the oven; 'tis lovely. Ye'd best eat it right away" the housekeeper said, and bustled off to fetch this product. Father O'Donnell, laughing, gave in, and cleared another chair for his new guest, as before piling up books to serve as tables.

"You'd better not miss Mrs. Bassett's sponge-cake, Mrs. Jamieson. Hers really are something" he said. Julia, smiling, sat down; the Father turned to Paddy Martin. "Yes, the cable came, and says everything you could wish—I'll show it to you. You needn't hesitate to talk about it in front of Mrs. Jamieson, because, when I learned that she was a friend of your wife's, I told her the whole story. I thought it best that she should know it."

"I'm glad you did. We've got to get the facts to Sally somehow." He looked questioningly at Julia. "Perhaps the lady might help?"

Julia was beginning to realise that she was going to be driven into precisely that position, inexorably; she looked doubtful, and was silent.

"I shouldn't stand much chance with Sally if I just walked up to the house and said—'I'm a good boy now; I want to come back'—would I?" he said, with a very beguiling grin.

Julia couldn't help smiling.

"Well no—I'll grant you that" she replied. Just then the sponge cake was brought in—it was indeed a noble sight, rising in a golden fluff above its smooth beige sides; and when Father O'Donnell had cut some slices, under Mrs. Bassett's watchful eye, it proved to be absolutely delicious.

"Take a slice out with you, Mrs. Bassett"—he said, cutting off another large piece. After this interruption they returned to the question of the best means of conveying the news of her husband's reform and return to Sally Martin. In the end, it was decided that the priest should write out a full account of what he had been told, accompanied by a note offering to come and see Mrs. Martin if she so wished, and that Julia should take this, together with the two cables, over to Achill. "Anyhow, now you can say you've seen me yourself" Paddy said to Julia, again with his grin—during all this discussion his manner of expressing himself, and his concern for Sally's feelings, made a very favourable impression on her. He was a *nice* person now; she was sure of it.

When she got back to Rostrunk the afternoon post was in, and there was another letter from Edina, giving more details about the formalities necessary for a Catholic wedding in Scotland: banns had to be posted for three weeks in the Church of Scotland Parish Church, "so that *all* may know of it," and also a notice of intent to marry in the local Registrar's office—"to inform the godless, one imagines" Edina wrote. "I can see to all that, if you *both* give me written authority to do so. But one of you must 'reside in the district' for fifteen clear days before you can even apply for the banns!—of course we hope you'll come to us for that, Julia. It looks as though we didn't exactly welcome non-Scots weddings up here! But not to worry—the Sheriff can grant a licence to marry in case of emergency—you just have to be interviewed by him and satisfy him that there is no impediment, and so on. Our Sheriff is a pet; I saw him at the Menteiths' cocktail-party last night and put your case to him, and he says of course he will help—it *is* an emergency for Gerald, he couldn't possibly leave his practice for weeks and weeks, and of course he'll want some honeymoon."

Julia rang Gerald up—luckily he was able to come in to Martinstown for lunch next day, when she passed all this information on to him, and also what she had learned from Father O'Donnell about the steps that he, Gerald, would have to get his own Parish Priest to take with the Priest at Glentoran. Then, more tentatively, she put to him her idea of being instructed and received into the Church *before* their marriage. "Obviously, there has got to be a lot of delay anyhow, with all these Scottish fusses" she said. "I thought perhaps Father O'Donnell could instruct me—I think I should like to be instructed by him."

"Did you mention that to him?"

"Oh yes—and he said to talk to you about it, and that he would think it over meantime."

But Gerald had another idea. "If you've got to spend so long at Glentoran for the civil business, perhaps there is some high-powered priest up there, or an Abbey or something not too far away, where you could get instruction while you

[245]

are doing this residence in the district. I'd rather it would have been Farm Street, though. Would your cousin know?"

"Edina? I don't suppose so, but she could find out. I'll ring her up tonight and ask."

"I should ask Father O'Donnell first—he might have some sort of Catholic directory that lists such places. Cost less, too. I see I shall have a wife with a tendency to extravagance!"

Father O'Donnell proved to have exactly that thing, and promised to ring Julia back after he had consulted it. Then— "Did you get to Achill yet?" he asked her.

"No, Father—I'm ashamed to say I didn't. I found this letter when I got back to Rostrunk, and I'm afraid I concentrated on my own affairs. I'll go tomorrow morning first thing. I'm very sorry," Julia said penitently.

The priest telephoned in about half an hour to say that there was a Benedictine Abbey within about twenty-five miles of Glentoran—"They run a school, so I am confident that you could get instruction there, if you could have the use of a car. Would you care for me to write to the Abbot?"

"Oh yes, please, Father. How good you are."

This time Julia did telephone to Sally Martin before setting out; she didn't want to risk running into O'Rahilly, in view of her errand. "I want to talk to you about something rather important," she said—she ventured on this in the hope of putting her friend in an enquiring state of mind.

"Oh, *what?*"

"Tell you when I see you—I'll be with you in an hour and a half."

Sally had got coffee ready when she arrived, and when they were sitting by the fire—"Now, what is this important thing you want to talk about?" she asked at once.

Julia pulled Father O'Donnell's account of his talk with Paddy Martin out of her bag. "I think you'd better read this first" she said, handing it over—no paving of the way would be of any use on this occasion, she felt. "It's from the priest at Lettersall."

"Who's he? And why does he write to me?" Sally looked a little frightened.

"Read it, darling—it's really good news" Julia said gently.

Sally Martin read for a moment or two—then she put the paper down, with a startled expression.

"But—he says he's seen Paddy!" she exclaimed. "He must be over here. This is awful!"

"Go on reading" Julia said. "Read it to the end."

Looking reluctant, Mrs. Martin read on. At last she put the Father's long letter down.

"I don't know this priest" she said. "I don't know whether I should believe what he says."

"Your husband thought of that, so he made Father O'Donnell send a cable to a priest who knows him—knows your Paddy, that is—asking for the facts. Here it is, and here is the reply he got" Julia said, pulling two more papers out of her bag. "Mr. Martin paid for the cables, of course. Read those now."

Sally Martin put her hands over her face. "I don't want to" she said, in a helpless tone.

"Sally dear, you *must*. It would be wicked not to. You can't want *not* to know that your husband has stopped being bad and become good" Julia said firmly.

"It's all so strange," Sally said. "I—I don't seem to be able to take it in."

Julia felt that she could understand that, and said so. "After living all these years with one idea of a person, to be told suddenly that he's turned into something quite different must be very puzzling and difficult to accept."

"That's it, exactly!" Sally said, with eager gratitude.

"But in honesty, and in fairness to yourself, as well as to him, you really ought to read these cables, now" Julia said, holding them out again.

This time Sally gave in, and did read them; she read both twice, slowly and carefully.

"It's fantastic" she said at last. "This one from that priest in Philadelphia makes Paddy—*Paddy!*—sound like some sort of holy person, doing all this work among boys and sick people."

"He's certainly turned into a very *nice* person" Julia said, smiling—"really a charmer."

"How do you know that? *You* haven't seen him, have you?"

"Yes, for a few minutes. He came in to Father O'Donnell's while I was there, to ask if the reply to the cable had come—and when the Father told him that I knew you, he wanted to know how you were, and when I had last seen you, and so on. He put a whole stream of questions, as eagerly as a boy," Julia said smiling. "You'll have to see him, Sally."

"Yes, I s'pose." A pause. "Would he want to go back to the States?" Sally asked.

At that question Julia knew that the battle was won.

"I don't know. He's bought a house here. You and he will have to settle all that" she said, getting up. She hurried out, and on the way back to Rostrunk rang up the Father, as usual, from the hotel at Mulranny.

"Yes, send him over. It will be all right" she said, confidently. As she was going out she ran into O'Rahilly. "Oh, hullo" she said.

"Been to see Sally?" he asked.

"Yes—to take her a splendid piece of news. Her husband has come back." It occurred to her that this was an excellent opportunity to simplify matters for Sally Martin in one direction, anyhow.

"*Is* it such good news, for her?" Billy asked doubtfully.

"Oh *yes!* Didn't you know? He's a completely reformed character—a teetotaller of years' standing, as well as being a most frightfully nice person" Julia said warmly.

"D'you mean to say you've *met* him?" Billy asked, startled.

"Oh yes—I liked him awfully" Julia said. "I must fly." She hastened out—how she knew of Paddy Martin's *bona fides* was no concern of Billy's; nor where she had met him, she felt.

Julia had another of her lunch-time meetings in Martinstown with Gerald, and first told him that Sally had been persuaded to accept the idea of Paddy's reformation and return. "Did she see him yet?" the man asked.

"I don't know. I telephoned to the priest and told him he could send him over, but that was only day before yesterday."

" 'Twould be nice to know that they are fixed up" Gerald said.

"Well, if she doesn't ring me, I'll ring her." Then she told him of the Benedictine Abbey within reach of Glentoran. "So that will be easy. I shall buy a car."

"Why not hire?"

"Well, I shall want my own car when I'm living here, so I might just as well buy it now. Then I shall be free to run over whenever it suits the Fathers, and not have to haggle with Edina over the car."

"Nor haggle with me over the car when you are at Rossbeg!" Gerald said laughing. "Well, I daresay it will make for harmony, and you can afford it. Shall you be received up there? I should like to be on hand when you are."

"Well, you'll be coming over for the wedding, won't you?"

Julia said, laughing too. "Couldn't I be received just a few days before it? I shall have to spend at *least* five weeks at Glentoran over this 'residence' business, perhaps more; and I suppose the Fathers could instruct me in that time, as with my own car I can go over as often as they want me to. Oh, kind Father O'Donnell has written to the Abbot about me—he is a dear man."

"He certainly is. When do you go?"

"Next week, I hope. I'm just waiting to hear from Edina about when she has been able to fix the actual date for the wedding with the Macdonalds; as we're borrowing their chapel, they must have some say."

"Isn't there a Parish Church?" Gerald asked.

"Yes, but nearly ten miles away! Think of the business of getting everyone to and fro by car! Whereas the Macdonalds' is just next door. That's why it's practically used as a parish Church, and Father Kennedy says Mass there on alternate Sundays. By the way, have you done all your business about getting Father Murphy to write and 'delegate authority' to Father Kennedy to marry one of his parishioners?"

"I'll check. I told him to, and I talked to the Bishop about it myself, so that ought to be all square."

That evening Julia had an ecstatic telephone call from Sally Martin—Paddy was at Achill, and they had decided to resume their marriage. "The children are thrilled to pieces to have a Daddy again—they love him already." They were going to stay in Ireland, but at Achill, because the school was so much handier there than at Ponticum Cottage, when they were not in Dublin. "Oh no"—in reply to a question from Julia—"we shan't sell the cottage; Paddy will keep it for the fishing. There's no fishing with this house." Julia gave affectionate congratulations at this happy outcome, and told Gerald.

Some weeks later Edina Reeder and Mrs. Hathaway were sitting in the library at Glentoran. The far end of the room looked like a rather high-class bazaar, being for the moment devoted to Julia's wedding-presents—Gerald's were, naturally, at Rossbeg. "They can go over in the lift-vans, so long as you don't mind housing them till the Philipino goes," Julia had said easily when they began to arrive. Julia had just gone off in her car on one of her almost daily visits to the Benedictine Fathers to receive her instruction, and her two friends were talking about her.

"She looks so happy now" Mrs. Hathaway said, with a half-wistful little sigh.

"Well, why wouldn't she, when she's on the point of getting married to one of the nicest men imaginable?" Edina said crisply. "But I wish she wasn't changing her religion— I don't see the point, at her age."

"Oh don't you, Edina? It seems to me so wise, as her husband is a Catholic. I always think it's better, and easier, if husband and wife belong to the same religion. And she's going to live in a Catholic country."

"I don't see what *that* has got to do with it" Edina said.

"Oh yes, surely. She'll be able to be of so much more help to the people round her, if they don't feel that she's alien in faith" Mrs. Hathaway said.

"Will they need much help? I thought Ireland was so rich and prosperous now."

"So it may be; but the less well-educated and less privileged are always the better of advice from the local gentry. Look what a lot of time your own Philip spends on that sort of thing!" Mrs. Hathaway stated firmly.

Philip Reeder came in at that moment and caught her last sentence.

"What do I spend a lot of time on, Mrs. H.?" he asked.

"Going about and talking to your tenants; and they come to you and ask for advice—I've heard them" the old lady said. "But I don't believe they would do that nearly so readily if you were a Roman Catholic."

"No, I don't suppose they would. But I'm not, nor likely to become one! What *can* you two be talking about?"

"Julia becoming an R.C." Edina said. "Mrs. H. thinks it is a good idea, because she's going to live in a Catholic countryside."

"So do I. And isn't her husband one? I should have thought there was everything to be said for it" Philip Reeder stated roundly.

"Oh well, obviously you win, Mrs. H." Edina said cheerfully. She got up. "I must go and lift the broodies" she said, and went out to the poultry-yard.

"I'm going up the Glen in the little car—I came to ask if you'd care to come too, for the spin, Mrs. H." Philip said. "I want to see how they're getting on with the new footbridge."

"Oh, I'd love to. My cloak's in the hall."

"There's nothing much to see just now; the azaleas are over."

"The Glen is always lovely. And the honeysuckle up on the high burn will still be nearly at its best" the old lady said, as she got up.

"How well you know this place!—every detail" he said, giving her his arm out to the hall.

"I've known it a long time, Philip," she said, putting on her cloak.

"And always loved it!" the man said.

What Philip called "the little car" was really hardly a car at all; it was more like a sort of motor bath-chair, small enough to go along quite narrow paths and tracks, into which a second person could *just* be squeezed if they were small enough. Mrs. Hathaway was not large and tucked in beside Philip Reeder very contentedly. The trees in the lower part of the Glen, nearest the house, were mostly sycamores, underplanted at wide intervals with species rhododendrons—Philip, looking about him, grunted discontentedly—"Those damned seedlings!" Indeed a dense growth of sycamore seedlings was springing up everywhere, threatening to smother the rhodos.

"Yes, they are a pest" Mrs. Hathaway agreed. "Years ago, I used to spend hours pulling them out, before they got quite as big as this. It was very sore on the hands."

"I bet it was. I must send the men up, to lift them before they get any bigger."

"Could you bear to pull up a moment here, Philip?"

"Yes, of course. What is it?"

"I do so love looking back at the Castle just from here, before the bend," the old lady said, twisting nimbly round in her seat as the small vehicle came to a halt. Philip turned round too, and looked back at his home. The sort of green tunnel formed by the trees over the road up the Glen did indeed frame a charming picture—the graceful grey stone structure with the tower at one end, the stretch of lawn beyond and flanking the building two large and beautiful trees, a lime on one side, a horse-chestnut on the other, the tone and texture of their foliage exquisitely contrasting. "It was really inspired to plan those particular trees just there" Mrs. Hathaway said.

"Who did plant them? Do you know?" Reeder asked.

"Oh yes—Edina's grandfather, old General Monro. He was always mad on planting trees. He inherited this place when he was only nine or ten, and he began planting at once —he had those two put in before he was eleven! And most of the ones down the drive and quite a lot of the Upper Glen was his doing. And he had a principle; of course one must cut down trees sometimes, but he never cut one down without planting two, *somewhere,* as a replacement."

"He must have been a remarkable chap. Did you ever know him?"

"Yes, when I was quite small. He was very splendid to look at, with a huge white beard, which I *hated!*" the old lady said with energy. "He was always kissing me, and it smelt awful of stale tobacco, as well as being bristly. I managed to put a stop to that" Mrs. Hathaway said, a look of self-satisfaction coming over her worn old face.

"How?" Reeder asked, with interest.

"I hid my Nannie's nail-scissors in the pocket of my pinafore and made my way into his study one morning; he was delighted to get a visit and when he began kissing me I took them out, and cut a piece off one side of the beard!"

"Well done!" Philip said, laughing.

"Yes, he was furious, and never kissed me again. In fact I don't think I was taken to Glentoran again till after he was dead. But the place owes him a lot" she said. "All right— drive on, Philip; I mustn't delay you with my chatter."

"I value your chatter—I learn a lot from it," her host said, letting in the clutch. And when they got back to the house he went to his study and jotted down what he had learned about the planting of trees at Glentoran in a book he kept of notes on the place which was his wife's inheritance, and which he had come to love dearly.